THE LAST GUNFIGHTER: THE DRIFTER

William W. Johnstone

ZEBRA BOOKS
Kensington Publishing Corp.
www.zebrabooks.com

ZEBRA BOOKS are published by

Kensington Publishing Corp.
850 Third Avenue

New York, NY 10022

Copyright © 2000 by William W. Johnstone

Zebra and the Z logo Reg. U.S. Pat. & TM Off.

First Printing:February, 2000
10 9 8 7

Printed in the United States of America

THE KID'S LAST WORDS

"Might as well get this over with," Frank said. He touched the brim of his hat in a salute to The Kid, a signal that he was ready, and stepped off the boardwalk and into the street.

Kid Moran did the same.

"Ride out of here, Kid," Frank called. "Don't throw your life away for nothing."

"It ain't nothin' to me, Morgan," the Kid called.

"Boy, the day of the gunfighter is nearly over. And as far as I'm concerned, it's past time."

"Frank Morgan done lost his nerve," The Kid yelled. "You beg me to let you leave and you can ride out of here, Morgan. Beg for your life, old man."

The distance between them was slowly closing. Little pockets of dust were popping up under their boots as they walked toward sudden death and destiny.

"Why don't you draw, old man?" The Kid yelled. "Come on, damn you. Pull on me!"

"It's your play, Kid," Frank said calmly. "You're the one challenging the law here in town. I'm ordering you to give this up and ride on out."

The Kid suddenly stopped in the middle of the street. Frank stopped his walking. There were maybe fifty or so feet between them. Plenty close enough.

"Draw on me, you old bastard," Kid Moran yelled, "so's I can kill you and have done with this."

"Drag iron, son," Frank replied. "I told you this is your play."

"Your afeared of me. I knowed you had a yeller streak up your back."

Frank waited, silent and steady—a man alone in the middle of the street, the tin star on his coat twinkling faintly in the last rays of the late-afternoon sun . . .

To Debbie and Dent Sigh

One

"Boy," the older man said, "I strongly advise you not to pull on me."

It seemed to those in the barroom there was not only a great weariness to the man's voice, but also a great sadness. Some of the spectators wondered about that. A few thought they knew why the sadness was there.

Outside, the early spring winds still had a bite to them on the late-afternoon day.

"You're nothin' but a damned old washed-up piece of coyote crap," the young man replied.

Old is right, the man thought. *Both in body and soul.*

"And you're a coward, too!" the young man added.

The older man smiled, but his eyes turned chilly. "Boy, you should really learn to watch your mouth."

The young man laughed. "You gonna make me do that, you old has-been?"

"I would rather not have to do that, boy. Besides, that's something your mother and father should have taught you."

"I never paid no mind to what they said."

"Obviously."

"Huh? Old man, you talk funny—you know that? You tryin' to insult me or something?"

"Not at all, boy. Just agreeing with you."

"I don't like you, old man. I mean, I don't like you at all. I think you're all talk and no do. And I don't believe all them stories told 'bout you, neither. I don't think you've kilt no twenty or thirty men."

"I haven't."

"I knowed it!"

"Closer to forty."

"You're a damn liar!"

"Boy, go home. Leave me alone."

"Naw. I'm gonna make you pull on me, Morgan. Then I'm gonna shoot you in the belly so's I can stand right here and watch you beg and cry and holler like a whipped pup 'til you die. That's what I'm gonna do."

"Is that really Frank Morgan?" a man in the crowd whispered to a friend.

"That's him."

"I thought he was a lot older."

" 'Nuff talk, old man!" the young man yelled. "Grab iron, you old buffalo fart!"

Frank Morgan did not move. He stood and watched the much younger man. "If you want a shooting, boy, you're going to have to start it."

"Then I will, by God!"

Frank waited.

"You think I won't?"

"I hope you don't, kid."

"I ain't no kid!"

"Pardon me?"

"I'm known around here as Snake."

"There is a certain resemblance."

Someone in the crowd laughed at that.

"What?" the young man yelled.

"I was just agreeing with you," Morgan said.

"Yore gonna die, Morgan!"

"We all die, kid. Some long before their time. And I'm afraid you're about to prove me right."

The kid cussed and grabbed iron.

Morgan shot him before the kid could even clear leather—shot him two times, the shots so close together they sounded as one. The kid's feet flew out from under him and he hit the floor, two holes in the center of his chest.

"Good God Almighty!" a man in the crowd said.

"He's as fast as he ever was," another man stage-whispered.

"You know Morgan?"

"I seen him once back in seventy-four, I think it was. He shot them two Burris brothers."

It was now April, 1888.

Frank slowly holstered his .45, then walked the few yards that had separated the two men. He stood for a moment looking down at the dying young man.

"I thought . . . all that talk 'bout you was . . . bull-crap," the young man gasped. Blood was leaking from his mouth.

"I wish it was," Frank said, then turned away from the bloody scene and stepped up to the bar. "A whiskey, please," he told the barkeep.

"I thought you only drank coffee, Mr. Morgan."

"Occasionally I will take a drink of hard liquor."

"Yes, sir. Mr. Morgan?"

Frank looked at the man.

"The sheriff and his deputies will be here shortly. Gunplay is not looked on with favor in this town."

"In other words, get out of town?"

"It was just a friendly suggestion. No offense meant."

"I know. None taken. Thank you." *Same old story,* Frank thought. *Different piano player, same song.*

Frank took a sip of whiskey.

"The kid's dead," someone said. "Reckon I ought to get the undertaker?"

"Not yet," a man said from the batwings.

Frank cut his eyes. Three men had stepped quietly into the saloon—the sheriff and two of his deputies. The two deputies were carrying Greeners—sawed-off, double-barreled shotguns.

No one with any sense wanted to take a chance when facing Frank Morgan.

Frank was standing alone at the bar, slowly taking tiny sips from his glass of whiskey.

"Frank Morgan," the sheriff said.

"Do I know you, Sheriff?" Frank asked. "I don't recall ever meeting you."

"I know you from dime novels, Morgan."

"I see."

"Them writers want to make you a hero. But I know you for what you really are."

"What am I, Sheriff?"

"A damn, kill-crazy outlaw."

"I've never stolen a thing in my life, Sheriff."

"You say."

Frank set the glass down on the bar and turned to face the sheriff. "That's right, Sheriff. I say."

The deputies raised the shotguns.

Frank smiled. "Relax, boys," he told them. "You'll get no trouble from me."

"You just can't keep that pistol in leather, can you, Morgan?" the sheriff said.

"I was pushed into this fight, Sheriff. Ask anyone here."

"I 'spect that's so, Morgan. The kid was a trouble-maker, for a fact."

"And now?"

"You finish your drink and get out of town."

"I've got a very tired horse, Sheriff, with a loose shoe. He's at the livery now. You don't like me—that's all right. But my horse has done nothing to you."

The sheriff hesitated. "All right, Morgan. You can stay in the stable with your horse. Get that shoe fixed first thing come the morning and then get the hell gone from here."

"Thank you. How about something to eat?"

"Get you some crackers and a pickle from the store 'cross the street. That'll have to do you."

"Crackers and a pickle," Frank muttered. "Well, I've eaten worse."

"Understood, Morgan?" the sheriff pressed.

"Perfectly, Sheriff."

"Some of you men get the kid over to the undertaker," the sheriff ordered. "Tell him he can have whatever's in the kid's pockets for his fee."

"Them guns of hisn, too?" a man asked.

"Yes. The guns, too."

Frank turned back to the bar and slowly sipped his drink. The sheriff walked over and leaned against the bar, staring at him.

"Something on your mind, Sheriff?" Frank asked.

"What's your tally now, Morgan? A hundred? A hundred and fifty dead by your gun?"

Frank smiled. "No, Sheriff. Not nearly that many. The kid there was the first man to brace me in several years."

"How'd you manage that, Morgan?"

"I stayed away from people. I mostly rode the lonesome."

"What made you stop here?"

"My horse. And I needed supplies. I lost my packhorse and supplies to some damned renegade young Indians last week. Down south of here."

"I heard about that. Got a wire from a sheriff friend of mine down that way. A posse went after those young bucks and cornered them. Killed them all."

Frank nodded his head. "They got what they deserved. That was a good horse they killed."

"Wilson at the livery's got a good packhorse he'd like to sell, if you've got the money. I don't think he wants much for him."

"I've got some money."

"I'll amble over there and drop a word on him to let you have the horse for his lowest price. Then you get supplies and ride on."

"Thanks, Sheriff."

Without another word the sheriff turned and walked away, his deputies following.

The swamper mopped up the blood on the floor and sprinkled sawdust over the spot.

The saloon settled down to cards and low talk. The excitement was over. Killings were rare in the town, but nobody had really liked the kid who called himself Snake. He had been nothing but a smart-aleck troublemaker. He would not be missed.

Frank Morgan pulled out early the next morning, after provisioning up at the general store. The man at the livery had tossed in a packsaddle for a couple of dollars, and Frank brought supplies, lashed them down, and pulled out before most of the town's citizens were up emptying the chamber pot.

Frank took it easy that morning, stopping often just to look around. It had been years since he'd been in this part of New Mexico territory, and things had changed somewhat. Hell of a lot more people, for one thing. Seemed like there were settlers nearly everywhere he looked.

For his nooning, Frank settled down in the shade by a fast-running little creek that came straight down from the mountains and had him a sandwich the lady at the general store had been kind enough to fix for him . . . for a dime.

Frank still wondered about the change in attitude of the local sheriff the day before. Some lawdogs could be real bastards, while others were fairly decent sorts once you got past all the bluster. But it had been many a year since any badge-toter had gotten too lippy with Frank Morgan. One tried to shove Frank around down in Texas—back around '75, he thought it was. Wasn't any gunplay involved that day, but Frank had sure cleaned the loudmouth's plow with his fists.

Frank ate his sandwich and then rested for a time while his horses grazed. Then he stood up and stretched. Felt good. Frank was just a shade over six feet, lean-hipped, broad-shouldered, with smooth, natural musculature. At forty-five years old, Frank was still a powerful man. Not the hoss he used to be, but close enough. His thick hair was dark brown, graying now at the temples. Pale gray eyes.

Frank wore a .45 Colt Peacemaker, right side, low and

tied down. He carried another Colt Peacemaker in his saddlebags. A Winchester rifle was stuck down in a saddle boot. On the left side of his belt he carried a long-bladed knife in a sheath. He occasionally used that knife to shave with. He was as handy with it as he was with a pistol.

Frank reluctantly left the peaceful setting of the creek and the shade and rode on slowly toward the north. He did not have a specific destination in mind; he was just rambling.

Frank had worked the winter in a line shack, looking after a rancher's cattle in a section of the high country. He still had most of his winter's wages.

Frank did have a dream: a small spread of his own in a quiet little valley with good graze and water. He occasionally opened a picture book in his mind and gazed at the dream, but the mental pages were slightly torn and somewhat tattered now. The dream had never materialized. Twice Frank had come close to having that little spread. Both times his past had caught up with him, and the local citizens in the nearest town had frozen him out. Nobody wanted the West's most notorious gunfighter as a neighbor.

Frank let part of his mind wander some as he rode, the other part remained vigilant. For the most part, Indian trouble was just about all over, except for a few young bucks who occasionally broke from the reservations and caused trouble. Those incidents usually didn't last long, and almost always ended with a pile of dead Indians.

The Wild West was settling down, slowly but surely.

Bands of outlaws and brigands still roamed the West, though, robbing banks and rustling cattle.

In the northern part of New Mexico it was the gangs

of Ned Pine and Victor Vanbergen that were causing most of the trouble. Frank Morgan knew both men, and they hated him. Both had been known to go into wild outbursts of anger at just the mention of his name.

Frank had, at separate times, backed each of the outlaw leaders down and made them eat crow in front of witnesses. They both were gutsy men, but they weren't stupid. Neither one was about to draw on Frank Morgan.

There were several names in the West that caused brave men to sit down and shut up. Smoke Jensen, Falcon MacCallister, Louis Longmont, and Frank Morgan were the top four still living.

Ned Pine and Victor Vanbergen had started their careers in crime when just young boys, and both had turned into vicious killers. Their gangs numbered about twenty men each—more from time to time, less at others—and they were not hesitant to tackle entire small towns in their wild and so far unstoppable pursuit of money and women . . . in that order.

Frank Morgan's life as a gunfighter had begun when he was in his midteen years and working as a hand on a ranch in Texas. One of the punchers had made Frank's life miserable for several months by bullying him whenever he got the chance . . . which was often. One day Frank got enough of the cowboy's crap and hit him flush in the face with a piece of a broken singletree. When the puncher was able to see again and the swelling in his nose had gone down some, he swore to kill the boy.

Young Frank Morgan, however, had other plans.

The puncher told Frank to get a gun 'cause the next time he saw him he was going to send him to his Maker.

Frank had an old piece of a pistol that he'd been practicing with when he got the money to buy ammunition. It was 1860, and times were hard, money scarce.

That day almost thirty years back was still vivid in Frank's mind.

He was so scared he had puked up his breakfast of grits and coffee.

Then he stepped out of the bunkhouse to meet his challenger, pistol in hand.

There was no fast draw involved in that duel. That would come a few years later.

The cowboy cursed at Frank and fired just as Frank stepped out of the bunkhouse, the bullet howling past Frank's head and knocking out a good-size splinter of wood from the rough doorframe. Frank damn near peed his underwear.

Young Frank acted out of pure instinct. Before the abusive puncher could fire again, Frank had lifted and cocked his pistol. He shot the puncher in the center of his chest. The man stumbled back as the .36-caliber chunk of lead tore into his flesh.

"You piece of turd!" the cowboy gasped, still on his boots. He lifted and cocked his pistol.

Frank shot him again, this time in the face, right between the eyes.

The puncher hit the hard ground, dead.

Frank walked over him and looked down at the dead man. The open empty eyes stared back at him. He struggled to fight back sickness, and managed to beat it. Frank turned away from the dead staring eyes.

"Luther had kin, boy," the foreman told him. "They'll be comin' to avenge him. You best get yourself set for that day. Make some plans."

"But I didn't start this!" Frank said. *"He* did." Frank pointed to the dead man.

"That don't make no difference, boy. I'll see you get your time, and a little extra."

"Am I leavin'?" Frank asked.

"If you want to stay alive, son. I know Luther had four brothers, and they're bad ones. They will come lookin' for you."

"They live close?"

"About a day's ride from here. And they got to be notified. So, you get your gear rolled up, son, and get ready to ride. I'll go see the boss."

"I'm right here," said the owner of the spread. "I was having my mornin' time in the privy." He paused for a moment and looked down at Luther. "Well, he was a good hand, but deep down just like his worthless brothers—no damn good." He looked at Frank. "You kill him, boy?"

"Yes, sir."

"Luther ain't gonna be missed by many. Only his sorry-assed brothers, I reckon. You got to go, boy. Sorry, but that's the way it has to be. For your sake. You get your personals together and then come over to the house. You got time comin', and I'll see you get some extra."

"I ain't even got a horse to call my own, Mr. Phillips," Frank said. "Or a saddle."

"You will," the rancher told him. "Get movin', son. I'll see you in a little while."

Frank rode out an hour later. He had his month's wages—twelve dollars—and twenty dollars extra Mr. Phillips gave him. He still had twenty-five dollars he'd saved over his time at the ranch, too. Frank felt like he was sort of rich. He had a sack of food Mrs. Phillips had fixed for him. He was well-mounted, for the foreman had picked him out a fine horse and a good saddle and saddlebags.

The other hands had gathered around to wish him farewell.

"You done the world a favor, Frankie," one told him.

"I never did like that sorry bastard," another told him.

"Here you go, Frankie," another puncher said, holding out Luther's guns. "You throw away that old rust pot you been totin' around and take these. You earned 'em, and you'll probably damn shore need them."

"What do you mean, Tom?" Frank asked.

"Frankie . . . Luther was a bad one. He's killed four or five men that we know of with a pistol. He's got himself a reputation as a gunman. There'll be some who'll come lookin' to test you."

"Test me?"

"Call you out, boy," the foreman said. "You're the man who killed Luther Biggs. They'll be some lookin' to kill you. Stay ready."

"I don't want no reputation like that," Frank protested.

"Your druthers don't cut no ice now, boy. You got the name of a gunman. Now, like it or not, you got to live with it."

Two

Frank drifted for a couple of months, clear out of Texas and up into Oklahoma Territory. He hooked up with two more young men about his age, and they rode together. Their parents were dead, like Frank's, and they just plain hadn't wanted to stay with brothers or sisters . . . as was the case with Frank.

By then the story had spread about the shoot-out between young Morgan and Luther Biggs. Frank never talked about it; he just wanted to forget it. But he knew he probably would never be able to do that . . . not completely.

The War Between the States was only a few months away, the war talk getting hotter and hotter. One of the boys Frank was riding with believed in preserving the Union. Frank and the other boy were Southern born. If war did break out, they would fight for the South.

The trio of boys separated in Arkansas when they received word about the beginning of hostilities between the North and the South. Frank joined up with a group of young men who were riding off to enlist in the Confederate Army. He never knew what happened to the other two boys.

For the next four years Frank fought for the Southern

cause and matured into a grown man. He became hardened to the horrors of war. At war's end, Frank Morgan was a captain in the Confederate Army, commanding a company of cavalry.

Rather than turn in his weapons, Frank headed west. During that time he had been experimenting with faster ways to get a pistol out of the holster. He had a special holster made for him at a leather shop in southern Missouri: the holster was open, without a flap, and a leather thong slipped over the hammer prevented the pistol from falling out when he was riding or doing physical activities on foot. Frank practiced pulling the pistol out of leather; he worked at it for at least an hour each day, drawing and cocking and dry firing the weapon. The first time he tried the fast draw using live ammunition, he almost shot himself in the foot. He practiced with much more care after that, figuring that staying in the saddle with just one foot in the stirrup might be a tad difficult.

By the time Frank reached Colorado, his draw was perfected. He could draw—and fire—with amazing accuracy, and with blinding speed.

And that was where his lasting reputation was carved in stone. He met up with the Biggs brothers—all four of them.

He was provisioning up in southeastern Colorado when he heard someone call out his name. He turned to look at one of the ugliest men he had ever seen: the spitting image of Luther Biggs.

"I reckon you'd be one of the Biggs brothers," Frank said, placing his gunny sack of supplies on the counter.

"Yore damn right I am. And you're Frank Morgan. Me and my brothers been trailin' you for weeks."

"I got the feelin' somebody was doggin' my back trail. Never could catch sight of you."

"Our older brother, Billy Jeff, run acrost a man who knowed you. I disremember his name. That don't matter. He said you come out of the war all right and was headin' up to the northwest. Tole us what kind of hoss you was ridin', and what you looked like now that you was all growed up. But here and now is where your growin' stops, Morgan."

"Take it outside, boys," the store owner said. "Don't shoot up my place. Gettin' supplies out here is hard enough without this crap."

"Shet up, ribbon clerk," Biggs said. Then his eyes widened when the store owner lifted a double-barreled shotgun and eared both hammers back.

"I said take it outside!"

"Now don't git all goosey, mister," Biggs said. "We'll take it outside."

"You do that."

"You comin', Morgan, or does yeller smell? I think I smell yeller all over you."

"Don't worry about me, Ugly Biggs. You go run along now and get with your brothers, since it appears that none of you have the courage to face me alone."

The storekeeper got himself a good chuckle out of that, and a very dirty look from Biggs.

"Don't you fret none about that, Morgan. I'd take you apart with my bare hands right now, 'ceptin' that would displease my brothers. They want a piece of you, too. And what is this ugly crap?"

"You, Ugly. You're so damn ugly you could make a living frightening little children."

The veins in Biggs's neck bulged in scarcely controlled

anger. He cursed, balled his fists, and took a step toward Morgan.

The store owner said, "I'll spread you all over the front part of this store, mister. Now back out of here."

"I'll be right behind you, Ugly," Morgan told him.

Cursing, Biggs backed out of the store and walked across the street to the saloon.

"You want to head out the back and get clear of town, mister?" the store owner asked.

"I would if I thought that would do any good," Frank replied. "But you can bet they've got the back covered."

"You can't fight them all!"

"I don't see that I've got a choice in the matter." Frank patted the sack of supplies on the counter. "I'll be back for these."

"If you say so."

"I say so." Frank looked at the shotgun the shopkeeper was holding.

The man smiled and handed it across the counter. "Take it, mister. I don't know you, but I sure don't like that fellow who was bracin' you."

"Thanks. I'll return it in good shape." Frank stepped to the front door, paused, and then turned around and headed toward the rear of the store. The shopkeeper walked around the counter and closed and locked the front door, hanging up the closed sign.

At the closed back door Frank paused, took a deep breath, and then flung open the door and jumped out, leaping to one side just as soon as his boots hit the ground. A rifle blasted from the open door of the out-house, and Frank gave the comfort station both barrels of the Greener.

The double blast of buckshot almost tore the shooter

in two. The Biggs brother took both loads in the belly and chest and the bloody, suddenly dead mess fell forward, out of the outhouse and into the dirt.

Suddenly, another Biggs brother came into view—a part of him, at least: his big butt.

That's where Frank shot him, the bullet passing through both cheeks of his rear end.

"Oh, Lordy!" he squalled. "I'm hit, boys."

"Where you hit, Bobby?"

"In the ass. My ass is on far, boys. It hurts!"

"In the ass?" another brother yelled. "That ain't dignified."

"The hell with dignified!" Bobby shouted. "I'm a-hurtin', boys!"

"Hang on, Bobby," a brother called. "We'll git Morgan and then come to your aid."

"Kill that no-count, Billy Jeff!" Bobby groaned. "Oh, Lord, my ass end burns somethang fierce!"

"Can you see him, Wilson?" Billy Jeff called.

"No. But he's down yonder crost the street from the livery. I know that."

"I know that better than you do," Bobby yelled. "I got the lead in my ass to prove it! Ohhh, I ain't had sich agony in all my borned days."

Some citizen started laughing, and soon others in the tiny town joined in.

"You think this is funny?" Wilson Biggs yelled. "Damn you all to the hellfars!"

Morgan had changed positions again, running back up past the outhouse and the mangled body of Wells Biggs. He was now right across the wide street from Wilson Biggs.

He had picked up the guns from Wells and shoved

them behind his gunbelt. He holstered his own pistol and, using the guns taken from the dead man, he emptied them into the shed where Wilson was hiding. The bullets tore through the old wood, knocking great holes in the planks.

Wilson staggered out, his chest and belly blood-soaked. The Biggs brother took a couple of unsteady steps and fell forward, landing on his face in the dirt. He did not move.

"Wilson!" Billy Jeff shouted. "Did you get him, Wilson?"

"No, he didn't," Frank called. "Your brother's dead."

"Damn you!" Billy Jeff called. "Step out into the street and face me, you sorry son."

"And have your butt-shot brother shoot me?" Frank yelled. "I think not."

"Bobby!" Billy Jeff called. "You hold your far and let me settle this here affair. You hear me, boy?"

"I hear you, Billy Jeff. You shore you want it thisaway?"

"I'm shore. You hear all that, Morgan?"

"I hear it, but I don't believe it. You Biggs boys are all a pack of liars. Why should I trust you?"

"Damn you, Morgan, I give my word. I don't go back on my word, not never."

"Step out then, Billy Jeff."

"I'm a-comin' out, Morgan. My gun's holstered. Is yourn?"

Before Frank could reply, Bobby said, "I'm a-comin' out, too. Let's see if he's got the courage to face the both of us!"

"Bring your bleeding butt on, Biggs!" Frank yelled. "If all your courage hasn't leaked out of your ass, that is." He checked to see his own pistol was loaded up full, then slipped it into leather, working it in and out several times to insure a smooth draw.

Bobby was hollering and cussing Frank, scarcely pausing for breath.

Frank walked up to the mouth of the alley and stepped out to the edge of the street.

Bobby stopped cussing.

Billy Jeff said, "Step out into the center of the street, Morgan, and face the men who is about to kill you."

"Not likely, Biggs. The only way scum like you could kill me is by ambush."

That started Bobby cussing again. He paused every few seconds to moan and groan about his wounded ass.

The residents of the tiny town had gathered along the edge of the street to watch the fight. Some had fixed sandwiches; others had a handful of crackers or a pickle.

This was exciting. Not much ever happened in the tiny village, which as yet had no official name.

"Make your play, Biggs!" Frank called.

Billy Jeff fumbled at his gun and Frank let him clear leather before he pulled and fired, all in one very smooth, clean movement. The bullet struck Billy Jeff in the belly and knocked him down in the dirt. Frank holstered and waited. He smiled at Bobby Biggs.

Bobby was yelling and groping for his pistol, which was stuck behind his wide belt. Frank drew and shot him in the chest, and forever ended his moaning and griping about his butt. Bobby stretched out on the street and was still. The bullet had shattered his heart.

Frank never knew what made him do it, but on that day he twirled his pistol a couple of times before sliding it back into leather. He did it smoothly, effortlessly, and with a certain amount of flair.

A young boy in the crowd exclaimed, "Mommy, did you see that? Golly!"

"I never seen no one jerk a pistol like that," a man said to a friend.

"He sure got it out in a hurry," his friend replied. "And a damned fancy way of holstering that thing, too."

Frank was certainly not the first to utilize a fast draw, but he was one of the first, along with Jamie MacCallister and an East Texas gunhand whose name has been lost to history.

Frank looked over at the crowd to his left. "This town got an undertaker?"

"No," a man said. "We ain't even got a minister or a schoolmarm."

"We just get the bodies in the ground as soon as we can," another citizen said. "Unless it's wintertime. Then we put 'em in a shed where they'll freeze and keep pretty well 'til the ground thaws and we can dig a hole."

"They ain't real pretty to look at after a time, but they don't smell too bad," his friend said.

"If you don't stay around 'em too long," another man added.

"You can have their gear and guns for burying these men," Frank told the crowd. "And whatever money they have. Deal?"

"Deal," a man said. "Sounds pretty good to me. They had some fine horses. The horses is included, right?"

"Sure."

"I hope they ain't stolen," a townsman said. "Say, I heard them call you Morgan—you got a first name?"

"Frank."

"You just passin' though, Frank?" There was a rather hopeful sound to the question.

"Just stopping in town long enough to pick up a few supplies," Frank assured the crowd.

"All right. Well, I reckon we'd better get these bodies gathered up and planted."

"I'll help," a citizen volunteered.

"I'll get their horses," another said. "I got a bad back, you know—can't handle no shovel."

"Sure you do, Otis. Right."

Frank turned and walked away, back to the store to get his supplies and to return the shotgun to the man.

"Hell of a show out there, Mr. Morgan," the shop-keeper told him.

"Not one that I wanted the leading role in, though."

"I suppose not. Where do you go from here?"

"Just drifting."

"Back from the war?"

"Yes." Frank smiled. "My side lost."

"We all lost in that mess."

"I reckon so. Thanks, mister."

"Take care, Mr. Morgan."

Frank rode out, heading toward the northwest, his growing reputation right behind him. . . .

Three

Frank rode on toward the north and tried to put old memories behind him. But there were too many memories, too many bloody shoot-outs, too many killings, too many easy women with powder and paint on their faces and shrill laughter that Frank could still hear in his dreams.

And of course, there was that one special woman.

Her name was Vivian. Frank had met her in the town of Denver early in '66, and had been taken by her charm and beauty. Frank was a very handsome young man, and Viv had been equally smitten by him. She was the daughter of a businessman and lay preacher.

Frank was working at the time on a ranch in the area, and doing his best to stay out of any gun trouble.

Theirs was a whirlwind courtship, and they were married just a few months after meeting. Viv's father did not like Frank, and he made no attempt to hide that dislike. But after the wedding, Frank felt there was little Viv's father could do except try to make the best of it.

Frank was wrong.

Six months after their marriage, Frank found himself facing a drifter hunting trouble.

"I heard about you, Morgan," the drifter said. "And I think it's all poppycock and balderdash."

"Think what you want to think," Frank told him. "I have no quarrel with you."

"You do now."

There were no witnesses to the affair. The drifter had braced Frank on a lonesome stretch of range miles from town. Frank had been resting after a morning of brush-popping cattle out of a huge thicket. He was tired, and so was his horse.

"How'd you know I was working out here?" Frank asked.

"I heard in town. I asked about you."

"No one in town knew."

"You callin' me a liar?"

"This isn't adding up, friend."

"I ain't your friend, Morgan. I come to kill you, and that's what I aim to do."

"Who paid you to brace me?"

The drifter smiled. "You better make your mind up to stand and deliver, Morgan. 'Cause if you don't, I'm gonna gut-shoot you and leave you out here so's the crows and buzzards can eat your eyes."

"That isn't going to happen, friend. Now back off and ride out of here."

"I keep tellin' you, Morgan, I ain't your friend."

"Tell me who paid you to do this madness."

The drifter smiled. "On the count of three, you better hook and draw, Morgan. One—"

"Don't do this, friend."

"Two—"

"I don't want to kill you!"

"Three!"

The drifter never even cleared leather. As his hand dropped and curled around the butt of his pistol, Frank's Colt roared under the hot summer sun. The drifter's mouth dropped open in a grotesque grimace of pain and surprise as Frank's bullet ripped into his chest. He dropped his pistol and stared at Frank for a couple of seconds, then slumped to his knees.

Frank walked the few paces to stand over the dying man. "Who paid you to do this?"

"Damn, but you're quick," the drifter gasped. "I heard you was mighty fast, but I just didn't believe it."

"Who paid you?" Frank persisted, hoping the name would not be the one he suspected.

But it was.

"Henson," the drifter said. "Preacher Henson." Then he fell over on his face in the dust.

Vivian's father.

Frank turned the man over. He was still breathing. "How much did he pay you to brace me?"

"Five hundred dollars," the drifter gasped. Then his eyes began losing their brightness.

"You have the money on you?"

"Half of it. Get . . . the other half . . . when you're dead." The drifter's head lolled to one side.

"Talk to me, damn you!"

But the drifter was past speaking. He was dead.

"Dear father-in-law," Frank whispered, rage and disgust filling him. "I knew you disliked me, but I didn't know your hatred was so intense."

Frank went through the drifter's pockets and then loaded the man's body across his saddle and lashed him down. Leading the skittish horse—who didn't like the smell of blood—Frank rode into the nearest town and up to the marshal's office. The much smaller town was miles closer than the fast-growing town of Denver.

Frank explained what had happened, sort of—leaving out who hired the drifter, and why.

"Any reason why this man would want to kill you, Morgan?"

"No. I don't have any idea. I've never seen him before. As you can tell by looking at me, and smelling me, I suppose, I've been working cattle most of the day."

The marshal smiled. "Now that you mention it . . ." He laughed. "All right, Morgan. Did you go through the man's pockets?"

"Yes, I did. Trying to find some identification. I didn't find any papers, but he had fifty dollars on him. The money is in his front pants pocket."

Frank had taken two hundred and left fifty to bury the drifter and to throw off suspicion.

The marshal did not question Frank further on the shooting. "We'll get him planted, Frank. Thanks for bringing in the body. Most people would have just left him."

Frank rode back home, arriving late that night. He did not tell Viv about the shooting—how could he? She wouldn't have believed him. He spent a restless night, wondering how to best handle the wild hate her father felt for him.

The next day he went to see his father-in-law. Frank tossed the two hundred dollars on the man's desk.

"There's your blood money, Henson. I left fifty dollars in the man's pockets to bury him."

The successful businessman/lay preacher looked up from his desk. Frank had never seen such hatred in a man's eyes. "You filth!" Henson said. "Worthless gunman. Oh, I know all about you, Morgan. You're a killer for hire."

"That's a lie, Mr. Henson. I've killed men, yes. I won't deny that. But it was in self-defense. Not for hire."

"You're a liar!" Henson hissed. "And you're not worthy to even walk on the same side of the street as my daughter. You're a hired killer, a gunman. You're filth, and always will be."

Frank stared at the man in silence for a moment. "I'm going to prove you wrong, Mr. Henson."

"No, you won't. You can't. I've had detectives tracing you all the way back to your miserable, hardscrabble beginnings, you white trash. And I know all about the rape charges that were brought against you in Texas."

"Rape!" Frank blurted. "What charges? There are no rape charges—there have never been any."

Henson smiled cruelly at Morgan. His eyes glinted with malevolence. "There will be when my men get through doing their reports."

Frank got it then. Viv's father was paying detectives to write false reports. He was speechless.

"Leave," Henson urged. "Leave on your own, and I won't use those reports against you. I give you my word on that. Just saddle up and ride away."

"Leave? Vivian is my wife. I love her."

"Love!" Henson's word was filled with scorn. "You don't know the meaning of the word. You're a damned rake! That's all you've ever been. I'll destroy your marriage, Morgan. I will make it my life's work. I promise you that."

Frank started to speak, and Henson held up his hand. "Don't bother begging, you trash. It won't do you a bit of good. Leave. Get out. Get out of my office, get out of my daughter's life, and get out of town." He smiled. "Before my detectives return and I have the sheriff place you under arrest."

"I'll tell Viv about this," Frank managed to say.

"Go right ahead. I'll just tell her I knew all about it and was trying to protect her. See who she will believe. Me, naturally."

"I can beat the charges."

"No, you can't. I'll see you tried, convicted, and carried away in chains, just like the wild animal you are. My detectives have found, ah, shall we call them 'ladies,' who will testify against you. And they will be believed."

Frank was boxed, and knew it. Henson had wealth and power and position, and could very easily destroy him. He sighed and said, "All right. But I have to know Vivian will be taken care of."

"Of course she will be. I'll see to that personally. She'll never want for anything. You're making a very wise decision, Morgan. Do you need money? A sum within reason, of course."

"I wouldn't take a goddamn dime from you, you sorry-assed, mealymouthed, self-righteous, sanctimonious son of a bitch!"

"Get out!" Henson flared. "Get out of town right now. Don't go home. Don't see Vivian. Just get on your horse and ride out of here. For Vivian's sake, if not for your own."

Frank almost lost it. He balled his big hard hands into fists, and came very close to tearing his father-in-law's head off his shoulders. Henson saw what was about to happen, and paled in fright. But at the last possible second Frank backed off.

Frank turned and walked out of the office.

Henson looked down at his trembling hands, willing them to cease their shaking. After a moment, he rose from his chair and got his hat. He just had time to go get his daughter and escort her to the doctor's office.

Vivian Morgan was pregnant.

"Come on," Frank muttered as he rode north. "Put the memories away and close that old door."

But that was not an easy thing to do. Even though it had been some twenty years since he had pulled out of Denver, twenty years since he had last seen Vivian, the memories were still very strong, and the image of her face was forever burned into his brain.

Frank had heard little bits of gossip about Henson: the man had become a millionaire through land deals in and around Denver, and a powerful voice in his church. He had sent his daughter, Vivian, back east to live with family. She had gotten married there (somehow her father had had her marriage to Frank annulled). She had a child by her second husband.

She and her husband had returned to Denver to take over her father's business when Henson's health began to fail. By that time, Frank had learned, the boy was in college somewhere back east.

Occasionally Frank ran across a weeks- or months-old Denver newspaper and read it. Sometimes there was something in there about Vivian Browning, and Frank would wonder what she looked like now, and for a time he would be lost in "what ifs?"

"Crap!" Frank muttered as he made camp for the evening in the timber of the Sangre de Cristos, east and a little north of Santa Fe. "Put it out of your mind, Morgan. Put her out of your mind. She hasn't thought about you in years."

But as many times as Frank thought that, he always wondered if it was true.

He certainly had never forgotten her.

Frank filled the coffeepot with water and set it on the fire to boil. He settled back with a book. Frank always made camp with an least an hour of daylight left him, so he could read. He was a well-read and self-educated man. There were always a couple of books in his saddlebags—history, government, sometimes poetry.

On this day he dug out a book by John Milton. He had bought the book weeks back from a traveling salesman. And while he would be the first to admit that sometimes he didn't know what the hell Milton was talking about; he nevertheless enjoyed his writings. Frank read for a time from something titled *Paradise Lost*. But he was not so engrossed that he did not know what was happening around him: the birds that had been singing so gaily had stopped, and the squirrels that had been chattering were silent. Frank put his hand on the stock of his rifle and pulled it close to him. Whenever he made camp for the night, he levered a round into the chamber of his rifle. All he had to do was ear back the hammer and let 'er bang.

"Easy, friend." The voice came out of the timber. "I don't mean no harm."

"Then why are you trying to slip up on me?"

" 'Cause I know who you are, and how quick you are on the shoot—that's why."

Frank smiled. "Fair enough. Come on into the camp."

"Let me get my horses—all right?"

"Bring them in."

The man looked to be in his sixties. He carried a rifle and wore a pistol at his side. He carefully propped his rifle against a tree and then saw to his animals. He joined Frank by the small campfire.

"If you ain't got no coffee, I got some in my gear."

"I have coffee. Waiting for the water to boil. What's on your mind?"

"Company for the evenin', that's all. If you don't mind."

"Not at all. I'm Frank Morgan."

"Jess McCready. I know who you are."

The water was boiling and Frank dumped in the coffee. "Be ready in a minute, Jess. What are you doing out here in the big lonesome?"

"Gettin' away from people, mostly." The older man sniffed at the heady aroma of coffee brewing and smiled. "I do like my coffee, Mr. Morgan."

"Frank. Just Frank."

"Thankee. Frank it is."

"Getting a little bit crowded for you, Jess?"

"A little bit?" The older man snorted derisively. "The territory is fillin' up. Towns sproutin' up ever'where you look. It's disgustin'."

Frank smiled and dumped in some cold water to settle the grounds. "I have noticed a few more people, for a fact." He got up and dug another cup out of his pack, then rummaged around and found the bacon and flour. "Stay for bacon and pan bread, Jess?"

"Oh, you betcha, I will. I got some taters we can fry up, and a couple cans of peaches in my gear. I'll fetch them, and we'll have us a regular feast."

"Sounds good to me."

Frank watched the man out of the corner of his eye as he got the peaches and potatoes. He made no suspicious moves and sat back down and started peeling the potatoes.

Jess grinned and held up an onion. "We'll slice this up and stick it with the taters. Gives 'em a good flavor."

"Sure does. I forgot to get me some onions when I provisioned up last stop."

"Frank, I ain't tryin' to meddle in your business. Believe me, I ain't. But are you by any chance headin' up toward Barnwell's Crossin'?"

Frank stopped his slicing of bacon to look at the man. "I never heard of that place."

"Well, it's called the Crossin', usually."

"Still never heard of it. What about it?"

"There was a silver strike there 'bout three years ago. Big one. Millions of dollars was taken out of them mines. But it was short-lived. Mines are about played out now."

"So? I've never mined for gold or silver."

"Ned Pine and Vic Vanbergen drift in and out of there from time to time."

That got Frank's attention. "Well, I see. You know about the bad feeling between Ned and Vic and me, eh?"

"Yep. I was there that time you made Vic back down. I know he's swore to kill you. And so has Ned."

"Those are old threats, Jess."

"But still holdin' true, Frank. Point is, one of the big company mines hit another strike. Got tons of damn near pure silver out and melted down. They're waitin' to transport the bars out. And the Pine and Vanbergen gangs are waitin' for them to try it."

"Why don't they hire some people to guard the shipment?"

"Don't nobody want the job. Ned and Vic done passed the word."

"I still don't see what that has to do with me, Jess."

"Well, I'll tell you. The minin company is the Henson Mine Corporation. It's owned by Mrs. Vivian Browning. Old man Henson's daughter."

Four

The next morning, Jess headed south and Frank headed north, toward Barnwell's Crossing. When Frank questioned the older man, Jess told him he had learned about Frank's marriage years back, from a pal of his who had worked for a man in Denver who knew Henson. Henson, Jess said, had not been well-liked. He was ruthless in his business dealings, and few had mourned his passing some years back.

Jess had told him that Barnwell's Crossing was a dying town, although it still had a couple of hundred people eking out a living there. The silver was just about all played out.

Frank didn't know how he would handle matters once he got to the Crossing. He sure didn't know how he would react if he came face-to-face with Vivian. He wondered if Vivian had told her husband about him.

Probably. Frank felt that a marriage built on a lie would not last.

Jess had given him directions on how to get to Barnwell's Crossing. After listening to the twisted route, Frank had commented that it sure seemed to be in a very isolated section of the territory . . . not in an area that he was at all familiar with.

"Wait until you get there," Jess had said. "You'll think you've fallen off the earth into hell."

"That bad, eh?"

"Worser. One way in, one way out"

"A perfect setting for Pine and Vanbergen."

"You betcha."

After a week of hard riding after leaving the company of Jess McCready, Frank reached a narrow, twisty road that led off into the mountains. Miles later, at a crossroads, he saw a crossing sign. A crudely painted arrow pointed off toward the west. The road was literally cut out of the mountains in some spots, and some of the drop-offs were hundreds of feet, straight down.

Frank remembered some long-ago campfire talk about the town as he rode. He had forgotten it until now. The town had been established some thirty-five years back; Frank couldn't recall the original name. The Apaches had raided the tiny town and burned it to the ground. It had been rebuilt, and the Apaches had raided and burned it once more. It had sprung to life again, Frank guessed, when silver had been found.

Frank had no idea where the name Barnwell came from, unless it belonged to the man who hit the latest strike of silver.

After he rode for several miles on the twisty road the town came into view. A dozen or so stores had not been closed and boarded up: a hotel, a large general store, a saloon, a doctor's office, a barbershop/undertaker's, a livery, and several other false-front stores. On all sides of the town the hillsides were dotted with mine entrances and narrow roads, all leading down to the town and the mill. Frank stared at the mill for a moment. It was still operating.

Frank rode into town, looking at the homes on either side as he rode. Some were very nice. Others were no more than shacks, thrown together. There were tents of varying sizes scattered among the houses and shacks.

No one paid the lone rider the slightest bit of attention as he rode slowly up to the livery and swung wearily down from the saddle. He wanted a hot bath, a shave and a haircut, and some clean clothing; his shirt and jeans were stiff with the dust and dirt from days of traveling.

"Take care of my horses," Frank told the young man, handing him some money.

"Yes, sir. Rub them down, curry, and feed?"

"Yes." Frank looked across the street. The livery was the last still operating business at this end of town. The reasonably nice houses across the street looked empty. "Any of those houses over there for rent?"

"All of them. See Mr. Willis at the general store, and he'll fix you up." The young man pointed. "That one is the best. Its got a brand-new privy just a few steps out back, and the man who just left installed a new hand pump right in the kitchen. It's nice."

Frank thanked the young man. "My gear be safe here, boy?"

"For a dollar, yeah. I can lock it up."

Frank smiled and gave him a couple of coins. "See that it is."

"You bet, sir. I'll do it. What's your name?"

Frank hesitated and then said, "Logan."

"Yes, sir, Mr. Logan."

Frank walked up to the general store and made arrangements to rent the house for a time, after making sure the place had a bed and a cookstove. While at the store, Frank bought some new clothes: underwear, socks, britches, shirts, and a suit coat that fit him reasonably well. He took his new purchases and walked over to the barber shop. There, he had a hot bath and a shave and a haircut while his old clothes were being washed and his new clothes pressed to get the wrinkles and creases out. He also had his hat blocked as best the man could do it.

Feeling like a new man, having washed away days of dirt and probably a few fleas, Frank walked the town's business district. The marshal's office was closed and locked, and showed signs of having been that way for a long time.

"Haven't had a marshal for several months now," said a man passing by. "Can't keep one."

"Why?" Frank asked.

"They get shot," the miner said, and walked on.

"That's one way to get rid of the law," Frank muttered, and walked on.

Frank stepped into the small apothecary shop and asked if there was anything new in the way of headache powders.

"You got a headache, mister?"

"No," Frank said with a smile. "But I might get one."

"We don't have anything new here. But I hear there is something being developed over in Germany. Supposed to be some sort of wonder."

"Oh. What's it called?"

"Don't know. Big secret. Being developed by the Bayer Drug Company. It'll be available in a few years, so I'm told.* I got some laudanum, if you want it."

----

*Aspirin went on sale in 1899.

"Maybe later," Frank said. "Thanks."

Frank walked on down the street, stepping carefully along the warped old boardwalk that still showed signs of the times when the town had been destroyed by fire. He came to a café called the Silver Spoon and went inside for a bite.

Frank had the Blue Plate Special: beef and beans and a piece of pie. He lingered at the table for a few minutes, enjoying a pretty good cup of coffee and a cigarette, watching the people in the small town as they went about their business.

"You working a claim here?" the cook asked, coming out to lean on the counter. There was only a handful of people in the café, for it was not yet time for the supper crowd.

"No," Frank replied. "Just passing through."

"You sure look familiar to me. I know you from somewheres?"

"Could be."

Frank was sitting at a corner table, his back to a wall, as was his custom. He had a good view of much of the street and everyone in the café.

A woman came up and whispered in the cook's ear. The cook's mouth dropped open, and his eyes bugged out for a few seconds. He stared at Frank for a couple of heartbeats. "Good God! It really is him!" the cook blurted, then beat it back to the kitchen.

The woman—Frank assumed she was the waitress—looked over at him and smiled. "Remember me, Frank?"

"Can't say as I do. You want to hotten up this coffee, please?"

"Sure." The woman brought the pot over and filled

his cup, then sat down uninvited across the table from Frank.

"I was married to Jim Peters," the woman said softly.

Frank paused in his sugaring and stirring. His eyes narrowed briefly; then he nodded his head. "I recall Jim Peters. He tried to back-shoot me up in Kansas."

"That's him," the woman said with a sigh. "Coward right to the end. I left him a couple of years before that shooting. Moved to Dodge. He followed me. I still wouldn't have anything to do with him. You did me a favor by killing him."

Frank sipped his coffee and waited, sensing the woman was not finished.

"That was five years ago, Frank. But the man who offered up five thousand dollars to see you dead is still alive, and the money is still up for your death—to anyone that's brave enough to go for it."

Frank set his cup down on the table. "I never knew anything about any five thousand dollars on my head."

The woman studied Frank's face for a moment. "You really don't know, do you?"

"No."

"He's a lawyer. Works for the Henson Enterprises."

"They own a mine here in Crossing."

"The biggest mine, Frank. No telling how many millions of dollars of silver was taken out of that mine. One more shipment to go, and the mine closes."

"But they can't ship it because of the Pine and Vanbergen gangs, right?"

"That's right, Frank. And then here you come riding in, getting set to get all tangled up in something that doesn't really concern you."

"It's a long story, Miss . . . ah—"

"It's still Peters. We were never divorced. And please call me Angie."

"All right, Angie it is. And I assure you, it does concern me, greatly."

Angie shook her head. "Because of Mrs. Vivian L. Browning, Frank?"

"You know a lot, Angie. The question is, why?"

"Why do I know? I've owned cafés all over the West. People talk in cafés as much or more as they do in saloons." She smiled. "And I am a real good listener."

"I bet you are." Frank returned the smile as he studied the woman. A good-looking woman. Not beautiful, but very, very attractive. Black hair, blue eyes, and a head-turning figure. Frank bet that when Angie took a stroll men looked . . . and wives got mad.

"How many men do Pine and Vanbergen have?"

"No one knows for sure. Thirty or forty at least. Probably more than that."

"Do any of them ever come into town?"

"Quite often. But never Pine or Vanbergen. The men who come in for supplies are not on any wanted list . . . that anyone knows about." Angie looked out the café window. "Frank, there are two members of the gang riding into town now."

Frank followed her eyes, watching as two rough-dressed men rode slowly up the main street. "I know them," he said. "They're related somehow. Cousins, I think. Both of them are wanted in Arkansas on murder charges. If this town had a marshal he'd be a thousand dollars richer by arresting those two."

Frank smiled and pushed back his chair. "As a matter of fact, I could use a thousand dollars right now."

"Frank . . ." Angie's voice held a warning note. "This isn't your fight. Don't get mixed up in this mess."

"Watch me," Frank replied, slipping the leather thong off the hammer of his pistol.

Five

Frank stepped out of the café and stood for a moment on the elevated boardwalk. It was built several feet off the ground due to a slope. The two riders stopped in front of the Silver Slipper Saloon and dismounted. They stood for a moment, giving the wide street the once-over. Their eyes lingered for a moment on Frank, and one said something to the other. The second man shook his head, and the pair of outlaws turned and walked into the saloon, apparently dismissing him as being someone who presented no danger to them.

Frank slipped the hammer thong free and walked across the street, his boots kicking up dust as he walked, his spurs rattling softly. He stepped up onto the old boardwalk and stood for a moment, thinking about his next move. He had some money on him, but he could also use a thousand dollars.

Frank was not a poor man by any means, but neither did he have money to throw around. He had some savings in a couple of Wells Fargo offices which were available to him by wire. He also had money sewn into a place behind the cantle of his saddle.

Frank was no stranger to bounty hunting. He'd done his share of tracking down wanted men for the prices on their heads. He did it only when he needed the money. The men he tracked down were always wanted for murder, and it nearly always ended in a shoot-out, for most of them would rather die from a bullet than dangle from the end of a rope with a crowd of gawkers looking on. Then Frank had to tote their stinking bodies back as proof, so he could collect the reward. It could be very unpleasant . . . and smelly.

Frank had been a lawman more than once. It was a job he liked. He'd carried a badge in towns in Kansas, Texas, and several other places. But once he'd cleaned up the towns, seems like the "good" people no longer wanted him around. Frank never argued about it—just collected what money was due him, packed up, saddled up, and rode away without looking back. He understood how they felt, and harbored no malice toward any of them. It was human nature, and Frank understood that well. Frank had done a lot of riding away without looking back in his life—most of his life, as a matter of fact.

Frank stepped up to the batwings and pushed them open, stepping inside the saloon.

The two outlaws were at the far end of the long bar, having whiskies. They did not turn around to look at Frank as he walked in. For that time of day the saloon was doing a good business. About half the tables were filled with drinkers and card players. The young man from the livery was seated at a table with several older men. Several heavily painted, rouged, and powdered-up soiled doves were working the crowd—without a lot of luck, Frank observed.

Frank walked to the bar and ordered a beer. He would have preferred coffee, but wanted to blend in for a few minutes without drawing undue attention to himself.

The talk was mostly about the mines playing out, the town slowly dying, and all the silver that was waiting to be shipped out. Frank could catch a few words here and there as he stood at the bar and sipped his beer.

Suddenly the talk died out, and the large room became silent. Frank sighed. He knew what had probably happened: somebody had recognized him.

"Hell," a man said, his voice unnaturally loud in the silence, "his name ain't Logan. I don't give a damn what he told you, Booker. That's Frank Morgan!"

Booker must be the young man from the livery, Frank thought. *Well, it's all out in the open now.*

The two outlaws at the far end of the bar turned to stare. Frank ignored them.

"Well, well," one of the outlaws said. "If it ain't the man all them books was writ about. I thought you had done up and died of old age, Morgan."

"Not hardly," Frank said softly, struggling to remember the man's name. Then it came to him: Davy something-or-another. Jonas was the other fellow's name. They were cousins.

"I know some folks who will be awful happy to hear you're in town, Morgan," Jonas said. He grinned, exposing a row of yellow teeth.

"I imagine so, Jonas. But how are you going to get the news to them?"

"Huh? Why I'll just ride out of here, you dummy!"

"You'll have to go through me to do that. You feel up to that?"

"They's two of us, Morgan," Davy said.

"I can count, Davy," Morgan replied, lifting the mug of beer with his left hand. His right hand stayed close to the butt of his .45. "But I don't care if there's five of you. You still won't get past me."

The men seated at the nearest tables began pushing their chairs back, getting away from what they were sure would turn into gunplay any second.

"You got no call to do this, Morgan," Jonas said. "We ain't done nothin' to you."

"Not personally, Jonas. But you both offend me."

"We both does what?" Davy asked, quickly adding, "What the hell does that mean?"

"You offend a lot of people, Davy. And you both are wanted by the law for murder."

"That's a damn lie!" Jonas said.

"No, it isn't, boys. I've seen the dodgers on you."

Davy's right hand started moving slowly toward the butt of his pistol. Frank's voice stopped him.

"Don't do it, Davy. I'll kill you where you stand."

Davy put his hand back on the bar.

Without taking his eyes off the two outlaws, Frank raised his voice and said, "One of you men go get the keys to the jail. Right now! Move!"

Several men rose from their chairs and left the saloon.

"What do you aim to do with us, Morgan?" Jonas asked.

"Put you in jail."

"Mayhaps we don't want to go to jail," Davy said. "What then?"

"Then I'll kill you," Frank replied, taking several steps closer to the pair of outlaws.

"You're just foolin' yourself, Morgan, if you think you're man enough to take both of us," Jonas told him.

Frank just smiled and moved closer.

"You stop right where you is!" Davy shouted. "We don't want no trouble, Morgan."

"That's up to you, boys," Frank said, stepping closer. "But if you don't want trouble, drop those gunbelts and stand easy."

"You go to hell, Morgan!" Jonas said, and he grabbed for his pistol.

Frank hit him with a fast, hard left, connecting squarely with the outlaw's jaw and dropping him to the floor.

Davy cussed wildly, then panicked and tried to run. Frank tripped him as he attempted to push past, and he hit the floor. Frank jerked the outlaw's pistols from leather and, using one of them, popped Davy on the noggin, dropping him into dreamland for a few minutes.

Jonas was groaning and trying to get to his boots. Using Jonas's gun, Frank laid it against the man's head, and Jonas joined his partner, unconscious.

Frank took Jonas's gun from leather and laid all three pistols on the bar. The batwings were shoved open, and the men who had hustled from the bar reentered, one of them carrying several sets of handcuffs.

"The jail's unlocked, Mr. Morgan," one of the men said, placing the cuffs on the bar. "The keys to the cells are on the desk."

"And the mayor's on the way to talk to you," another citizen added.

"What's he want?" Frank asked, bending down and fitting the cuffs on the outlaws.

"Durned if I know. But he'll be along any minute now."

"Name's Jenkins," another citizen said, looking down at the two murderers.

"He's president of the bank," the third man offered.

"Wonderful," Frank said. "We'll wait until these two yahoos can walk, then escort them to the jail. There's a telegraph office in this town, isn't there?"

"Oh, you bet, Mr. Morgan. If the wire's up, that is."

"It's up," a citizen called from the tables. "I seen Mrs. Browning send some wires this mornin'."

Vivian, Frank thought as something invisible and soft touched his heart. . . .

"And that damn brat son of hers was with her," the citizen added.

"Way he keeps that snooty nose of his stuck up in the air, he's gonna drown if he's caught out in a hard rain," another citizen said.

"Sort of an uppity young man, is he?" Frank asked.

"Uppity?" one of the men blurted. "Conrad thinks he's better than everyone."

"Conrad?" Frank questioned.

"Conrad Browning. Sixteen or seventeen years old, I'd say. Big kid. And doesn't treat his mother with the proper respect, neither."

Another man summed it up. "He's a turd."

Vivian's father must have had a hand in raising the boy, Frank thought.

"You know, Mr. Morgan," a citizen pointed out, "them outlaws is rumored to be part of the Pine and Vanbergen gangs?"

Frank shrugged. "I know both of those no-counts. Why hasn't the law around here done something about them?"

"For one thing, the law can't catch them. For another, nobody is willin' to step up and point the finger at any of them. They always wear masks and dusters when they're robbin' people. The third thing is, law is scarce in these parts. We ain't had a marshal here in this town for months."

"And the pay is real good, Mr. Morgan. I'm Will Moncrief, a member of the town council. The town may not have long to live as a silver boom town. Another two, three months, maybe. But while it does, we pay good money for a badge-toter. Why don't you take the job? You've wore a badge before."

"And I'm on the council, too," another citizen said. "You want the job, Mr. Morgan?"

"Maybe. But it'll take more than the two of you to OK me, won't it?"

"There's four of us on the council, and the mayor," Moncrief said. "And—"

The batwings were pushed open, interrupting Moncrief. A man stepped inside the saloon. "And I'm the mayor of Barnwell's Crossing," the neatly dressed man said. "Mayor Jenkins. What's going on here?"

The crowd hushed up, and all eyes turned toward Frank.

"These two hombres on the floor are wanted men, Mayor," Frank said. "They're both murderers. Rewards out for them. I want to hold them in your jail until they're picked up."

"Sounds all right to me," Jenkins said. "You took them without firing a shot?"

"Yes."

"I know you. Seen your picture. You're Frank Morgan."

"That's right. You have a problem with that, Mayor?"

"Oh, no. Not at all. You're not an outlaw. You've never

been wanted anywhere for anything, as far as I know. And you've worn a badge a number of times, as I recall."

"Yes, I have."

"Want to wear another one?"

Frank paused dramatically, for effect. "If the money's right, yes."

"The money will be right—I can assure you of that."

"Let me lock these two no-counts up, and we'll talk about it, all right?"

Frank jerked the two members of the Pine and Van-bergen gangs to their feet and shoved them toward the batwings. He would send a wire to Arkansas just as soon as he locked the two down. What the state of Arkansas did after that was up to them.

Crossing the street, Davy said, "The boys will come in here and tear this town apart, Morgan. They won't let us be held for no hangin'."

"If Pine or Vanbergen and their gangs come riding into this town hell-for-leather, there's a good chance they'll be buried here."

"You say!" Jonas's words were filled with contempt.

"That's right, Rat Face. I say."

"Rat Face!"

"Yeah. You look like a rat to me."

"You go to hell, Morgan!"

Frank laughed and opened the jail office door. He shoved the pair inside and over to the door that led to the cell block. He carefully removed the cuffs from each and shoved them into a cell.

"I'll find blankets for both of you before night. And I'll build a fire in the stove that'll get the place warm before I leave."

"How about some food, you bastard?" Davy asked. "Or are you gonna let us starve to death?"

"You'll be fed. Probably from the Silver Spoon Café. The cook over there fixes good meals."

Frank took the time to inspect the jail. It was as solid as the rock it was made of—shaped rock two or three feet thick. The bars were thick and solid, set deep in the rocks. Davy and Jonas would not be prying or digging out. That was a dead certainty.

Frank found a rag, sat down at the battered desk in the front office, and wiped the several months' accumulation of dust from the top of the desk. He looked around the big room. Several rifles and shotguns were in a wall rack. He would inspect and clean them later. Frank began opening the desk drawers. He found dozens of dodgers and laid them off to one side. Two pistols and several boxes of .45 ammunition. The jail log book. The last entry was a drunk and disorderly, dated several months back. He found an inkwell, empty, and several pens and pencils. That was it.

The front door opened and the mayor stepped in, followed by a group of men. Frank was introduced to the town council. He shook hands, sat back down, and waited for the mayor to say something.

"We talked it over, Frank," the mayor said. "And we think you're the right man for the job of marshal."

"I'm honored," Frank said.

The mayor smiled and named a monthly salary that was astronomically high for the time and place, and Frank accepted the offer. Frank stood up to be sworn in by the mayor, and a badge was pinned to his shirt.

"If you can find a man to take the job, you're entitled

to one deputy," the mayor told him. "Congratulations, Marshal. Welcome to Barnwell's Crossing."

The mayor and town council trooped out, closing the door behind them, and that was that.

"Marshal Frank Morgan," Frank whispered. "Too bad the town is dying. I might have found a home."

"Hey, Morgan!" Davy shouted from the cell area. "We're hungry. How about some food?"

"I'm cold!" Jonas yelled. "Where's them blankets you promised us?"

Frank ignored them and got up to set and wind the office wall clock. It had stopped at high noon. Frank wondered if that was somehow significant.

Six

Frank went to Willis's General Store and bought a few supplies for his rented house—coffee, sugar, bacon, flour, and the like—then began strolling the town, letting the townsfolk see him and get used to the badge on his chest. The Crossing was larger than Frank had first thought. There was another business street, angling off like the letter L, and many more houses than Frank realized, at the end of the second business street. The other business street had several smaller stores—including a leather shop, a ladies' store right on the corner, a smaller and rougher-looking saloon, and the doctor's office.

Frank smiled and touched his hat when meeting ladies, and he gave the men a howdy-do. Most of the people returned the greeting; a few did not. At the end of the street, Frank saw a sign for Henson Enterprises dangling from a metal frame.

The building was one story, and nice. Even though it was getting late in the day, with shadows already creeping about, darkening this and that, the office was bustling with people bent over ledgers and scurrying about.

Frank forced himself to walk on. He would run into Vivian sooner or later, and he had very mixed feelings about the inevitable meeting.

Frank had just stepped off the boardwalk when a very demanding voice behind him said, "You there, Constable. Come here."

Frank stopped and turned around. A young man, eighteen at the most, was standing in the doorway of the Henson building, wagging his finger at Frank. "Yes, you!" the young man said. "I'm not in the habit of speaking to an empty street."

Frank stared at the young man for a few seconds, stared in disbelief. He was dressed at the very height of fashion . . . if he were in Boston or New York City, that is. In the rough mining town of northern New Mexico territory he looked like a damned idiot.

"Well, come here!" the young man said.

Frank stepped back onto the boardwalk, his hackles already rising at the kid's haughty tone. "Can I help you?" Frank asked.

"I certainly hope so. You're the new constable, aren't you?"

News travels fast in this town, Frank thought. "I'm the marshal, yes."

"Marshal, constable . . . whatever," the almost a man said, waving his hand in a dainty gesture that would damn sure get him in trouble if he did it in the wrong place. "There is a drunken oaf staggering about in our offices, cursing and bellowing, and I want him removed immediately."

"All right," Frank said. "Although I was just passing by, and didn't hear a thing."

"He's calmed down for the moment, but I suspect he'll be lumbering about and swearing again at any moment."

"Oh? Why do you think that?"

"Because he's that sort—that's why. Now will you please do your duty and remove that offensive thug?"

"Lower-class type, huh?"

"Certainly. He's a laborer. They really should learn their place."

"Oh, yes, quite." Frank hid his smile and stepped into the offices. The front office seemed as calm as when Frank had first looked in only a couple of moments ago.

"In the middle office," the snooty kid said. He pointed. "That way."

"Thank you," Frank said, just as acidly as he could. Just then the shouting started.

"By God, you owe me a week's wages, and I ain't leavin' 'til I get it, you pukey-lookin' little weasel!"

"Do you?" Frank asked the young man. There was something about the kid that was vaguely disturbing to Frank. Something . . . well, familiar.

"Do I what?"

"Do you owe him money?"

"Heavens! I don't know. Take that up with the accounting department."

Frank walked to the middle office and shoved open the door, stepping inside. A big man in dirty work clothes stood in the center of the room, shouting at several men seated behind desks. When the door was opened the man paused and looked at Frank, his eyes taking in the star on his shirt.

"I eat two-bit marshals for supper," the miner told Frank.

"This one will give you a bad case of indigestion," Frank responded.

"This company owes me several days' pay," the miner

said. "And I'll either get my money or I'll take this office apart."

Frank looked at one of the bookkeepers. "Do you owe him money?"

"He was off work for two days," the bookkeeper said. "He was paid for four days, not a full six."

"I got hurt in the mine!" the miner shouted. "That ain't my fault."

"Is that right?" Frank asked the bookkeeper.

"That doesn't make any difference, Marshal. He worked four days. He gets paid for the time he was on the job."

Frank looked at the miner. "Did you agree to those terms before you took the job?"

"I knew how it was," the miner said sourly. "But that don't make it right."

"I agree with you. It doesn't make it right. But you agreed to the terms. You got no quarrel. Get on out of here and cool off."

"And if I don't?" the miner challenged him.

"I'll put you out. Then I'll take you to jail. The doctor can see you in your cell."

The miner laughed. "You and how many others are gonna do that, Marshal?"

"Just me," Frank said softly.

"You really think you can do that, huh?"

"Oh, I know I can."

"With or without that pistol?"

"Either way. But if you want to mix it up with me, you'll be liable for any damage to this office."

The miner laughed at that. "How would you collect the money?"

"A day in jail for every dollar of damage. You really

want to spend months behind bars? Then there will be your medical expenses. And they will be many—I assure you of that."

"You got a name, Marshal?"

"Frank Morgan."

The miner paled under his dark stubble of whiskers. He slowly nodded his head. "I reckon I'll leave quietly."

"Good," Frank told him. "You know the way out."

The miner didn't tarry. He nodded in silent agreement, left the office, and walked out of the building without saying another word.

"You certainly calmed that situation down in a hurry, Marshal," one of the bookkeepers said. "Are you really Frank Morgan?"

"Yes." Frank no longer wondered how so many people knew about him. He'd seen several of those penny dreadfuls and dime novels that had been written about him. Most of them were nothing but a pack of lies.

And he had never gotten a nickel for all the words in print about him.

"Have you really killed five hundred white men and a thousand Indians?" another office worker asked, his eyes big around.

Frank smiled. "No. Nowhere even close to either number."

"I do so hate to interfere in this moment of juvenile adoration," said the young man who had first hailed Frank. "But it's time for everybody to get back to work."

Frank had just about had enough of the kid, and came very close to telling him where to stick his lousy attitude. The only thing that saved the moment was the miner who had just left. He came storming back inside, yelling and cussing.

"No man orders me around like I was some damn stray dog!" he hollered. "Gunfighter or no, by God, let's see what you can do with your fists!"

He ran over and took a wild swing at Frank. Frank ducked the blow and stuck out one boot. The miner's forward momentum could not be halted in time, and he tripped over Frank's boot and went butt over elbows to the floor, landing with a tremendous thud. He yelled and cussed and got to his feet.

"You afraid to fight me kick, bite, and gouge, gunfighter?" he threw down the challenge.

"No," Frank said calmly. "But my warning still holds. Whatever this fight breaks, you pay for."

"I boxed in college," the haughty kid said. "And I was quite good. Allow me to settle this dispute. I can do it rather quickly, I assure you."

Frank and the miner looked at the young man, then at each other, and both suddenly burst out laughing, all animosity between them vanishing immediately.

"Are you laughing at me, you lumbering oaf?" the young man asked the miner.

Frank verbally stepped in. "Boy, this isn't a boxing match with rules. Out here there *are* no rules in a fight. It's kick, gouge, bite, and stomp. I don't think you understand."

"I can take care of myself, Marshal. And I don't appreciate your interference."

"Fine," Frank said. "Then by all means, jump right in, boy."

It wasn't a long jump, and the young man didn't have but a few seconds to realize he had made a horrible mistake. He didn't even have time to get his feet planted and his dukes up before the big miner hit him twice, left and right. The young man bounced on the floor and didn't move.

The miner backed up and looked at Frank. "What else could I do?"

"Nothing. He attacked you." Frank knelt down and checked out the young man. He was all right, pulse strong and breathing normal. He was just unconscious, and probably would be for several minutes.

Frank stood up and told the miner, "Get out of here and stay out of sight for a few days. You might want to hunt for another job."

"I've 'bout had enough of this town, anyways," the miner replied. "At least for a while, even though I don't believe anyone's found the mother lode yet. It's out there. I know it is. I can feel it. But you're right. I'm gone for a while. No hard feelin's?"

"None at all."

"See you around, Morgan."

The miner left, and Frank looked at the office workers. They were all smiling, looking down at the young man sprawled unconscious on the floor. Frank was sure the kid was the son of Vivian—had to be. And he wasn't well-liked, for a fact.

Suddenly there was a shout coming from the street, followed by several other very excited shouts. Someone yelled, "They found it! Found it at the Henson mine. It's big. My God, it's big!"

"What's big?" Frank asked.

"They've hit another vein," one of the office workers said. "Has to be it. Our engineers said it was there. Said it was just a matter of time."

"Who is this kid?" Frank asked, pointing to the young

man on the floor, who was just beginning to moan and stir.

"Conrad Browning," a man said. "Mrs. Vivian L. Browning's son."

"I thought so. Snooty, isn't he?"

"That's one way of putting it, for a fact."

"Where is Mrs. Browning?"

"She should be along any moment now. She always comes in just at closing time to check on things."

"Let's get Junior on his feet and walking around," Frank suggested. "If Mrs. Browning sees him like this she'll likely have a fit."

"Doubtful," an office worker said. "Mrs. Browning is well aware of her son's predilection for haughtiness. Conrad has been a sour pickle all his life."

Frank smiled as he heaved Conrad Browning to his feet. "A sour pickle . . . that's a very interesting way of putting it."

"Mrs. Browning's carriage just pulled up at the rear," a man said.

Frank plopped Conrad down in a chair and turned to make his exit—too late. The door to the rear office opened and Vivian stood there.

She recognized Frank instantly and gasped, leaning against the doorjamb for a moment.

Conrad broke the spell by blurting, "Mother, I have been assaulted by a hoodlum. I am injured."

"Oh, horsecrap!" Frank said.

Seven

Frank and Vivian stood for several silent seconds, staring at each other, before Frank took off his hat and said, "Ma'am. Your son is not hurt much. He just grabbed hold of a mite more than he could handle, that's all."

"It was not a fair contest," Conrad objected. "That thug struck me before I was ready."

"What thug?" Vivian asked.

"Mr. Owens," one of the office workers said. "He was in here again about his money."

"The man I spoke with yesterday?" Vivian asked.

"Yes, ma'am."

"Did you give him his money, as I instructed?"

"Ah . . . no, ma'am. We didn't."

"I told them not to pay him," Conrad said. "He was adequately compensated for the work he performed."

Vivian closed her eyes just for the briefest second and shook her head. "Conrad, you go see Dr. Bracken. Your jaw is bruised and swelling a bit."

"Mother—"

"Now!"

"Yes, Mother."

"I'm pretty sure it isn't broken, ma'am," Frank said.

"Just get some horse liniment and rub it on the sore spot. That'll take care of it."

"Horse liniment?" Conrad blurted. "I think not. I'll be back in a few minutes, Mother." He left the middle office, walking gingerly, rubbing his butt, which was probably bruised from impacting with the floor.

Outside, the excited shouting was still going on.

"A new strike, Mrs. Browning?" a bookkeeper asked.

"Yes. A big one. We'll be hiring again. And we need Mr. Owens. If he comes back in, pay him for the days he missed while hurt and put him back to work."

"Yes, ma'am."

"I'll probably see him around town, ma'am," Frank said. "I'll tell him to check back here."

"Thank you, Marshal. Would you please step into my office? I'd like to speak with you for a moment."

"Certainly, ma'am."

In the office, behind a closed door, Vivian grasped Frank's hands and held them for seconds. Finally she pulled back and sat down in one of several chairs in front of her desk. Frank sat down in the chair next to her.

"It's been a long time, Frank."

"Almost eighteen years."

"You know my father is dead?"

"I heard."

"Frank, I want you to know something. I knew within days that my father made up all those charges he was holding over you back in Denver. I also knew that you left to protect me—"

"Water under the bridge, Viv. It's long over."

"No. Let me finish. I did some checking of my own, and found out father had paid those detectives to falsify charges against you. I confronted him with that knowledge. At first he denied it. Then, finally, he admitted what he'd done. He hated you until the day he closed his eyes forever. He threatened to cut me off financially if I didn't do his bidding. I didn't really have much choice in the matter. Or, more truthfully, I thought I didn't have a choice. When I finally realized father was bluffing, it was too late. You were gone without a trace, and I was pregnant."

That shook Frank right down to his spurs. He stared at Vivian for a long moment. "Are you telling me that . . . Conrad is my son?"

"Yes."

Frank had almost blurted out, *You mean to tell me that prissy, arrogant little turd is my son?* But he curbed his tongue at the last possible second. He stared at Viv until he was sure he could speak without betraying his totally mixed emotions. "Did the man you married know this?"

"Yes, Frank. He did. My late husband was a good, decent man. He raised Conrad as if he were his own."

"Does the boy know?"

"No. He doesn't have a clue."

"Your father had a hand in raising him, didn't he?"

"Quite a bit. He spent a lot of time back east with us. Several years before he died, father was with us almost all the time."

"Viv, ah . . . the boy . . ." Frank paused and frowned.

"Doesn't fit in out here? I know. He probably never will. He hates the West. He loves to ride. He's really very good. But he won't ride out here."

"Why not?"

"The way he rides, his manner of dress. He just doesn't fit in."

"He rides one of those dinky English saddles?"

"Yes."

"Don't tell me wears one of those silly-looking riding outfits."

"Yes, he does."

"I bet he got a laugh from a lot of folks the first time he went out in public, bobbing up and down like a cork with a catfish on it."

Vivian smiled despite herself. "I'm afraid he did."

"I can imagine. Wish I'da seen that myself."

Viv's smile faded. "Why'd you come here, Frank? To this town, I mean."

"Oh, I didn't have anything else to do. Besides, I heard you were in trouble up here. Had a lot of silver to ship, and nobody would take it out for you."

"Tons of it, Frank. Tons and tons of it. Worth a fortune. But getting it out of these mountains and to a railroad has proven to be quite a chore."

"How many shipments have been hijacked?"

"Several. You have any ideas on how to get it out?"

"Oh, I imagine I could get some boys in here to take the shipments through. But they don't come cheap."

"I think I can afford them."

Frank smiled. "I 'spect you can, at that."

"Look into that for me, will you?"

"I sure will. I'll send some wires first thing in the morning."

"I would appreciate it. Frank? How are we going to handle this? You and I, I mean."

"How do you want to handle it, Viv?"

"I . . . don't know. I'm not sure."

"Did you love him? Your late husband."

She averted her eyes for a few seconds and said, "No. I liked him. But I didn't love him."

"There has never been another woman for me, Viv."

"Nor another man for me, Frank. Not really."

"And there it stands, I suppose."

"I suppose so, Frank."

"It would cause talk if I came calling, wouldn't it?"

"If you don't come calling, Frank, I'll have some of my miners come looking for you."

Frank smiled at her. Vivian had lost none of her beauty. She had matured—that was all. "I'll drop by tomorrow, Viv. What time will you be in the office?"

"From seven o'clock on. We'll be working long hours for a while, now that the new strike is in."

"I'll try to get by at midmorning. You'll be ready for a coffee break by then."

"I'll be here waiting, Frank. And don't be surprised at how I'm dressed."

"Oh?"

"I've set many a tongue wagging in this town by occasionally dressing in men's britches."

"Really?" Frank smiled as he met Viv's eyes. "Now *that* I'd like to see." Viv was a very shapely lady.

Vivian returned his smile. "Midmorning tomorrow it is, Frank."

Frank picked up his hat from the carpeted floor by his chair and stood up. He looked at Vivian for a moment, then said, "What about Conrad, Viv?"

"Let's just let that alone for the time being. It's much too soon to even be thinking about that."

"As you wish, Viv. Tomorrow, then."

"Yes."

Frank left the office, closing the door behind him, and walked the length of the building to the front, ignoring the curious looks from the office workers. He stood on the boardwalk for a moment, listening to the excited whooping and hollering from the milling crowds on the main street. By this time tomorrow, the town would be filling up again. Closed and boarded-up stores would be reopening, and new merchants coming in. Surely there would be a couple more saloons. And there would be a lot of riffraff making their way to the town.

It was going to be a money-making place for some people for a while and, above all, a place where trouble could erupt in a heartbeat.

Frank had seen it all before, in other boom towns where precious metals were found.

Big strikes were both a blessing and a curse.

Frank's thoughts drifted back to Vivian, and he struggled to get the woman out of his mind. He could dream about her in quiet moments, but now was not the time. He had his rounds to make. And any marshal in any Western town who walked the streets at night and didn't stay alert ran the possibility of abruptly being a dead marshal.

Frank walked up to the corner of the main street and stood for a moment. He rolled a cigarette and smoked it, while leaning up against a hitchrail. It was full dark now, and both saloons were doing a land-office business. Pianos and banjos and guitars were banging and strumming and picking out melodies. Occasionally Frank could hear the sounds of a fiddle sawing away.

Frank walked up to the Silver Spoon Café and ordered supper for the prisoners, then carried the tray over to the jail. While they were eating, he made a pot of coffee and sat at his desk, smoking and drinking coffee. Then he took down the rifles and shotguns from the wall rack and cleaned and oiled them. He took out the pistol he'd found in the desk drawer and cleaned it, then loaded it up full with five rounds. It was a short-barreled .45, called by some a gambler's gun. It was actually a Colt .45 Peacemaker, known as a marshal or sheriff's pistol. Frank tucked it behind his gunbelt, on the left side. It was comfortable there.

A little insurance was sometimes a comfort.

Frank took the tray back to the café, then went over to the general store and bought some blankets for the cell bunks, charging them to the town's account. Back at the jail, he blew out the lamps and locked the front door. He did not build a fire in the jail stove, for the night was not that cool. Besides, if they both caught pneumonia and died that would save the state of Arkansas the expense of sending someone out here to take them back, plus the cost of hanging them.

He walked away, putting the very faint yelling and cussing of the two locked up and very unhappy outlaws behind him. They would settle down as soon as they realized there was no one to hear them.

Frank first stepped into the Silver Slipper Saloon and stood for a moment, giving the crowd a slow once-over. He spotted a couple of gunslicks he'd known from way back, but they were not trouble-hunters, just very bad men to crowd, for there was no back-up in either of them.

Frank walked over and pushed his way to a place at the bar, between the two men. "Jimmy," he greeted the one his left.

"Morgan." Jimmy looked at the star on Frank's chest and smiled. "I won't cause trouble in your town, Frank."

"I know it. I just wanted to say howdy. Hal," he greeted the other one.

"Frank. Back to marshalin' again, huh?"

"Pay's good."

"I don't blame you, then."

"You boys bring your drinks over to that table in the far corner—if you've a mind to, that is. I may have some work for you both."

"If it's marshalin', count me out, Frank," Hal said.

"It isn't."

"OK, then. I'll listen."

At the table, Frank laid out the problem of getting the shipments of silver to the spur rail line just across the border in Colorado.

"I heard Vanbergen and Pine was workin' this area," Jimmy said.

"Big gangs," Hal added.

"That worry you boys?" Frank asked.

"Hell, no," Jimmy said. "You let me get some boys of my choosin' in here, and let us design the wagons, we'll get the silver through. Bet on that."

"All right. Get them in here."

"It'll take a while. They're all scattered to hell and gone," Hal said.

"We've got the time. And Mrs. Browning's got the money."

"Who is this Mrs. Browning, anyways?" Jimmy asked.

"Old Man Henson's daughter. He died some years back, and she's running the business."

"Any truth in the rumor I heard years back, Frank?" Jimmy asked. " 'Bout you and Old Man Henson's daughter?" He held up one hand before Frank could say anything. "I ain't pushin' none, Frank, and I sure ain't lookin' for trouble. But the rumor is still floatin' around."

"Whatever happened was a long time ago, boys. Her

father hated my guts. Now he's gone, and she's in a spot of trouble. That's why I'm here."

"That's good enough for me," Jimmy said. "I won't bring it up no more."

"I'll get some wires sent in the mornin'," Hal said. "Then we'll see what happens."

"Good deal," Frank said, pushing his chair back. "Where are you boys staying?"

"We got us a room at the hotel," Jimmy told him. "We picked us up a bit of money doin' some bounty huntin' work. Brought them two in alive, we did."

Hal grinned. " 'Course they was sorta shot up some, but they was alive."

"What happened to them?" Frank asked.

"They got hanged," Jimmy said.

Frank smiled and stood up. "See you boys tomorrow."

"Take it easy, Frank," Hal told him.

Frank left the saloon, very conscious of a few hostile eyes on him as he walked. He had spotted the young trouble-hunters when he first pushed open the batwings: three of them, sitting together at a table, each of them nursing a beer.

Frank did not want trouble with the young hotheads who were—more than likely—looking for a reputation. All three were in their early twenties—if that old—and full of the piss and vinegar that accompanies youth. But the youthful piss was going to be mixed with real blood if they tangled with Frank Morgan.

Frank walked up and down both sides of the main street of town. All the businesses except the saloons, the two cafés, and the hotel were now closed for the night. Frank turned down the short street that angled off of Main and paused for a moment, standing in the shadows.

The street and the boardwalk were busy, but not overly crowded with foot traffic. Judging from the noise, the Red Horse Saloon was doing a booming business. A rinky-dink piano was playing—only slightly out of tune—and a female voice was singing—also out of tune. Everything appeared normal.

But Frank was edgy. Something was wrong, something he couldn't quite put his finger on, or name. He had learned years back to trust his hunches. Over the long and violent years, that sixth sense had saved his life more times than he cared to remember.

Frank stepped deeper back into the shadows and waited, his pistol loose in leather, his eyes moving, watching the shadows across the street.

There! Right there! Frank spotted furtive movement in the alley between two boarded-up buildings across the street.

Frank squatted down in the darkened door stoop, presenting a smaller, more obscure target. His .45 was in his hand, and he did not remember drawing it. He eared the hammer back.

He watched as the shadows began to move apart and take better shape. Frank could first make out the shapes of three hats, then the upper torsos of the men as they stepped out of the alley and onto the boardwalk. He could not hear anything they were saying, if they were talking at all, because of the music and song from the Red Horse Saloon.

But he did catch a glint of reflection off the barrel of a rifle.

"They ain't huntin' ducks this time of night," Frank muttered.

But are they hunting me? he questioned silently. *And*

if so, why? He was sure they weren't the three young hotheads he'd seen back in the saloon.

He was further intrigued as he watched the men slip back into the alley and disappear from sight. Just then a door opened on Frank's side of the street and bright lamplight flooded the street and illuminated the alley he'd seen the men walk into.

But they were gone without a trace.

"What the hell?" Frank muttered. "What in the hell is going on here?"

The door closed, and Frank sprinted across the wide street and darted into the alley. He paused, listening. He could hear nothing.

He moved on, to the end of the alley, stopping as he heard the low murmur of men's voices.

"I told you that bitch wasn't in her office this late. I told you both that."

What bitch? Frank asked himself.

"So OK, so you was right. We'll grab her tomorrow night."

"Oncest we get the big boss lady, that brat kid of hern will gladly hand over the silver."

"Yes," the third man said. "Shore a lot easier than waitin' for them to ship it."

Viv! They're after Viv.

"So what do we do now?"

Frank stepped out of the alley, his hands wrapped around the butts of both .45's. "You stand right where you are, is what you do."

The three men whirled around and the night exploded in gunfire.

Eight

As soon as the words left Frank's mouth he side-stepped back into the alley. The three men fired where Frank had been, their bullets hitting nothing but the night air.

Frank hunkered down next to the boarded-up building and fired at the shadows to his right. One man screamed and went down to his knees. The other two fired at the muzzle flashes, and Frank was forced to duck back.

He crawled under the building. Built about two feet off the ground, it was damp, smelled bad, and was littered with trash. He slithered along like a big snake until he was only a few feet away from the two men still left standing.

"I think we got him!" one said.

"Think again," Frank said from the darkness under the building, and opened fire.

The two men went down in an awkward sprawl. Frank rolled out from under the building and got to his boots.

"My leg's broke," one of the men moaned. "Oh, crap, it hurts bad."

"I'm hard hit," another one said. "Where is that bastard?"

"Right here," Frank said. "And if either of you reaches for a gun you're dead."

"Sam?" said the one with a broken leg said. "Sam? Answer me, boy."

There was no response. The only person Sam was going to answer to was God.

"He's dead," Frank told the would-be kidnapper just as a crowd began to gather, some of them with lanterns.

"Who the hell are you?" The other outlaw groaned the question.

Frank ignored that. "Get the doctor." He tossed the command to the gathering crowd. "And someone else get the undertaker."

"Who are these men?" someone in the crowd asked. "And what did they do?"

"They're part of the Pine and Vanbergen gangs," Frank told him. "They were attempting to kidnap Mrs. Browning for ransom."

"Good God!" a man said.

"How the hell did you know that?" one of the wounded outlaws asked. "And who the hell are you?"

"Somebody talked," the other outlaw said. "That's how he knew. Man . . . Ned is gonna be pissed about this."

"Who are you?" the outlaw persisted.

"Frank Morgan."

"Oh, hell!"

The town's doctor pushed his way through the growing crowd and ordered lamps brought closer to the wounded men. "That one's dead," he said, pointing. "This one's got a broken leg." He moved over to the third man. "Shot in the side. Bullet went clear through.

Some of you men carry these men over to the jail. Where is Mr. Malone?"

"Right here," a tall thin man said, pushing his way through the crowd. "How many dead?"

"One. The other two will live, I'm sure."

"One is better than none," Malone the undertaker said. "If he's got the money to pay for my services."

"You bastard!" the outlaw with the broken leg said. "You give him a decent sendin' off, damn you."

"He'll get planted," Malone said. "How solemn and dignified will depend on the cash in his pockets."

"Get the living out of here," the doctor told the volunteers.

Frank spotted Willis in the crowd. "I'm going to need some extra blankets from your store."

"I'll get them and bring them over to the jail," the store owner said. "Anything else?"

"Laudanum," the doctor said.

"I'll get it from Jiggs at the apothecary."

Doc Bracken stood up. "I've done all I can do here."

"I'll be at the jail," Frank told him.

When the wounded outlaws were patched up and locked down, Frank went looking for Hal and Jimmy. He found them in their room at the hotel.

"Big doin's, huh, Frank?" Jimmy asked.

"Shaping up that way. How tired are you boys?"

"Not tired at all," Hal replied. "Matter of fact, we had just finished washin' up and was thinkin' of findin' us an all-night poker game."

Frank told them about the planned kidnapping, and that got their attention.

"What can we do to help?" Jimmy asked. "Name it, Frank. We owe you more'un one favor."

"You'll be well paid for this, I assure you. Want to stand guard at the Browning house?"

"Consider it done. Have you talked to Mrs. Browning about it?"

"I'll do that right now. You boys get dressed and we'll walk over together." Frank smiled. "That is, as soon as I find out where she lives."

It was the grandest house in the town, naturally, with a sturdy iron rail fence around it. The gate was locked. A cord was hanging out of a gap in the fence, and Frank pulled on it.

A man dressed in some sort of uniform came out and stood on the porch. "Yes? What do you want?"

"I'm Marshal Frank Morgan. Here to see Mrs. Browning on a matter of great urgency."

"I'll tell her, sir."

"Got to be one of the servants, I guess," Frank said to Hal and Jimmy.

"Must be nice," Hal said.

"I reckon," Frank replied.

"I never been in a house this grand," Jimmy said. "Y'all stomp your boots a couple of times to get any horseshit off of 'em."

Frank smiled. "Good idea. We don't want to leave tracks on the carpet."

Conrad came out onto the porch and down the walkway to the gate, and he took his time doing it. As he was unlocking the chain he said, "I do hope this is important, Marshal. We were in the middle of dinner."

"Hell, it's eight o'clock," Hal said. "Y'all hadn't et yet?"

"Eight o'clock is when most civilized people sit down for dinner," Conrad told him.

"Pardon the hell outta me," Hal muttered.

The interior of the home was elaborately furnished. There were paintings on the walls, and vases and various types and sizes of sculptures on itsy-bitsy tables and pedestals.

"La dee da," Jimmy muttered, looking around him as they were led into the dining room.

"Don't knock nothin' over, you clumsy ox," Hal told his partner. "And don't touch nothin', neither."

"Speak for yourself, you jumpy moose," Jimmy responded.

Vivian rose from the longest table Frank had ever seen outside of a banquet hall. The chandelier over the table must have cost a fortune. Its glow made the room as bright as day. Vivian smiled and said, "Marshal Morgan."

"Evening, ma'am," Frank said, taking off his hat. "We're sorry to disturb you, but something came up I thought you ought to know about. This is Hal and Jimmy."

"How do you do, gentlemen?"

"Fair to middlin', ma'am," Hal said.

"OK, I reckon, ma'am," Jimmy told her. "Shore is a nice place you got here."

"Thank you. Would you gentlemen like something to eat, or some coffee?"

"Coffee would hit the spot," Hal said, ignoring the dirty look he was getting from Frank.

Viv picked up a little silver bell from the table and shook it. A servant appeared almost instantly. "Coffee for the gentlemen, please, Marion."

"Yes, mum."

"Sit down, please," Viv said. "Do make yourselves comfortable." She looked at Frank. "What is the matter of great urgency, Fra"—she caught herself—"Marshal?"

"Yes," Conrad said, entering the dining room and sitting down. "Do enlighten us."

Frank resisted an impulse to slap the snot out of Conrad. "Jimmy and Hal here are going to be your bodyguards for as long as you stay in this area, Vi"—Damn, but it was catching—"Mrs. Browning."

"Oh?" Vivian said, staring at Frank. "Don't you think I should have something to say about that? And what makes you think I want or need bodyguards?"

"Yes. And I must say I quite resent your coming in here and giving orders. I am perfectly capable of looking after my mother," Conrad said haughtily.

"Shut up, boy!" Frank told him. "You couldn't look after a lost calf."

Conrad's mouth dropped open, and he started sputtering and stuttering.

"Close your mouth," Frank said, "before you swallow a fly." He turned his gaze to Vivian. "I just shot three men tonight, Mrs. Browning. Killed one, and wounded the other two. They were planning to kidnap you."

Nine

Terms of employment were quickly agreed to, and Frank stayed with Vivian while Hal and Jimmy returned to the hotel to get their belongings. Vivian wanted them to stay in the house, but both gunhands shook their heads at that suggestion. They would stay in the carriage house, behind the main house.

Conrad, his feathers ruffled by Frank's blunt comments concerning his ability to protect his mother, stalked off to bed, leaving Frank and Vivian alone in the dining room. The candles and lanterns had been trimmed, leaving the room in very subdued light.

"If you had not heard I was having trouble shipping the silver—" Viv said. She shook her head. "I shudder to think what would have happened had you not been here."

"Well, I'm here, Viv. And Hal and Jimmy are good men. They'll get some wires off in the morning to some friends of theirs, and before you know it your silver will be safely shipped. Hal and Jimmy will design the wagons, and they'll be built right here in town. Until Vanbergen and Pine are taken care of, Hal and Jimmy will be your shadows, around the clock."

"And you, Frank?"

"I'll be around—you can bet on that. You couldn't run me off if you tried."

She touched his hand. "I'm counting on that."

"You've got it."

"Hal and Jimmy are certainly . . . well, capable looking. I have to admit that."

"They're both tough as wang leather. They're not the prettiest pair in the world, but they're one hundred percent loyal. They ride for the brand, Viv. And they're quick on the shoot. They'll stick no matter what."

"Why doesn't the law do something about this gang, or gangs, I should say?"

"You were living back east a long time, Viv. You've forgotten this is the West. It's slowly being tamed, but its still pretty much wild and wooly and full of fleas. There isn't much law out here, not in most places. And it'll be some time before there is."

"I suppose so."

"I taught you how to shoot, Viv. Do you still have a pistol?"

"No. My husband didn't like guns."

"Can Conrad use a gun?"

"No. He doesn't like guns either."

Frank shook his head. "Maybe that's for the best. He'd probably brace somebody and get himself shot."

"He's lonely, Frank. That's his biggest problem. And I don't know what to do about that."

"He wouldn't be, Viv, if he wasn't such a stuck-up fussbucket."

Vivian tried her best to look offended at that, but couldn't quite pull it off. She gave up, and with a half-smile said, "He just doesn't fit in out here, Frank. I don't believe he ever will."

"Some folks never do. But those that can't are the folks who want someone else to do for them. You were raised out here, Viv. You know all this."

"The settled East is an ideal place to forget all that," she said gently.

"I guess so. Don't know much about the east. Never wanted to go there." Frank fiddled around with his empty coffee cup for a few seconds.

"More coffee, Frank?"

"No. thanks. This will do me. Soon as the boys get back I've got to start making my night rounds and check on the wounded at the jail."

"What will happen to those men?"

"They'll be held here for trial. I'll be checking dodgers to see if they're wanted anywhere else . . . and I'm sure they are."

"What if their gang tries to break them out?"

"I'll do my best to prevent that."

"You're just one man, Frank. The combined strength of those gangs, so I'm told, can be as high as forty."

Frank shrugged his shoulders. "I can't help that. I was hired to enforce the law and keep the peace. I intend to do just that."

The gate bell rang, and Marion went outside to let Hal and Jimmy in. Frank stood up. "I'll see you tomorrow, Viv. About midmorning, for coffee."

Frank stood outside the Browning estate for a moment and rolled and smoked a cigarette, then strolled up the boardwalk and stepped inside the Red Horse Saloon for a look around. It was noisy and rowdy, but that was a joyful sound. There were a few sour expressions at the sight of Frank, but that was to be expected whenever a badge showed up at a party.

Frank looked around for a moment, then quietly left the saloon without speaking to anyone. He walked the business area of the town, checking the doors of the closed-for-the-night businesses, making sure they were all secure. He stopped in at the Silver Slipper Saloon and stayed only a couple of minutes before walking over to the jail and checking on his prisoners.

The men were all asleep—the wounded ones in a laudanum-induced slumber. Frank quietly stepped back and closed and locked the heavy door leading to the cell area. He checked on his horses at the livery and then walked across the street to his rented house and went to bed. He had missed supper, but it wasn't the first time Frank Morgan had missed a meal—nor, he suspected, would it be the last.

He went to sleep and dreamed about Vivian, frowning whenever Conrad entered his dreams. Frank felt no closeness or affection for the young man. He felt nothing, and his sleep became restless because of that. As the boy's father, shouldn't he feel some sort of blood bond, some sort of paternal sense or awakening . . . something, anything?

Frank awakened with silent alarm bells ringing in his head. Men who constantly live on the razor edge between life and sudden, bloody death develop that silent warning system—or die very young—in their chosen, violent lifestyle.

Frank lay very still and listened. He could hear nothing. Perhaps, he thought, the sounds of silence were what woke him. No. He rejected that immediately. He didn't think that was it. Then . . . what?

Frank slipped from bed and silently pulled on his britches and slipped his bare feet into an old pair of moccasins he'd had for a long time. He picked up his gunbelt and slipped it over one shoulder. Frank had learned years back that it was not wise to run out of ammunition in a gunfight. The loops on his gunbelt always stayed filled. He didn't bother pulling on a shirt.

He padded noiselessly to the rear of the darkened house and looked out through the window. He had not yet purchased material for some seamstress to make him curtains. He could see nothing in the rear of the house.

He walked to the front of the house and looked out. Nothing. He pulled his pocket watch from his jeans and clicked open the lid. A few minutes after four o'clock. This was the time when people were snuggling deeper into bed and blankets for that final hour or so of good, deep sleep. The best time of the night for murder.

He should get going. By the time he heated water and took a shave and a spot bath it would be five o'clock. Then he had to get over to the jail and make coffee and empty and rinse out all the piss pots from the cells. Then he had to see about breakfast for himself and the prisoners. After that, he had to see if there was any reply from Arkansas about the reward money. He would be busy for a couple of hours, at least. And he didn't want to forget to check on any bounty on the men he'd locked up last night and the one he'd killed. Yes, it was shaping up to be a busy morning.

Banker Jenkins, also the mayor, had told him as soon as he received conformation about the reward money he would advance Frank the money and have Arkansas authorities send it directly to his bank. That sounded good to Frank.

Walking about the still dark house, Frank bent down to pick up some kindling wood from the box by the stove. He heard a tin can rattle in the backyard, followed by a soft curse.

OK, Frank thought. *Whoever you are and whatever you want, boys, you just queered the deal.*

Frank slipped to the back door and waited. There was no way he was going to open that door and step into a hail of bullets. He heard the soft creak of boards as someone stepped onto the small back porch. Frank carefully backed up until he could get the large stove between the door and himself. He eased the hammer back on his .45.

Frank heard the sound of someone carefully trying the doorknob. It was loose, and rattled when touched. "Come on in," he whispered.

But the man on the porch obviously had other ideas. He backed away, stepped off the porch, and silently faded into the coolness of night.

"Now just what in the hell was that all about?" Frank questioned.

The night was silent, offering no explanation.

Frank slipped through the house to the front room and peered out. The street was silent and empty.

He decided he'd shave at the jail. He did not want to risk lighting a lamp. He finished dressing. Then, taking a change of clothing with him, he slipped out the back of his house and cautiously made his way up the side of the house to the street. He neither saw nor heard anyone.

"Strange," Frank muttered. "Very odd, indeed."

At the jail, he rolled out the prisoners and collected the bed pots. Then he made coffee and shaved and dressed: black trousers, new red-and-white-checkered shirt buttoned at the collar, string tie, and the suit coat he'd bought at the general store the day before.

"How about some coffee and some breakfast, Morgan?" a prisoner called.

"Coffee is almost ready. I'll get your breakfast in a few minutes."

At the café, which was doing a brisk business, he asked Angie to fix some trays—beef, fried potatoes, cornmeal mush—and to cut up the meat and leave only a spoon for each prisoner to eat with.

"You going to feed them lunch, Frank?" she asked.

"Biscuits and coffee. I'll be back around noon."

The prisoners fed, Frank turned up the lamps, sat down at his desk, and brought his jail journal up to date. Then he wrote several wires to send about his new inmates and the dead man.

Dawn was busting over the mountains when he finished. Frank checked on the prisoners, then walked over to the café for his own breakfast. He took the empty trays with him, after carefully checking to make sure all the spoons were there. With a little work a spoon could be turned into a deadly weapon.

It was past six now, and the café had cleared out some.

Frank ordered breakfast and sat at a corner table, drinking coffee until the food arrived. It was pointless to ask Angie if she'd seen any strangers in town, for the town was full of newcomers. And during the next few weeks, there would be hundreds more streaming in.

Frank made up his mind to hire a deputy, and he asked Angie if she knew anyone.

"Yeah . . . I think I do, matter of fact. He ought to be coming in here anytime now. He's a man in his mid-fifties, I'd guess, and he's steady and dependable. I think he's done some deputy work in other places."

"Sounds good to me. What's his name?"

"Jerry. Jerry Dobbs."

"Introduce me when he comes in."

"I'll do that."

Frank was just finishing his breakfast when Angie called out, " 'Mornin', Jerry. Got someone here who wants a word with you."

"Oh?" the big man said just as Frank was pushing his chair back and rising to his boots.

The men shook hands, and Jerry sat down at the table with Frank. A few minutes later, Frank had hired a deputy.

"I'm no miner," Jerry explained while eating his breakfast. "Didn't take me long to figure that out. I've worked a lot of things in my life, but lawing is something I enjoy the best."

"It can be rewarding," Frank said. "Until the town is cleaned up. Then the people want to get rid of you."

"For a fact," Jerry agreed. "I've sure seen that happen a time or two."

"This town is going to boom for a while," Frank said. "I'm going to ask the mayor if I can hire a second deputy."

"Might not be a bad idea. I've seen these boom towns go from a hundred people to five thousand in a matter of days. The way I heard it, this is a major strike, too."

Frank liked the older man almost instantly. Jerry was big and solid and well-spoken. Frank could sense he had plenty of staying power, and once he made up his mind it would take a steam engine to move him.

Frank told Jerry about the planned kidnapping attempt against Vivian and his hiring of two bodyguards for her.

"Hal and Jimmy are known throughout the West as men who'll brook no nonsense," Jerry replied. "Not killers, but damn sure quick on the shoot. They'll take care of her."

"I'm counting on that. Jerry, there's a small living area in the jail. You want to use it?"

"Yes," the big man said quickly. "Sure beats payin' a weekly rate for a room with two other guys."

"As soon as you finish your breakfast we'll go over to the jail and see what you need for your living quarters, then go to the store for provisions."

"Sounds good to me."

"By that time the mayor should be in his office at the bank, and we'll get you sworn in. Jerry, you haven't asked about salary."

Jerry smiled. "I know what boom towns pay their lawmen. It will be more than adequate, I'm sure."

"I'll see that it is."

Angie came over and refilled their cups. The customers all had been served and were chowing down, and no one was calling for anything, so she pulled out a chair and sat down.

"Gonna be a law dog again, Jerry?" she asked.

"Beats the mines, Angie."

"I'm sure. Unless you're the owner."

"Frank Morgan!" the shout came from out in the street. "Get out here, you bastard!"

"What the hell?" Jerry asked.

Frank got up and looked out the window. A man was standing in the center of the wide street. He was wearing two guns, something that was becoming a rarity in the waning days of the so-called Wild West.

"You know that man, Frank?" Angie asked, standing just to Frank's left.

"I never saw him before, but he sure as hell is no kid."

Jerry joined them at the window. "I've seen him around town a time or two. Don't know his name."

"Morgan!" the man called. "You murderin' pile of coyote puke. Get out here and face me!"

"I don't think that fellow out there likes me very much," Frank said.

Jerry looked at Frank and smiled and shook his head at the marshal's calmness. "I think you'd be safe in sayin' that, Frank."

"Did you see anyone with the guy, Jerry, anyone at all?" Frank asked.

"No. Never. I never even seen him talkin' to anyone."

Both sides of the street had cleared of people within seconds. The few horses at hitch rails that early in the day had been quickly led away by their owners in anticipation of lead flying about.

"You either come out and face me or I'm comin' in there and drag you out, you yellow bastard!" the man in the street hollered. "By God, I mean it, Morgan!"

Frank slipped his pistol in and out of leather a couple of times. He didn't have to check to see if it was loaded. He knew it was. "Time to go see what that fellow wants," Frank said.

"Hell, Frank!" Jerry blurted. "You know what he wants. He wants to kill you!"

"Lots of people have tried that over the years, Jerry. I'm still here."

Angie put a hand on Frank's arm. "He may have some-one in hiding, Frank. Not many men would face you alone. It's something to consider."

Frank cut his eyes to her. "I always take that into con-sideration. That's one of the reasons I'm still alive. But I'm marshal here. I can't afford to let something like this get out of hand. And it could, very easily. If it did, that would be the end of law and order in this town."

Angie opened her mouth to speak. Jerry held up a hand. "He's right, Angie. I know you've got a shotgun behind the counter. Give it to me, and I'll back him up."

"All right." Angie hurried behind the counter and re-turned with a long-barreled scattergun.

"It's got light loads in it," the cook said. "But at close range they'll sure put someone out of commission."

"Good enough," Jerry said, breaking open the scatter-gun to make certain both chambers were loaded up. He looked at Frank. "You ready?"

"You sure you want to do this, Jerry? Hell, man, you're not even on the payroll yet."

Jerry grinned at him. "Maybe you can arrange a bonus for me."

"Count on it."

"Come on out, you chicken-livered has-been!" the loudmouth in the street hollered.

"That does it," Frank muttered through suddenly clenched teeth, and moved toward the café door.

None of the principals noticed the young man across the street stop on the boardwalk and stand and stare. Dressed in his stylish business suit, he was as out of place as a buffalo turd in a crystal punch bowl.

"What in the world is going on?" he asked a clerk who had been sweeping the boardwalk.

"There's gonna be a gunfight."

"Why doesn't someone call the marshal?"

"Someone just did, boy. That fellow standin' in the street."

"My word!" Conrad said.

Ten

Frank stepped out the front door of the café, taking his time while Jerry hustled out the back door and made his way to the street, coming up the narrow space between the two buildings. The small crowd that had gathered on the boardwalks moved left and right, out of the line of fire . . . they hoped.

Frank looked more closely at the man in the street. He did not recognize him, and did not believe he had ever seen him before. "What is your problem?" Frank called.

"You! You're the problem, Morgan."

"Why? I've never seen you before. I don't know you."

"I know you."

"How?"

"You killed my brother up in Wyoming. Jim Morris was his name . . . remember?"

"Can't say as I do. What's your name?"

"Calvin. The man who's gonna kill you, Morgan."

"Doubtful, Calvin, very doubtful."

"You callin' me a liar? Damn you, you back-shootin' lowlife!"

"I never shot anyone named Morris. Not in the back or anywhere else."

"You're a liar, Morgan. You ambushed him one night and shot him in the back!"

"Not me, Calvin. You have the wrong man."

"You're both a liar and a coward, Morgan!"

"You're wrong on both counts. Think about it. Don't throw away your life."

"Enough talk, Morgan. Walk out here and face me if you've got the guts."

That settled the question in Frank's mind about a second, hidden gunman. He and Morris were in full, open view of each other. So the hidden gunman must not, as yet, have a good shot at Frank. He hoped Jerry got the message.

"What's the matter, Calvin?" Frank asked. "Can't you see me? You need glasses, maybe?"

"I can see you, Morgan," Calvin said sullenly. "I don't need no damn glasses."

"Then let's get this over with. I'm tired of trying to save your life."

"Huh?"

"You seem determined to end your life this morning. I've tried to keep you from doing that. But you won't listen. So let's do it, Calvin. Enough talking."

Calvin looked up for just a second. That was all the signal Frank needed. The second gunman was on the roof of the café, or one of the buildings just left or right of the café. As long as Frank stayed under the awning, he was safe from the sniper.

"I knowed you was yeller, Morgan. I'm challengin' you to stop all this talk and step out here and face me."

"Hook and draw, Calvin," Frank said easily. "You can see me."

"You're yeller. I knowed all along you was yeller. Told everybody I'd prove it."

"And you're a loudmouth son of a bitch," Frank said without raising his voice.

That got to Calvin—if Calvin was his real name, which Frank doubted. The man tensed, and Frank could see his expression change.

"You'll pay for that, Morgan."

"How? You going to have your buddy on the roof shoot me in the back?"

"Take him, Lou!" the man on the roof shouted. "Take him now. He's on to us!"

Calvin/Lou hesitated for just a second, then grabbed for his pistol.

Frank shot him twice just as he was clearing leather. He placed his shots fast but carefully, knocking both legs out from under the man. Jerry's shotgun boomed, and there was a scream from the gunman on the roof.

"Oh, my ass!" the sniper squalled. "You done ruint me. Oh, sweet Baby Jesus!" Then he fell off the roof, crashing through the awning and landing on the board-walk.

Frank took a quick look at the man. His ass was a bloody mess. He had taken both barrels of Jerry's scatter-gun in the butt. He had landed on his belly on the boardwalk, and the wind had been knocked out of him.

Jerry stepped out of the alley, a six-gun in his hand. "Watch him," Frank said, pointing to bloody butt. Then he walked over to the fallen man in the dusty and now bloody street.

"Calvin, or Lou?" Frank asked him.

"Lou. You bastard! You done broke both my legs."

"That was my intention."

"Damn your eyes!"

"Lou what?"

"Lou Manning."

"Well, well, now. I have a dodger on you over in the office. Another five hundred dollars in my pocket."

"That's an old dodger. It's a thousand now."

"That's even better. How about your buddy over there?"

"Bud Chase. He ain't got no money on his head. You gonna get me a doctor, Morgan?"

"I see him coming now. Was that you prowling around outside my house this morning?"

"Huh? No." He groaned in pain. "I don't even know where you live, Morgan. I wish to God I'd never seen you. Where is that damn sawbones?"

"Taking a look at your buddy's butt. He's got two loads of bird shot in his ass."

"To hell with Bud's butt! My legs is busted, goddamn it."

Doc Bracken came over and looked at Lou's wounds. "Neither leg seems to be broken, but you won't be doing much walking around for a while."

"I really hurt something fierce, Doc," Lou said. "Can you give me something for the pain?"

"When we get you settled in the jail," the doctor told him.

"How's the other one?" Frank asked.

"Very uncomfortable," Bracken said with a half-smile. "And he's going to be even more so when I start probing around for those shot."

Frank waved at some men. "Get these two over to the jail," he told them. He looked at Doc Bracken. "Unless you want them in your office."

Bracken shook his head. "Jail will be fine. Neither one of them are in any danger of expiring. Your jail is getting full, isn't it, Marshal?"

"I'll have two cells left after these two are booked."

"Ummm," Doc Bracken said. "What happens if your jail gets full?"

"I'll chain prisoners outside to a hitch rail."

Bracken gave him a hard look. "And you would too, wouldn't you, Marshal?"

"Bet on it."

The doctor chuckled. "I think you'll be the best marshal this town has ever had, Morgan. Providing you live long enough, that is."

"Thank you, Doc. How soon can I ask these two a few questions?"

"A couple of hours, maybe. Probably longer. I'm going to sedate them heavily. I'll let you know."

"Good enough."

The wounded were carried off to the jail. Dirt was kicked over the bloody spot in the street, and Frank told Jerry to locate one of the town's carpenters and have him get busy repairing the awning and the broken boardwalk. He sent another man to find the mayor and arrange for a meeting.

Conrad had not moved from his spot in the doorway across the street. Frank spotted the young man and walked over to him.

"How is your mother this morning, Conrad?"

"Very well, Marshal. Thank you for inquiring. That was quite a performance a few moments ago. Do you always twirl your pistol after a shooting?"

Frank did not remember doing that. It was just something he did automatically. "I suppose so, Conrad. It's just a habit."

"Very impressive, I must say. You are quite proficient with that weapon."

"I try."

"Tell me, Marshal, if you will, how long have you known my mother?"

Frank had no idea what Viv had told the young man, but he wasn't going to start off whatever relationship that might develop with a lie. "I knew her years ago, Conrad. For a very brief time."

"Before she married my father?"

"Oh, yes."

"I see. Well, at least you both have your stories straight. Good day, Marshal." Conrad turned away and walked off toward the Henson Enterprises office building without another word.

"Boy damn sure suspects something is not quite right," Frank muttered. He also knew that he and Viv had better get their heads together and plan something out, and do it quickly.

Mayor Jenkins strolled up, all smiles. "Well, Marshal," he said, grabbing Frank's hand and shaking it, "congratulations. I was just informed about the incident. I was told that was quite a dandy bit of shooting on your part. Knocked the pins out from under that gunman quicker than the eye could follow. And I'm told you have a new deputy. Jerry, ah, what's his name? Consider him on the payroll." He named a very generous monthly sum of money—about twice the going rate, even for a boom town. "You can swear him in. That goes with the office, Marshal. I should be hearing something from Arkansas in about a week. I'll let you know immediately. Good day, Marshal. Great job you're doing. Yes, indeed."

"Most happy fellow," Frank muttered. He went in search of Jerry to swear him in.

Frank did not notice Conrad peeping around the corner of a building, watching his every move.

Eleven

Frank swore Jerry in as deputy marshal and pinned a badge on him. Then they went over to Willis's store and bought provisions for the small private room at the jail. Back at the jail, Frank fixed a pot of coffee and the two men talked while Doc Bracken worked on the wounded in the cell block.

"Never married, Jerry?"

"Once. Had two kids. Boy and a girl. She didn't like the West, and she really didn't like me, I guess. We lived in Kansas. Took the kids and left one day when I was out with a posse. I've not seen hide nor hair of any of them since. That was twenty years ago. Don't know where they are. You, Frank?"

"A long time ago. Right after the war. We weren't married long. It didn't work out. I've been drifting ever since."

"Yeah, me too, but I don't blame that on her. I reckon I'm just meant to wander, that's all." Jerry stood up. "I need to go back to the roomin' house and get my things, Frank. OK with you?"

"Sure. Go ahead. I've got an appointment to see Mrs. Browning this morning. I'll probably be gone time you get back."

"That's a nice lady."

"Yes, she certainly is."

Jerry left and Frank looked in on Doc Bracken and his assistant. "You going to be much longer, Doc?"

" 'Bout ten more minutes. I've got all the shot out of this man's butt that I can. The rest will have to stay. Some will work out in time, but he'll be sitting on a lot of bird shot for the rest of his life."

"I'll kill that son of a bitch who shot me," the butt-shot Bud groaned through his laudanum-induced haze.

"Shut up," Doc Bracken told him. "You'll have lots of time to think up threats while you're in prison. You'd better be thankful it wasn't buckshot that hit you, fellow. You wouldn't have any ass left."

"Gimmie some more laudanum," Bud mumbled.

"You've had enough," the doctor told him.

Frank closed the door and sat down at his desk, bringing his jail book up to date. He checked all his dodgers for one on Bud Chase. There were no wanted fliers on Bud, but he did find the dodger on Lou Manning. He wrote out a wire to send to the Texas Rangers.

He glanced at the wall clock. He still had a few minutes before he was due to meet Viv. Frank leaned back in the wooden swivel chair. He did not delude himself about the likelihood of getting back with Viv. His chances were slim to none. Their worlds were too far apart now, and Frank was man enough to admit that. But they would enjoy each other's company while they had the opportunity. After that? Well, only time would tell.

Frank looked in on the prisoners, giving them a cup of coffee if they wanted it, then closed and locked the door to the cell block. He had given Jerry a set of keys to all doors, so he locked the front door upon leaving, too.

He strolled down the boardwalk, taking his time and looking over the town in broad daylight. A few of the stores that had been boarded up were already in the process of being reopened, getting ready to rent. He had been told the bank owned them. Mayor Jenkins didn't miss a bet. If there was a dollar to be made, as banker he was going to get a part of it.

Already new people were coming in from tiny communities that were close by, all of the newcomers riding in. Soon the wagons would be rolling in, and when the permanent structures were all taken—which wouldn't be long—wooden frames would be erected, and canvas fastened in place, forming roofs and sides. There would be a dozen makeshift saloons and eating places and what have you thrown up in less than a week. Hurdygurdy girls would be working around the clock, and so would the gamblers, and both spelled trouble with a capital T.

Frank walked into the Henson Enterprises building and past the workers in the front office just as Viv was coming out of her rear office. She saw him and smiled.

"Be with you in a moment, Marshal," she called.

All very proper and correct, Frank thought. He looked behind him. Hal was standing in the outer office. They nodded at each other. Jimmy would be working the outside, Frank figured. Every hour or so the men would swap up.

Viv motioned for Frank to come into her office. She closed the door and stood facing him. "Are you all right, Frank?"

"I'm fine."

"Conrad told me about the shooting incident."

Frank shrugged that off. "Where is Conrad?"

"At the mine. For his age, he's really a very responsible young man. He knows the business."

"I'm sure he is, Viv, and I'm sure he's a big help. He just doesn't much care for me, that's all."

"Give him time. Maybe things will change."

"Maybe they will. We'll see. Ready to take a stroll through town?"

"That will set some tongues wagging."

"That bother you?"

"Not in the least. I'll get my parasol."

With Hal and Jimmy hanging back a respectable distance, the two began their leisurely walk. *The gunfighter and the lady,* Frank thought with a smile. *That would make a good title for a dime novel.*

Heads did turn as the two walked slowly toward the Silver Spoon Café. Vivian was dressed in the height of Eastern fashion, and was a beautiful woman. Frank wondered why women toted around little parasols and didn't open them. What the hell was the point, anyway? The sky was a dazzling, clear blue, and it sure wasn't raining. Besides, he didn't figure the dainty little thing would even do much to keep off rain.

He concluded that he would never understand women.

"Town's being reborn," Viv remarked.

"Sure is. This your first boom town, Viv?"

"Yes."

"You ain't seen nothing yet. If this strike turns out to be as big as people are saying, there'll be a thousand more people packed in here before it's all over. Maybe more than that. It'll be a great big, sometimes uncontrollable, mess."

"You've worn a badge in other boom towns, Frank?"

"Yes. Several of them."

"I've tried to keep track of you over the years. But it hasn't been easy."

"I'm sure. I did move around a lot."

"And often disappeared for months at a time. Where did you go, and what did you do during those times?"

"Sometimes I worked on a ranch, under a false name."

"For thirty dollars a month?"

"Less than that a few times."

"But somebody would always come along who recognized you." It was not posed as a question.

"Yes. Or someone would get their hands on one of those damn books . . . all of them nothing but a pack of lies."

"I've read all of them."

Frank cut his eyes to the woman walking by his side. "You're joking, of course?"

"No. I swear it's the truth. I had to hide them from my husband, and from Conrad." She smiled. "It was a deliciously naughty feeling."

"Oh? Reading the books about me, or hiding them from your family?"

She poked him in the ribs and giggled. "Did you really take up with a soiled dove named Hannah?"

"Oh, hell, no!" Frank chuckled. A few seconds later he said with a straight face, "Her name was Agnes."

This time Viv laughed aloud and grabbed Frank's arm. "And she died in your arms after stepping in front of a bullet that was meant for you?"

"Slowest bullet since the invention of guns, I reckon. Took that writer a whole page to get that bullet from one side of the room to the other."

"You read them, Frank?"

"Parts of some of them. I haven't read any of the newer ones."

"I have a confession to make."

"Oh?"

"The man who writes those novels was a good friend of my husband. He lives in Boston. He used to come over to the house quite often for croquet and dinner."

"Ummm. Is that so? How difficult was it for you to keep a straight face?"

"Terribly difficult."

Their conversation ground to an abrupt halt when they met a gaggle of ladies coming out of Willis's General Store. The ladies had to stop and chat for a few minutes with Vivian and oohh and aahh about her dress and hat. Frank stepped over to one side, rolled a cigarette, and smoked and waited for the impromptu hen party to end.

When the gossiping was over and the town's ladies had sashayed on their way, Viv smiled at Frank. "Sorry about that, Frank."

"It's all right. What in the world did you ladies talk about?"

"You, mostly."

"Me!"

"Yes. They wanted to know how I knew you."

"And what did you tell them?"

"The same thing I told Conrad: that I knew you years ago when you were a young cowboy."

"Conrad doesn't believe that."

"You know something?"

"What?"

"Those ladies didn't, either."

* * *

By nightfall, thanks in no small part to the ladies who had chatted with Viv earlier, it was the talk of the town that Mrs. Vivian L. Browning, president of Henson Enterprises, was seeing the town marshal, Frank Morgan. Tongues were wagging in every store, home, saloon, and bawdy house.

Frank and Jerry saw that the prisoners were fed and locked down, and then made their early evening rounds.

"There is the first wagon coming in," Jerry said, looking up the street. "They must have traveled all night after hearing the news off the wire."

"There'll be a hundred more by week's end," Frank opined. "We're going to have our hands full."

The sign on the side of the gaily painted wagon read:

DR. RUFUS J. MARTIN
DENTIST EXTRAORDINAIRE

"What the hell does 'extraordinaire' mean?" Jerry asked.

"Extra special, I suppose, would be one definition."

"What's so special about gettin' a tooth pulled?"

Frank did not reply to the question. His gaze was on a man riding slowly up the street. His duster was caked with trail dirt, and his horse plodded wearily. Rider and horse had come a long way.

Jerry had followed Frank's eyes. "You know that man, Frank?"

"Yes. That's Robert Mallory. Big Bob. From out of the Cherokee Strip."

"I've heard of him. He's a bad one, isn't he?"

"One of the worst. He's an ambusher, a paid assassin.

He's probably got three dozen kills on his tally sheet . . . at least. From California to Missouri. Most of them back-shot. He rides into an area, someone is found dead, he rides out."

"He's never been charged?"

"No proof that he ever did anything. Dead men don't talk, Jerry."

"But I've heard he's a gunfighter."

"He is. He's quick as a snake if you push him. Big Bob is no coward. Believe that. But he'd rather shoot his victim in the back."

"Frank, no one just rides into this town by accident. It's too far off the path."

"I know."

"You think he's after Mrs. Browning?"

"Only God, Big Bob, and the man who is paying him knows the answer to that. But you can bet your best pair of boots he's after somebody."

"Let's see where he lands for the night."

"The best hotel in town—that's where. Bob goes first-class all the way. That's his style."

"Frank . . . he might be after you."

"That thought crossed my mind."

"You two know each other?"

"Oh, yes. For many years. And he dislikes me as much as I do him."

"Why?"

"The dislike?"

"Yes."

"We're opposites, Jerry. He'll kill anyone for money. Man, woman, or child. And has. He doesn't have a conscience. There isn't the thinnest thread of morality in the man. And he doesn't just kill with a bullet. He'll throw a victim down a deep well and stand and listen to them scream for help until they drown. He'll set fire to a house and burn his victims to death. He'll do anything for money."

"Sounds like a real charmin' fellow."

"Oh, he is. He swore to someday kill me. Swore that years ago."

"Why?"

"I whipped him in a fight. With my fists. Beat him bloody after he set a little dog on fire one night up in Wyoming. He still carries the scars of that fight on his face, and will until the day he dies. And I hope I'm the person responsible for putting him in the grave."

"Why did he do that? That's sick, Frank. Decent people wouldn't even think of doing that."

"Because he wanted to do it—that's why. He's filth, and that's all he'll ever be. Besides, I like dogs. If I ever settle down somewhere I'll have a dozen mutts."

"I've had a couple of dogs over the years. Last one died about five years ago. You know, it's funny, but I still miss that silly animal."

"I know the feeling. What was his name?"

Jerry laughed. "Digger. That was the durnedest dog for diggin' holes I ever did see." Jerry was silent for a moment. "Let's take a walk over to the hotel and see what name Mallory registers under," he suggested.

"His own. He always does. He's an arrogant bastard. He knows there are no dodgers out on him. He likes to throw his name up into the face of the law."

"If he isn't after you, Frank, I'm surprised he came here, knowing you're the marshal."

"I doubt if he knows."

A man came running up. "Trouble about to happen at the Red Horse, Marshal," he panted. "Gun trouble."

"Go home," Frank told him. "We'll handle it."

"I'm gone. I don't like to be around no shootin'."

The man hurried away.

"Let's go earn our pay, Jerry," Frank said.

No sooner had the words left his mouth than a single shot rang out from the direction of the Red Horse Saloon.

"Damn!" Jerry said, and both men took off running.

Twelve

Frank and Jerry pushed open the batwings and stepped into the smoke-filled saloon. A man lay dead on the dirty floor. Another man stood at the end of the bar, a pistol in his hand. Frank noted that the six-gun was not cocked. The crowded saloon was silent. The piano player had stopped his playing, and the soiled doves were standing or sitting quietly.

"Put the gun down, mister," Frank ordered.

"You go to hell, Morgan!" the man told him.

"All in due time. Right now, though, I'm ordering you to put that gun away."

"And if I don't?" The man threw the taunting challenge at Frank.

"I'll kill you," Frank said softly.

"Your gun's in leather. I'm holdin' mine in my hand, Morgan."

"You'll still die. Don't be a fool, man. If I don't get you, my deputy will."

Jerry had moved about fifteen feet to Frank's right.

"What caused all this?" Frank asked the shooter.

"He called me a liar, and then threatened to kill me. I don't see I had no choice."

"He's right, Marshal," a customer said. "I heard and seen it all."

"All right," Frank replied. "If it was self-defense, you've got no problem. Why are you looking for trouble with me?"

" 'Cause you ain't takin' me to jail—that's why."

"I didn't say anything about jail, partner. I just asked you to put your gun away."

"You ain't gonna try to haul me off to jail?"

"No. Not if you shot in self-defense. Now put that pistol back in your holster."

"All right, Marshal," the shooter said. "I'm doin' it real easy like."

The man slipped his pistol back into leather and leaned against the bar. Frank walked over to the dead man on the floor and knelt down. The dead man's gun was about a foot from the body, and it was cocked. Obviously he had cleared leather when he was hit. Frank stood up. "I need some names."

"My name's Ed Clancy," the shooter said. "I don't know the name of the guy who was trouble-huntin'."

"Anybody know who he is?" Frank asked. "Or where he's from?"

No one did.

"Get the undertaker, Jerry," Frank said.

Jerry left the saloon, and Frank walked over to the shooter by the bar. "Where are you from, Ed?"

"Colorado. I come down here to look for gold."

"Gold?"

"Yeah. But there ain't none. Not enough of it to mess with, anyways."

The bartender was standing close by, and Frank ordered coffee. "You have a permanent address, Ed?"

"Not no more. You want me to stick around town for a day or so?"

"If you don't mind."

"I'll stay. I don't mind. Reason I got my back up was I figured you was gonna kill me, Morgan. I'm sorry I crowded you."

"That's all right, Ed. I understand. Where are you staying in town?"

"Over at Mrs. Miller's boardin'house."

"Thanks, Ed. I'll probably have all the paperwork done by tomorrow, and you can pull out after that if you've a mind to."

"Thanks, Marshal. You're all right in my book."

Undertaker Malone came in, and Frank and Jerry watched as he went through the dead man's pockets looking for some identification. There was nothing.

Malone stood up. "He's got enough money to bury him proper, Marshal. But no name."

Jerry had circulated through the crowd in the Red Horse, asking about the dead man. No one knew who he was.

"Put his gun and everything you found in his pockets on the bar, Malone," Frank said. "I'll hold it at the office."

"How 'bout his boots?" Malone asked. "They're near brand-new."

"Bury him with them on."

"That seems a shame and a waste to me, Marshal."

"Did I ask you?"

"No, sir."

"Then get him out of here. Jerry, start poking around and see if you can locate the man's horse. I'll be here for a few more minutes."

Frank drank his coffee and watched while the body was carried out. The saloon swamper came over and mopped up the blood, then sprinkled sawdust over the wet spot. Frank waited by the bar until Jerry returned.

"Man's horse was over at the livery, Frank. But no saddlebags, and no rifle in the boot."

"All right. We'll check the hotel and the rooming houses tonight. If we don't have any luck there, we'll start checking the empty houses and tents in the morning."

"Might not ever know who he is," Jerry opined.

"That might very well be true, Jerry. The West is full of unmarked graves." *I've put a few men in those unmarked graves myself,* Frank added silently.

Frank and Jerry drew a blank at the hotel and the town's several rooming houses. At the hotel, Frank pointed out a name on the register: Robert Mallory.

"Big as brass," Jerry said.

"He's proud of his name, for sure. Loves to flaunt it in the face of the law. Let's call it a night, Jerry. We'll start checking the town tomorrow."

"OK, Frank. You off to bed?"

"In a little while."

"You want me to make the late rounds? I'll be glad to do it."

"No. I'll do it. Thanks for the help tonight, Jer. See you in the morning."

Frank stepped into the Silver Slipper Saloon and ordered coffee. He stood at the far end of the bar and drank his coffee, looking over the now thinning-out crowd—a quiet crowd, as many had gone home for the night. A few people spoke to Frank; most gave him a wide berth, accompanied by curious glances. By now everyone in town, newcomer and resident alike, knew that one of the last of the west's most famous, or infamous, gunfighters was marshal of the town.

Frank stayed only a few minutes, and when he left he used the back door, stepping out into the broken bottle and trash-littered rear of the saloon. He stood for a moment in the darkness, further deepened by the shadow of the building.

He heard the outhouse door creak open and saw a man step out, buttoning up his pants. Frank knew who it was, for few men were as tall as Big Bob Mallory.

"Big Bob." Frank spoke softly.

Bob paused for just a couple of seconds, then chuckled. "I know that voice for sure. Heard you was law doggin' here at the Crossin', Morgan."

"You heard right, Bob. What are you doing in town?"

"None of your goddamn business, Morgan—that's what!"

"I'm making it my business. Now answer the question."

"Takin' a vacation, Morgan. Just relaxin'."

"A vacation from what? All you do is back-shoot folks a couple of times a year. Doesn't take much effort to pull a trigger. I don't think you've ever had a real job."

"Ain't nobody ever proved I shot anyone, Morgan. And you damn sure can't do it. And I do work now and then, and can prove it. I do odd jobs here and there to get by. Doesn't take much for me to live on."

"Don't screw up in my town, Bob. You do, and I'll be on you quicker than a striking snake."

"You go to hell, Morgan!"

"If you've a mind to, we can sure settle it right now."

"You must be tired of livin', Morgan."

"Anytime you're ready to hook and draw."

"I think I'll let you worry and stew for a while longer."

"What's the matter, Bob? Would it help you reach a decision if I turned my back?"

Frank watched the big man tense at that. For a few seconds, he thought Bob was going to draw on him. Then Mallory slowly began to relax.

"Good try, Morgan," Bob said. "You almost had me goin' then."

"What stopped you?"

Bob refused to reply. He stood there, silent.

"Don't cause trouble in this town, Bob. Any bodies show up without explanation, I'll come looking for you and I'll kill you on sight."

"That's plain enough."

"I hope so."

"Mind if I go back in the saloon?"

"I can't legally stop you, Bob. I could order you out of town. But"—Frank paused—"I won't do that. Not yet."

"Getting soft in your old age?"

"You want to keep running that mouth and find out?"

Bob laughed. "I don't think so. Maybe later."

"Anytime. Face-to-face, that is."

"It'll be face-to-face, Frank. When the time comes. You can count on that." Bob walked up to and then past Frank without another word. He opened the back door of the saloon and stepped inside, closing the door behind him. The night once more enveloped Frank.

"Getting real interesting around town," Frank muttered. "Hope I can stay alive long enough to see how it all turns out."

Thirteen

Frank slept well that night, and no one came prowling around his house in the quiet of darkness. Jerry had fed the prisoners when Frank reached the jail the next morning. There had been no new additions to the cell block during the night. The two men walked over to the Silver Spoon to have breakfast.

"Any luck on finding out the dead man's name?" Angie asked, filling their coffee cups.

"Not yet," Frank told her. "We're going to try again after breakfast. But I have my doubts about whether his rifle and saddlebags will ever show up."

"Another unmarked grave," Angie said before moving off to take the order from another customer. "People ought to carry something on them in the way of identification."

"She's right about that," Jerry said.

"I reckon so," Frank replied, sugaring and stirring his coffee. "There might even be a law about that someday."

The men ate their breakfasts and watched as the town's population grew by about fifty people in just the time it took them to eat their food.

Several men, their clothing caked with the dirt of hard traveling, stepped into the café. "Where's the gold strike?" one of them demanded in a very loud and irritating tone.

"What gold strike?" Angie asked.

"Lady, don't act stupid," the second man said. "We've come a long way for this."

"There is no gold here," Frank said in a low voice. "Silver, not gold."

"Who the hell asked you?" the man asked.

"And this is only a small sample of what we'll be facing in the weeks ahead," Frank whispered to his deputy. He pushed his chair back and stood up, facing the two men. Their eyes flicked briefly to the star on Frank's vest. "I didn't know I needed an invitation to speak."

"That two-bit star don't mean a damn thing to me," the man said.

"Yeah," his partner said. "Why don't you sit down and be quiet, Marshal?"

"I don't believe this," Jerry muttered, pushing back his chair and standing up.

"Back off, mister," a customer said softly. "That's Frank Morgan."

Both miners went suddenly slack-jawed and bug-eyed for a few seconds. They exchanged worried glances. The bigger of the pair finally found his voice. "Sorry, Marshal Morgan. I guess we stepped over the line there."

"It's all right, boys," Frank told them. "Sit down and have breakfast and cool down. The food is mighty good here."

"Good idea," the other miner said. "I am hungry as a hog. Ain't neither one of us et since noon yesterday. After we eat maybe we can talk about the big gold strike."

"Right," Frank agreed with a small smile. "The big gold strike."

Frank and Jerry sat back down and Jerry said, "We're really in for it if there is a rumor about gold here."

"More than you know, Jerry. I've been in towns after several hundred very angry miners learned strike rumors were false. It can get real ugly in a hurry."

"Look there," Jerry said, cutting his eyes to the street.

Frank turned his head and watched as a dozen or so riders, all leading packhorses, rode up the street. "Yeah. And it'll get worse."

"At least they're not gunslicks."

"Not yet," Frank said. "They'll come next, with the gamblers and con artists and whores."

"There's Mrs. Browning's son," Jerry said. "Sneakin' around like he's been doin' for the past couple of days. He seems to be watchin' you, Frank."

Frank looked and shook his head. "I thought I saw him yesterday snooping around. That boy is mighty curious about me."

"Any reason he should be?"

Before Frank could reply, the front door burst open. "It's the Pine gang!"

"Here?" Frank blurted, jumping to his feet.

"Well . . ." the man said. "One of them."

Frank relaxed just a bit. "One?"

"Who is it, Pete?" Angie called.

"That Moran kid. I seen him personal on the edge of town. He's just sittin' his horse and watchin'."

"Kid Moran?" Frank asked. "Here? Part of the Pine gang?"

"Yes," Jerry replied. "But that can't be proved. At

least no one's ever come forward. I don't think there are any dodgers out on him, either."

"Why would he be comin' here?" a customer asked.

"Probably to try me," Frank said. "He's a gun-happy kid looking for a reputation.

"He's already killed five or six men," said the man who brought the news. "Maybe more than that."

"About that," Frank said. "Wounded two, three more. He's quick, so I hear."

Jerry had a worried look. "Moran is young and fast, Frank."

Frank smiled. "And I'm older and faster, Jerry. But maybe it won't come to that. We'll see." Frank picked up his coffee cup and drank the last couple of swallows. Then he walked toward the door.

"Frank," Angie called.

With his hand on the door handle, Frank cut his eyes.

"It might be a setup," she said.

"Might be, Angie. We'll see." Frank stepped out onto the boardwalk and looked up the street. The Kid was still there, sitting his horse. Frank leaned against a support post and waited for The Kid to make the first move.

Kid Moran spotted Frank and began slowly walking his horse toward the center of town. Frank got his first good look ever at the young man with the growing reputation as a gunslick. The Kid was of average height and weight, and slender built.

As he drew closer, Frank could see only two things that were menacing about the Kid: the matched pair of .45's belted around his waist. But Frank also knew that some people saw beauty in a scorpion, a tarantula, and a rattlesnake.

Kid Moran was as deadly as they came, Frank knew, and he also knew that The Kid was lightning fast.

The Kid rode slowly toward Frank. He touched the brim of his hat and smiled at Frank as he rode past. *More of a smirk than a smile,* Frank thought as he held up one hand in return greeting.

He watched The Kid rein in at a hitch rail in front of the general store and dismount. Frank decided against going over to the store . . . at least not yet. He did not want to provoke an incident with The Kid. Frank felt The Kid would try him, sooner or later.

Conrad Browning walked up the boardwalk—Frank had not seen him cross the street—and stopped just to Frank's left. "Good morning, Marshal Morgan."

" 'Mornin', Conrad. You always up this early?"

"Always. I like to open up the office for mother. It's just one less thing for her to do."

"Very conscientious of you."

"Marshal? May I ask you a question?"

"Sure."

"Sometimes you speak as if you had attended some sort of institution of higher education. Other times you don't. Why is that?"

Frank smiled at the question. "I read a lot, Conrad. I always have at least one book in my saddlebags. I enjoy reading."

"I see. Who is your favorite author?"

"I don't think I have one. A while back I did get interested in this fellow Plato. He has quite a way with words."

"Plato? Ummm. Yes, I would say he does."

Hal was across the street, watching Conrad as he chatted with Frank. Jimmy and Hal were taking no chances, figuring that if the outlaws couldn't grab Vivian they might try for her son. Kid Moran was still inside the general store.

"Who is that young man that just rode into town, Marshal?" Conrad asked. "He seems to be of great interest to you."

"A gunfighter. Calls himself Kid Moran."

"Kid Moran. How quaint. He appears to be still in his teen years."

"He's about twenty, I reckon. But he's shot more than his share of men."

"Why?"

"I beg your pardon?"

"Why did he shoot them?"

"I reckon 'cause he wanted to. Trying to build himself a reputation as a gunslick."

"And that's important out here?"

Again, Frank smiled. "Well . . . it is to some folks, Conrad."

"Sort of like being the town bully, I suppose."

Frank nodded his head. "Yes, that's a very good way of putting it."

"But with a gun."

"Yes."

"Thank you, Marshal. I believe I have a better understanding of the West now. You have a nice day." Conrad strolled off toward the Henson office building.

"Strange boy," Frank muttered. "In many ways, more man than boy."

Kid Moran stepped out of the general store and leaned against an awning post. He stared across the street at the marshal.

What's wrong with this? Frank thought. *Something isn't right, but I can't put my finger on it.*

Frank looked up at the buildings across the street. Was there a second shooter on a rooftop somewhere? If so, was it in front or behind him? Had Pine or Vanbergen sent The Kid in to check out things, or had The Kid come in on his own?

The café door opened behind him and Jerry asked, "What's wrong, Frank?"

"I don't know, Jer. Maybe nothing. But I've got a funny feeling about this thing."

"Far as I know, this is the first time The Kid has ever ridden in alone."

"He's been here before, then?"

"Oh, yes. But always with others. Never alone. Frank, I'm goin' to check out the back of this block of buildings. Don't step out until you get a signal from me."

Jerry exited the rear of the café while Frank waited on one side of the street, Kid Moran on the other. They leaned up against awning support posts and stared at each other without speaking.

As it nearly always happened in Western towns, the word spread fast and the main street became quiet—no riders, no one walking up and down.

"All clear back here, Frank," Jerry called from one end of the block.

"OK, Jer." *Then why am I so edgy?* Frank wondered. He wasn't afraid of facing The Kid in a hook and draw situation. Frank made it a point to find out all he could about any and all gunfighters, new and old, and he knew that while The Kid was very quick, it was reported that he almost always missed his first shot. Frank used to be the same, until he began spending countless hours practicing, making that all important first shot count.

Fear wasn't a factor in the edgy feelings Frank was experiencing.

Frank again searched the rooftops of the buildings across the street. As near as he could tell, there was no one up there. The Kid was still leaning against the post across the street, staring at him.

"All right," Frank muttered. "I've had enough of this. I'm going to find out what The Kid has on his mind." He stepped off the boardwalk and into the street.

The Kid immediately straightened up and began walking away from Frank, heading down toward the end of the street. Frank signaled Jerry to stay put, and began following The Kid. He didn't have a clue as to what was going on . . . but something was up—he was sure of that.

The Kid suddenly stopped and looked around him—everywhere but directly at Frank. Then he crossed the street.

Frank was now standing in the middle of the wide street.

"Well, damn!" Frank muttered.

Half a dozen fast shots blasted the early morning air, as near as Frank could tell, coming from near the Henson office building. He looked for The Kid, but Kid Moran had vanished.

"Goddamn it!" Frank yelled, and took off running.

Fourteen

Frank rounded the corner of the street just as Hal went down in another roar of lead from several pistols in the hands of men standing in the middle of the street in front of the Hanson building. The bodyguard spun around, hit several times, and slumped to the dirt. Frank shot the first assailant in the belly, and his second round knocked another down in the street, hip-shot. Frank was forced into an alley as several hidden gunmen opened fire, the bullets howling and whining all around him. The third gunman in the street jumped behind a water trough.

Frank had caught a quick glimpse of Conrad, huddled in the doorway of the office building. He didn't appear to be hurt, but was apparently too frightened to seek better cover. And Vivian was due to arrive at any moment.

Frank snapped a quick shot at a man standing in a doorway.

The bullet knocked a chunk out of the door stoop and sent splinters into the face of the man. Screaming in pain as one of the splinters stuck in his eye, he stepped out of cover. Frank put a bullet in the man's guts that doubled him over and sent him stumbling into the street. He collapsed facedown in the dirt, and was still.

Jerry's six-gun cracked from the other end of the

street, and a man yelled and went off the roof of a boarded-up building. Anyone within earshot could hear his neck break as he landed in the street.

"This ain't workin!' " a man yelled. "Let's get the hell outta here!"

Frank and Jerry waited.

"How?" another man shouted.

"Through the pass, you nitwit. Just like we planned."

There was silence for a moment, then the sounds of several horses being ridden hard away from the edge of town.

Jerry ran over to Frank, a pistol in each hand. "Are you hit?"

"No. Let's see about the boy. I don't think he's hurt, just scared."

Conrad was getting to his feet when Frank and Jerry reached him. His face was ashen, and he was trembling. "They were going to kidnap me!" Conrad blurted. "Hal pushed me down and stood in front of me." He looked at Hal, bloody and dead in the street. "Oh, my God!" Conrad started to move toward Hal, and Frank stopped him.

"Easy, boy. No point. He's beyond help."

"You don't know that!"

"I know, boy. I saw him take three rounds in the center of the chest."

"I liked that man. I didn't at first. But I really liked him. He saved my life."

"That's what he was paid to do, Conrad."

Jerry was checking the dead and the wounded. "Two alive, Frank. And one of them ain't gonna be for long."

"Good," Frank said. "The jail's gettin' full." A crowd had gathered at the mouth of the street. "One of you get

Doc Bracken, and someone get the undertaker. Move!" He turned to Jerry. "See if you can locate Kid Moran. Don't brace him, Jerry. Just see if he's still in town."

"Will do."

Jimmy and Vivian walked up. Vivian was pale with shock, and Jimmy was killing mad. Frank could read it in his eyes. "Settle down, Jimmy. They're gone."

"Me and Hal been pards for a long time, Frank. I ain't likely to forget this."

"See to Mrs. Browning and her son, Jimmy. Right now!"

Jimmy nodded and took Viv's arm, leading her and Conrad toward the front door of the office building and inside. Jimmy stood in the doorway for a moment, looking at the bloody and still body of his longtime friend. The man touched the brim of his hat and walked inside the office, closing the door.

Someone called that the doctor had been roused out of bed and was on his way, as was Malone, the undertaker. Frank walked over to the hip-shot gunman. On closer investigation, he recognized him—Max Stoddard. He was wanted in several states for murder, and there was a hefty reward for his arrest.

"You boys are making me a princely sum of money, Max," Frank told him.

"Go to hell."

Frank smiled at the outlaw. "Time I get through here, I'll be near'bouts able to retire, I reckon."

"Damn you, Morgan!"

Frank reached down and slipped an over-and-under derringer from the outlaw's left boot. "Were you thinking I'd forget about this little banger, Max?"

"I was hopin' you would, you bastard."

Frank laughed at him and took a long-bladed knife from the sheath on the outlaw's belt. "Not likely, Max. I haven't stayed alive this long by being careless."

"Ned or Vic will get you, Morgan. You can count on that. They'll get you 'fore this is over."

Doc Bracken was pushing his way through the still gathering crowd, cussing loudly and ordering the gawkers to get the hell out of his way.

Mayor Jenkins was right behind him, both of them looking as though they had jumped into their clothes, unshaven and with disheveled hair.

"What the hell happened here?" the mayor shouted.

"These men tried to kidnap Conrad Browning," Frank said, pointing to the dead and wounded in the street. "Conrad's bodyguard was killed. Conrad and his mother are safe. They're in the office building."

"My God!" the mayor whispered. "Do you know any of these men, Marshal?"

"I know this one. Max Stoddard. He's wanted for murder in several states. All these men are part of the Pine and Vanbergen gangs."

The mayor patted Frank on the arm. "Wonderful job, Marshal. Superb."

The mayor wandered off into the crowd. Frank turned his attention to the doctor, watching him work on Stoddard for a moment.

"No permanent damage to the hip," the doctor said. "But he won't be walking for a while. Some of you men take this hombre over to the jail." Doc Bracken moved quickly to the other outlaws. "Dead," he said twice. "And this one won't last long. Some of you men make him as comfortable as possible. He'll be dead in a few minutes."

"Damn you to hell, Morgan!" the dying man said.

"Here, now," Dr. Bracken admonished him. "That's enough of that. You best be making your peace with God."

The outlaw started cussing, spewing out a stream of profanity. Suddenly he began coughing. He arched his back, and then relaxed in a pool of blood.

"He's gone," Doc Bracken said.

Frank went with the undertaker and searched the pockets of the dead men. They had no identification on them. He took their guns and walked back to his office. Jerry met him on the way.

"Kid Moran left town when the shooting started, Frank. Half a dozen people seen him hightail out."

"All right. What about this pass the outlaws took to get out of town?"

"Cuts through the mountains yonder," he said, pointing. "But it's tricky, so I'm told. If you don't know the way, you can get all balled up and lost and find yourself dead-ended on a narrow trail."

"Can't go forward, and you have hell going back?"

"That's it."

"You been up there?"

"No. It's outlaw controlled on the other side of the mountains. Only the outlaws use it, and they don't use it very often. Men and horses have been killed up there, slippin' off the narrow trails."

"So the Pine and Vanbergen gangs are headquartered just over those mountains?"

"Yep. Not five miles away, as the crow flies. But they might as well be plumb over on the other side of the moon, if you know what I mean."

Frank nodded his head. "I do. Let's go see about our new prisoner and then arrange a nice service for Hal."

* * *

A week after the shoot-out in which Hal was killed, a deputy U.S. Marshal came by train to Denver and then took the spur line down to the border and went from there by horse to the Crossing and picked up two of the prisoners Frank was holding. Frank's bank account grew substantially. Ten days later another deputy U.S. Marshal rode in and promptly rode out with Max Stoddard. Stoddard had a two thousand dollar reward on his head, and so did one of the other dead men. Frank gave half of the money to Jerry, and Jerry almost pumped his arm off shaking his hand. Frank's bank account grew even larger.

Hal was buried in the local cemetery, and Vivian bought a nice headstone for the grave.

Barnwell's Crossing grew by almost a thousand people in two weeks. Most were coming in because of the rumor of a major gold strike, and nothing anyone could say would make them believe it wasn't true.

"Hell with them," Frank told Jerry one morning. "When they get tired of digging they'll leave."

The county now had a judge—Judge Walter Pelmutter—assigned to the town of Barnwell's Crossing, and that made the disposition of those arrested a lot faster. The marshal's office got two dollars out of every fine, and Frank split that with Jerry. Judge Pelmutter was a no-nonsense, by-the-book judge who cut no slack to anyone for anything. The jail was usually full at night and emptied out the next morning after court.

Frank checked the wall clock. Eleven o'clock. He had a lunch date with Vivian at her home in half an hour. After lunch they were to go riding and spend the afternoon together. Conrad would stay at the office. That would give Jimmy a much needed break. Frank had offered to hire another bodyguard, but Jimmy had said he didn't want to work with anyone else . . . not for a time yet. Jimmy was gradually working his way out of his grieving over the loss of his saddle pard, but he still had a ways to go.

"I'm going to go home and wash up some and change clothes, Jerry," he told his deputy. "Then I'm over to Mrs. Browning's house. We're going riding down in the valley."

"Don't worry about a thing, Frank. I'll take care of any problem that comes up. Y'all have fun and relax."

At his house, Frank cleaned up and changed clothes— black trousers with a narrow pinstripe, black shirt. He tied a red bandanna around his neck and slipped on a black leather vest. He combed his hair, put on his hat, and then inspected himself as best he could in the small mirror he'd bought at Willis's General Store.

"Well, Morgan," he said to the reflection. "You're not going to win any contests for handsome. But you don't look too bad, considering what you have to work with."

He buckled on his gunbelt and stepped out onto the small front porch. The day was sunny and cloudless, the sky a bright blue—a perfect day for a ride in the country.

He rode the short distance over to the Browning estate and talked with Jimmy for a few minutes before walking up to the porch and being admitted inside the grandest house in town.

"You look lovely," he told Vivian, as she opened the door and he stepped inside.

"You wouldn't be the least prejudiced, now would you, Frank?" she teased.

"Not at all. You're as pretty as the day we married."

"And you tell great big fibs, Frank Morgan. But do continue."

Lunch was fried chicken, hot biscuits, mashed potatoes and gravy.

"Did you fix this?" Frank asked.

"I certainly did. The servants have the afternoon off. And I told Jimmy to take off as soon as you got here."

"How about Conrad? Is Jimmy going to the office?"

"No. I asked a couple of my miners to look after him. Those men have been with me for years. Completely trustworthy."

After lunch, over coffee, Vivian said, "I'm going to change clothes, Frank. I hate to ride sidesaddle. Will you be shocked if I change into britches?"

Frank chuckled. "I knew you pretty well a long time ago, Viv. I think I'm past being shocked by anything you do."

She laughed. "Don't say I didn't warn you."

She came out of her bedroom a few moments later wearing very tight-fitting men's jeans and a checkered shirt, open at the collar. Frank almost choked on his coffee.

"Damn, Viv!" he managed to say, wiping a few drops of coffee off his chin.

"You don't approve, Frank?" she teased him.

" 'Approve' is . . . not quite the word."

"Come on, let's get saddled up and get out of this town. I want to forget business for a few hours. I want us to be totally alone, and I want a good, hard ride."

Frank grinned and held his tongue on that one . . . but oh, what he was thinking.

She caught his smile. "You're naughty, Frank. But don't ever change."

"I'm too old to change now, Viv."

Five minutes later they were riding out of town, heading toward the mountains and a pretty little valley that lay in the shadows of the mountains.

Shortly after they rode out of town, four men dressed as miners rode out. They occasionally exchanged smiles as they followed the man and woman. They had traveled a long way to get to the town of Barnwell's Crossing. The five thousand dollars that Vivian's father had placed on Frank's head had grown to ten thousand over the years, and the man who was overseeing the bounty, controlling the purse strings—a close friend of the family, and legal advisor—had added ten thousand, plus a substantial bonus if the body was never found, for Vivian's death.

The four paid assassins had been lounging around town for a week, staying out of sight and waiting for the right moment . . . and this was it.

Fifteen

The valley was an oasis of green surrounded by mountains, a profusion of multicolored wildflowers and gently waving grass in the slight breeze.

"It's lovely," Viv whispered as she and Frank rested their horses at the mouth of the valley. "So beautiful and peaceful."

Frank had carefully checked out the valley a few days before, and had been pleasantly surprised to find it as Vivian had just described it.

"A little creek is over yonder," Frank said, pointing. "Water is cold and pure. I had me a drink, and it numbed my tongue."

"Large enough to take a swim?"

"No. If you're brave you could stick your feet in it, though. But you won't leave them in there for long."

"I'm thirsty."

"We'll ride down and have us a drink. Fill up our canteens."

"I wrapped up some of that chicken and biscuits."

"I'm so full now I'm about to pop, Viv. But it'll sure taste good later."

Vivian took off her fashionable boots and put her feet into the fast-running creek . . . for about one second. She squealed, jerked her feet out, and immediately began rubbing them. "I have never felt water that cold!"

"I warned you," Frank said with a laugh. He quickly cut his eyes to the horses, grazing a dozen yards away. Their heads had come up quickly, and their ears were pricked. The nostrils on Frank's horse were flared, and his eyes were shining with a wary and suspicious light.

"Stay put, Viv. Don't move unless I tell you to. And if I tell you, get behind that clump of trees just to your left."

"What's wrong, Frank?"

"I don't know. But the animals suddenly got jumpy, and I've learned to trust that big horse of mine. He's saved my skin more than once."

Frank stayed low and worked his way over to his horse. Using the big animal for cover, he pulled his rifle from the boot. He opened a pocket on the side of the boot and took out a box of cartridges and slipped them in his back pocket. Frank preferred the rifle because it packed a hefty wallop and had excellent range.

He crawled back to Viv and motioned for her to head for the copse of trees he had pointed out.

In the trees, she looked at him through worried eyes. "What's wrong?" she repeated.

"I saw one man, maybe two, slipping around on that ridge over there, dead in front of us."

"The Pine and Vanbergen gangs?"

"Maybe. Can't be certain about that. But folks who slip around are damn sure up to no good."

"Conrad!"

"The boy will be all right, Viv. You've got people looking out for him, and Jimmy will be in town and so will Jerry. Don't worry about him."

She peered through the weeds at the ridge. Frank felt her stiffen beside him.

"What's wrong, Viv?"

"I just caught a glint of sunlight off of something."

"Where?"

"Way over there to our right. In those rocks."

"That's three men, then. At least."

"We're in deep trouble, aren't we, Frank?"

"Well . . . yes and no. To get behind us would take some doing. It's all nearly wide-open meadow for a long way on either side of us. An Indian could do it easy enough, but these men aren't Indians."

"The question is, who are they and what do they want?"

"You or me, or both of us."

"So we do . . . what?"

"We wait, Viv. By now they're sure to have figured out we've spotted them, so surprise is out of their plans. That's a plus for us."

"The minus is, there appears to be only one easy way into this valley, right?"

Frank smiled. "You're still a very observant lady, Viv. That's right. There are a half-dozen ways in and out, but only one easy way. And they've got it covered."

"And the other ways out?"

"Rough. Danger of slides, mostly. To the north is completely out of the question. That pass is controlled by the Pine and Vanbergen gangs."

"Well . . . we've got a little food and plenty of water. I can stand to lose a few pounds, anyway."

Frank chuckled. "You're a tough lady, Viv. Tougher now than when we first met."

"Dealing with male heads of business and shifty attorneys can do that."

"I 'spect you're had plenty of practice in dealing with both over the years."

"Running a conglomerate of businesses is tough enough for a man in a man's world, Frank. Being a woman makes it doubly tough."

The ugly whine of a bullet put an end to that conversation. The bullet slammed into a tree behind the pinned-down pair and tore off bits of bark.

"They sure know where we are," Viv remarked, raising her head and looking around.

Frank did not immediately reply. He was trying to determine where the bullet came from. He had a hunch it came from the location of a fourth man. Finally he said, "I'm sure there is another man behind the rocks near the entrance to the valley, Viv. That makes four."

"The odds just keep getting worse."

"We've got good cover, and that bullet came nowhere near us. I'm not even sure they know exactly where we are. They may be just trying to flush us."

"You will excuse me if I don't share your cool calmness, Frank. I'm a stranger to this type of thing."

"You're doing fine, Viv." He looked up at the sun. About five hours of good daylight left, maybe less. "If it comes to it, Viv, I can lead us out on foot come dark."

Another bullet bowled into the copse of trees; then several more came whistling in.

"I think they have guessed we're here, Frank."

"I think so, too. This was the logical place for us to take cover."

"I counted four rifles."

"Yes. Me, too. I think someone is using a .32-.20. Another sounds like a .45-.70."

"Is all that supposed to mean something to me?"

Frank grinned at her. "When we get out of this pickle I'll give you a short course in firearms."

"I can hardly wait. In more ways than one."

The gunmen on the ridges and in the rocks opened up again, and Frank and Vivian could do nothing but huddle behind cover, all thoughts of talk obliterated by the roar of gunfire and the bowling of bullets.

"This is beginning to make me mad," Frank muttered, when the gunfire ceased for a moment.

Viv looked at him in astonishment. She had taken off her hat, and her hair was just slightly disheveled. Her white blouse was spotted with dirt and grass stains. "You're just now getting angry, Frank?"

"Yeah. That bunch of yellow bastards over yonder is really annoying me now." He lifted his rifle to his shoulder and mentally figured the range before squeezing off a round. The bullet was low, and he compensated for that before squeezing off another round. This time the bullet must have come very close to the hidden sniper, for both Frank and Viv heard a yelp of surprise.

"You hit?" the question was shouted.

"Naw. But that bastard can shoot."

"We all knowed that startin' off, Dick."

There was more conversation between the snipers, but it was so faint neither Frank nor Viv could make out the words.

Then one of the gunman called, "This ain't workin' out, boys."

Frank and Viv looked at each other.

"What do you mean, Rob? We got 'em cold. All we got to do is wait 'em out."

Another voice was added. "Yeah? But for how long?"

"That's right. Them two got good cover, and we can't get to them to finish this."

"He's right 'bout that," another called. "It's all open twixt us and them."

"Goddamn it, no names, you idgits!"

"Rob and Dick," Frank muttered. "Remember those names, Viv."

"Forever," she whispered.

There was more murmuring of words between the gunmen, again so faint that Frank and Viv could not make them out. They waited in the copse of trees.

Then there was nothing but the gentle sighing of the wind in the valley.

"Have they gone?" Viv asked.

"I don't know, honey. It may be they just want us to think they've left."

"If wishes were horses . . ."

"What?"

"Nothing," she said with a quiet laugh. "Don't pay any attention to me. I'm babbling."

"Babble on, Viv. I'm going to ease out of here and take a look around."

She cut her suddenly alarm-filled eyes to him. "Frank—"

"Relax. I'm not going far, and I'm not going to take any chances. Take it easy, Viv. I'll be right back."

"Promise?"

"Cross my heart. You want to spit in my palm?"

She smiled, and Frank could see her tension ease. "Get out of here, you nut!"

Frank eased out of the trees and wormed his way down to and over the creekbank, then worked his way about fifty feet. Easing up behind a clump of weeds, he gave the rocks and ridges a good visual going-over. He could see nothing moving. His and Viv's horses had moved a few yards during the gunfire, but were now grazing calmly. His big horse was showing no signs of being alarmed.

Frank crawled over the creekbank and quickly got to his feet, running toward the horses. No shots boomed; no lead came howling in his direction. He led the horses over to the thick copse of trees.

"They're gone, Viv. Come on. I want to take a look at the ridges. I might find some sign that I can use."

Frank found some brass from a .45-.70 and a .32-.20. But it was the butt-plate markings that caught and held his attention. They were strange looking.

"What's wrong, Frank?"

"The butt-plate on this rifle. It's the strangest I've ever seen." He snapped his fingers. "I know what it is. It loads through the buttstock. I'll bet you it's a bolt-action military rifle."

"Are they rare?"

"They are out here."

"And if you find a man in town who has one, it's a good bet he's one of the men who attacked us."

"That's it, Viv. Come on, let's ride. It's a good hour back to town, and we're not taking the same trail back we used to get up here."

Frank found the tracks of the men who'd attempted to kill them, and there were four horses. The hoofprints led straight toward town. Frank cut across country, and they made it back to town in just over an hour. Frank saw Vivian back to her house, where Jimmy was waiting on the porch.

Jimmy saw the dirt and grass stains on their clothing and asked, "Trouble?"

Frank explained what had happened.

"I bet that's one of those Winchester-Hotchkiss so-called sportin' rifles," Jimmy said. "The army has some of them, but they're rare out here."

"Keep your eyes open for one, Jimmy."

"Will do."

At the office, while Jerry made a fresh pot of coffee, Frank told him about the events of that afternoon.

"You think they were after you, or Mrs. Browning?"

"Both of us. And I'm getting damn tired of it."

"You think the Pine and Vanbergen gangs were behind the ambush?"

Frank shook his head. "I don't think so, Jerry. They want to kill me, yes. But I believe there are other forces working to kill both of us."

"Who?"

Frank explained in as much depth as he knew about Viv's father and his deathbed desire to have him killed. He ended with, "This attorney, whoever he is—and Viv told me they have a couple of dozen lawyers, maybe more than that, working for the company—has some big ideas, I think. Ideas about controlling the various companies that make up Henson Enterprises. But first he has to get rid of Vivian."

Jerry slowly nodded his head. "OK. But that still leaves the son."

"Who is not twenty-one years old, and legally can't do a damn thing until he is."

"Ah! Yeah. I'm getting the picture now. But you have no proof of any of this."

"Not a bit. It's all speculation on my part."

"Now what?"

"Now I go visit the saloons."

"You saw the men who attacked you?"

"No. But if I show up where they are, one of them just might get nervous and tip his hand."

"Could be. Want me to tag along?"

"No. You do the early business check on Main Street. I'll handle this on my own."

The men sat for few minutes and drank a cup of coffee. The cell block area of the jail, for the first time in a long time, was empty. Frank finished his coffee and stood up to leave. He really wanted another cup, for Jerry made good coffee, but he had a lot to do, and wanted to get started. He could get a cup in one of the saloons, although theirs usually tasted the way horse liniment smelled.

Frank tucked the short-barreled Peacemaker behind his gunbelt, butt forward on the left side, and headed out. He had filed the sight off so it would not hang up.

His first stop was the Silver Slipper Saloon, and it was doing a booming business. He walked through the saloon, speaking to a few of the patrons. Just as he was about to exit out the back way, he cut his eyes over to a far corner table and stopped. Big Bob Mallory was sitting alone. Frank had thought Big Bob was long gone, for he hadn't seen him in a couple of weeks. He walked over and sat down.

"Make yourself right at home, Frank," Bob said. "Un-invited, of course."

"I was hoping I'd seen the last of you, Bob. I thought you'd long rattled your hocks."

"I been here and there, Frank. But I'll leave when I get damn good and ready."

"Where were you this afternoon?"

"Not that it's any of your damn business, but I was playin' poker over at the Red Horse. All afternoon. Check it out if you don't believe me."

"I will, and I don't believe you. I wouldn't believe anything you had to say even if you were standing in the presence of God."

Bob smiled at him. "You're not goin' to rile me into pullin' on you, Morgan. Not now. I'm tellin' you the truth 'bout this afternoon. You'll see."

"Don't screw up in this town, Bob. I told you before, and I'm telling you now."

Bob smiled at him and said nothing.

Frank pushed back his chair and walked away, exiting out the back door, stepping into the night. The darkness was broken only by the faint glint off the many empty whiskey bottles that littered the ground. Someone was grunting in the outhouse. Frank ignored that and walked on, up the alley and back onto the street. He stood in the mouth of the alley for a moment.

The foot traffic was heavy early in the evening—mostly miners wandering from saloon to saloon to whorehouses located at each end of the town, just past the town limits.

Frank stepped out of the alley and starting walking toward the Red Horse Saloon. He hadn't gone a dozen steps before three shots blasted the air. The sound was muffled, and Frank knew they came from inside a building. Probably the Red Horse.

"Here we go again," Frank said, and began running toward trouble.

Sixteen

Just before Frank reached the entrance to the Red Horse, a man staggered out, both hands holding his bloody stomach and chest. The gut-shot man fell off the boardwalk and collapsed on the edge of the street. He groaned in pain and tried to rise. He didn't make it. He died in the dirt before Frank could reach him.

Frank pushed open the batwings and stepped inside the smoky saloon. The large crowd had shifted away from the bar, leaving the long bar empty except for two young men dressed in black, each of them wearing two guns, tied down low. Frank guessed them to be in their early twenties. The music and singing had ceased; the crowd was still, and gunsmoke hung in the air.

Trouble-hunting punks, Frank thought. *Well, they've damn sure found it.* "What happened here?" Frank said.

"Who the hell are you?" one of the young men at the bar asked belligerently.

"The marshal. I asked what happened here."

"He got lippy and wanted trouble—that's what. We gave it to him."

"Both of you shot him?"

"Yeah," the other young trouble-hunter mouthed off. "What's it to you, Mr. Marshal?"

"Sonny boy," Frank said, taking a step closer to the young men. "I've had all the mouth I'm going to take from either of you. I'll ask the questions, you answer them. Without the smart-aleck comments. Is that understood?" Frank took a couple more steps toward the pair.

One of the punks feigned great consternation at Frank's words. "Oh, my! I'm so frightened I might pee my drawers! How about you, Tom?"

"Oh, me, too, Carl. The old-timer's words is really makin' me nervous."

Both of them burst out laughing.

Frank took several more steps while the pair were braying like jackasses and hit Tom in the mouth with a hard straight left. The punch knocked the punk clean off his boots and deposited him on the floor. Frank turned slightly and drove his right fist into the belly of Carl. Carl doubled over and went to his knees, gagging and gasping for air.

Frank reached down and snatched the guns from Tom, tossed them on a table, and then pulled Carl's Colts from leather. He backed up, holding the punk's twin pistols, and waited.

Tom got to his feet first, his mouth leaking blood. He stood glaring at Frank.

Someone out on the boardwalk yelled, "Here comes Doc Bracken. Get out of the way, boys!"

"Get your friend on his feet," Frank told Tom. "Right now!"

Jerry pushed open the batwings just as both young trouble-hunters were on their feet, wobbly, but standing.

"Jerry," Frank said, "I want you to get statements from as many people as you can about this shooting. Get their names and tell them to drop by the office in the morning to verify and sign all they told you."

"Will do, Frank."

Frank motioned with the muzzle of the right hand Colt. "Move, boys. To the jail."

"It was self-defense, Marshal!" Tom shouted. "He was pesterin' us."

"That's a damn lie," a miner said. "It was them pesterin' the other guy. They goaded him into a gunfight. They pushed him real hard. I wouldn't have tooken near'bouts as much as that other feller took. He had to fight. That's all there was to it. They didn't give him no choice in the matter. None a'tall."

"Yore a damn liar, mister!" Carl said.

"Give your story to my deputy," Frank told the man. "Move, boys."

"You're makin' a mistake, Marshal," Carl said.

"Shut up and move. If the other man started the trouble, you can ride on out of town."

"You son of a bitch!" Tom cussed him.

"Be careful, boy," Frank warned him. "Don't let your ass overload your mouth."

Frank locked the pair up and once more hit the streets. He began prowling the new makeshift saloons, and there were about a dozen wood-frame, canvas-covered drinking spots that had sprung up since the new silver strike and the rumors of a major gold strike.

The evening's rambling and searching produced nothing. Frank could flush no one. He finally gave it up and returned to the office.

"Any luck?" Jerry asked.

Frank shook his head as he poured a mug of coffee.

"If I did see them, they're mighty cool ole boys. I didn't produce a single bobble."

"I might be on to something," Jerry said.

"Oh?"

"Four men are living in a tent 'bout a mile out of town." He pointed. "That way. Off the west trail. They staked a claim, but no one's ever seen them working it. Man I've known since I come to town told me about them. Only reason he brought it up was 'cause those ole boys is real unfriendly and surly like. I questioned him some and he said he seen them ride out 'bout noon today, and they didn't come back 'til late afternoon."

"You did good, Jerry. I appreciate it."

"There's more, Frank. My friend thinks one of them has a bolt-action rifle."

Frank sugared his coffee and stirred slowly. "I'll pay those ole boys a visit first thing in the morning. Going up there tonight would be asking for trouble."

"It sure would. And it isn't against the law to be unfriendly."

Frank smiled. "You're right about that. If it was, half the population would be in jail. How did the questioning over at the saloon go?"

"Those two trouble-hunters we have locked up started the whole thing. They needled the other fellow into pulling on them. But the other guy did go for his gun first."

"They'll probably get off, then. If the other man drew first, I don't know of any major charges that could be brought against them. But we'll keep them locked up until the judge opens court. It's his mess to deal with now. You go on to bed, Jerry. I'll make the late rounds."

"You sure, Frank?"

"Oh, yeah. I'm not a bit sleepy. Besides, I need to go

over to the funeral parlor and find out what I can about the dead man."

"See you in the morning, Frank."

" 'Night, Jer."

At the funeral parlor, Frank walked into the back, where the nude body of the stranger was on a narrow table. Malone was preparing the body for burial. He looked up as Frank strolled in.

"No identification on the body, Marshal. He had fifty dollars on him. Ten dollars in silver, the rest in paper. His gun and clothes and boots are over there on that table next to the wall."

Frank carefully inspected the dead man's boots and gunbelt for a hidden compartment. There was nothing. "I'll pick up the gun and rig in the morning," he told Malone.

Malone nodded his head and kept working on the body. Frank got out of there. He walked over to the livery and asked if anyone fitting the dead man's description had stabled his horse there. The night holster nodded and pointed to a roan in a stall.

"Where's his saddle?" Frank asked.

"In the storeroom. Saddle, saddlebags, and rifle in a boot. Far right-hand corner."

Frank carried the gear over to the office and stored it as quietly as possible. Jerry was already in his room, in his bunk, snoring softly. Frank would go through the saddlebags in the morning, but he didn't expect to find anything in the way of identification. The grave would be just another unmarked one in a lonely cemetery. The West had hundreds of such graves. On the Oregon Trail, it was said, there were two or three graves for every mile of the pioneer trek westward. And still the people came, hundreds every week.

During his wanderings, Frank had seen countless abandoned cabins. He wondered how many of the pioneers gave up after a few years and went back east.

Frank locked up the office and walked over to the Silver Spoon for a cup of coffee. The place was dark, closed for the night.

He began making his rounds of the town, checking the doors of the businesses. He cut up the alley and came out near the Henson Enterprises building. He watched the building for a moment, then decided to check the windows and back door. The back door was unlocked.

Frank pushed open the door and saw the faint glint of lamplight under the door, coming from Viv's office. Frank put his hand on the butt of his .45.

Then the door opened and Conrad stepped out. He spotted the dark shape of Frank and gasped, "Oh, my God! Don't shoot!"

"Damn, boy!" Frank said. "What the hell are you doing down here this time of night?"

"Marshal! Well . . . doing some necessary paperwork. Mother neglected her duties this afternoon. Mr. Dutton arrived on the stage, and was displeased to find mother gone gallivanting about the countryside while so much work was left unattended here."

"Who the hell is Dutton?"

"Our company's chief attorney."

"What business is it of his what the president of Henson Enterprises does in her spare time?"

"I resent your tone, Marshal!"

"I don't give a damn what you resent. Your mother and I are old friends—a friendship that goes back twenty years. If she wants to go riding and relax, that's her business—none of yours, and sure as hell none of this Dutton fellow's. Is that clear, Conrad?"

"If you're such 'old friends' "—the young man put a lot of grease on the last two words—"why weren't you mentioned before now? Personally, I think you're both lying. What is it between you and my mother?"

"We're friends, Conrad. That's all. As to why I wasn't mentioned years back . . . well, after all, I do have something of an unsavory reputation. In very polite Boston society it just wouldn't do for your mother to let people know she was friends with a gunfighter."

"Ummm. Well, you're certainly correct in that assumption. But I still believe there is more . . . a lot more than either of you are willing to tell. And I shall make it my business to find out what."

Frank sighed. The young man was a bulldog, no doubt about that. "Whatever, Conrad. Where is this Dutton fellow?"

"At the hotel."

"Come on, then. Close up the place, and I'll escort you back to the house."

"I am perfectly capable of seeing myself home, Marshal. I bought a pistol today."

"God help us all," Frank muttered.

"Beg pardon?"

"Nothing, Conrad. What kind of pistol?"

"This one," Conrad said, reaching inside his coat and hauling out a Colt Frontier double action revolver. He pointed it at Frank, and Frank quickly pushed the muzzle to one side and took the weapon.

Frank stepped closer to the light streaming through the

open door and inspected the pistol. A .45 caliber. "It's a good pistol, Conrad. Have you fired it yet?"

"Certainly not! And I won't until it becomes necessary."

"I . . . see. I think."

"It shouldn't take too much expertise to discharge a firearm. One simply points the weapon and pulls the trigger. Right, Marshal?"

"Well—"

"So, considering this recent firearm purchase, I shall now take over the job of protecting my mother. Your services will no longer he needed. If indeed they ever were."

"Is that right?"

"Quite."

Resisting a sudden urge to jerk a knot in the boy/man's butt, Frank instead suggested, "Why don't we let your mother decide that, Conrad?"

Conrad didn't speak for several seconds, then said, "Oh, very well, Marshal. Let's don't go into a lot of folderol about it. Now I have to lock up."

"I'll wait for you, Conrad."

"Very well, Marshal. If you insist."

Conrad blew out the lamps and locked the back door. Frank waited in the darkness of the alley. When Conrad turned around, Frank said, "Have you eaten, Conrad?"

The young man looked at Frank. Even in the darkness, Frank could feel Conrad's attitude toward him soften. "Why . . . yes, I have, Marshal. Thank you for asking."

"Come on, let's get out of this alley."

On the boardwalk, in a bit more light from newly installed oil lamps along the way, Conrad asked, "Who were those gunmen after today, Marshal—you or my mother?"

"I don't know, Conrad." Frank knew very little about the why of those wanting Vivian out of the way, but he did know he was not going to discuss it with Conrad. "Has your mother said anything?"

"Precious little. But something is weighing very heavily on her mind. I can tell that. She just won't open up to me. Perhaps she will, in time."

"I'm sure she will, Conrad."

They walked on for a half block. Frank felt his guts tighten as four men stepped out of an alley. They were lurching along as if they were drunk, but Frank wasn't sure about that. When they began singing, he was certain they were pretending.

"When I tell you to run, Conrad, don't argue with me, and for God's sake don't hesitate. Just run like the devil is after you. You understand?"

"Yes, sir. Those men up ahead of us?"

"Yes. I'm sure they're going to pull something. Get ready to flee, boy."

The four men began to separate until they were covering the whole boardwalk. Frank watched as one slipped his hand under his coat. When the hand came out holding a six-gun, Frank yelled, "Go, boy! Run!"

Conrad took off, and Frank snaked his Colt out of leather.

Seventeen

Frank dived behind a water trough just as the quartet opened up, the lead howling all around him. He managed to snap off one shot that brought a yelp of either pain or surprise from one of the gunmen—Frank wasn't sure.

He was astonished when a shout came from the other side of the street.

"You filthy savages!" Conrad shouted. "Damn you all!" Conrad pointed his big .45 in the general direction of the quartet of gunmen and pulled the trigger.

The bullet tore the hat off one of the men and sent him hollering and scampering toward a doorway stoop. "Jesus Christ!" he yelled.

Conrad's next shot knocked the heel off the left boot of another man and sent him sprawling to the boardwalk. "My leg!" he squalled. "I'm hit, boys!"

Jiggs from the apothecary shop came running up the boardwalk, a shotgun in his hand, just as Conrad cut loose again. The bullet whined past Jiggs's head, missing his nose by about one hot half-inch.

"Oh, shit!" the druggist whooped, and he ran for cover into the general store . . . right through the closed and locked front door. Jiggs took the door with him.

"Get that punk!" one of the gunmen yelled.

Conrad pointed the .45 at the man and triggered off another round. The bullet took off a tiny piece of the man's ear, and the assassin started jumping up and down and yelling as if he'd been touched by a hot branding iron.

"I been shot in the head, boys. Oh, Lordy, I'm done for, I reckon."

Conrad shot him again . . . or at least came really close to upsetting the man's evenings for a long time to come. The bullet nicked the gunman's inner thigh, just a microscopic distance from his privates.

"Oh, good God!" the man screamed. "I'm ruint, boys. He's done shot me in the balls!"

Conrad took that time to reload with a handful of cartridges from his coat pocket. Fully loaded, he continued his cussing, shouting insults, and firing.

"You rotten scalawags!" Conrad shouted. "You all belong in a cage!"

"Then put me in a cage!" yelled the man who thought he'd been shot in the doo-das. He had both hands between his legs, holding onto his precious parts . . . what he thought was left of them. "Anywhere! Just get me away from that crazy kid!"

"I'm out of here," the fourth outlaw yelled, running up to where Frank lay crouched behind the water trough.

Frank reached out and grabbed the man's ankle, spilling him onto the boardwalk. The man lost his pistol on his way down, banged his head on the rough boards, and knocked himself goofy for a few minutes.

Conrad fired again, the bullet knocking splinters into the face of the man who had lost his hat to Conrad's first shot.

"I yield!" the man yelled, throwing down his gun. "Don't shoot no more."

"Somebody get me a doctor!" shouted the man who thought he'd been violently deprived of his private parts as hot blood from the nick on his thigh ran down his leg. "Oh, Lord, get me to a doctor."

Frank then realized what the man was so upset about. He got to his boots, trying to keep from laughing at the total absurdity of the entire situation, and told the man who thought he'd been shot in the gonads, "What do you think the doctor's going to do, you idiot, sew the sac back on?"

That really set the man off. He began wailing and moaning so loudly windows began glowing with lamp-light all up and down the street.

Jiggs stepped out of the general store, his shotgun covering the two would-be kidnappers who were still standing and in one piece, more or less.

Jerry had showed up, and had talked Conrad into giving him his .45.

"Thank God," Frank muttered.

Doc Bracken walked up. "What in the world is going on here?"

"Here's the doctor, buddy," Frank told the man who was making moaning sounds . . . sort of like a train whistle with a stopped up valve.

"What's his problem?" Doc asked.

"He thinks his balls have been shot off."

"Good Lord! That's terrible. Did you find them?" Doc asked, after glancing at the man's bloody britches. He began looking all around him on the boardwalk and in the street. "I might be able to sew them back on. I've heard it's been done."

"Do they stay on?" Frank asked.

"Not so far. Infection always sets in, and they rot off."

That really got the mournful sounds cranked up from the would-be kidnapper who thought his cojones were gone forever, and they echoed around the mountain town. A dozen bound dogs joined in from various parts of town, and the noise brought a hundred or more people out of their homes and into the street.

Conrad was shaking so much Jerry had to lead him over to the boardwalk on the opposite side of the street and sit him down.

"Oh, my God," Conrad said, his voice shrill from nervousness. "Did I actually hit somebody?"

"Way I heard it, you shot a feller's balls off," Jerry told him.

"Oh, my goodness!"

"That's him over yonder, wailing like a train whistle. I reckon he's a mite upset." Jerry paused and reflected for a few seconds. "I damn sure would be."

"I think I'm going to be sick," Conrad said, putting a hand to his mouth.

"Let me back up 'fore you puke," Jerry said quickly. "These are brand-new boots."

Frank was trying to get matters settled. He finally told everyone not involved in the shooting to go home, clear the street. After a few minutes the crowd began to disperse.

Jerry told Conrad, "You stay right here, boy, until you get to feelin' better. Then you come over and join Frank and me, OK?"

"Yes, sir," Conrad said softly. "This has really been a very traumatic experience for me."

"I'm sure it has, son. Whatever that me—

put, now." Jerry walked across the street and handed Conrad's gun to Frank, butt first. "The boy's cannon. That's a hell of a pistol, Frank. Where'd he get it?"

"Bought it today, I think." Frank smiled. "But he sure played hell with these four rounders, didn't he?"

Jerry grinned. "That he did. How about the feller with no balls? He quieted down in a hurry."

"He's all right. The bullet nicked the fleshy part of his inner thigh just below his privates. Gave him a good scare, that's all."

The four assailants were sitting on the edge of the boardwalk, guarded by several citizens with shotguns, while Doctor Bracken worked on them. All their wounds were very minor ones.

"These the four men who attacked you and Mrs. Browning?" Jerry asked.

"No. These men heard about the attempted kidnapping, and tried a copycat attempt. All they'll be getting out of it is long prison terms."

Jerry took off his hat and wiped his brow with a bandanna. "Stupid of them."

"Very stupid. I'll send some wires in the morning, see if they're wanted anywhere else. But I doubt they are. How's Conrad?"

"Scared, shook up some, and sort of sick to his stomach. But he's not hurt. I told him to stay put over yonder until he got to feeling better."

"Here come Vivian and Jimmy," Frank said, looking up the street as a carriage came rolling up. A servant was handling the reins, and Jimmy was sitting in the back with Viv.

Frank walked out into the street as the carriage came to a halt. "Conrad's all right, Vivian. He didn't get a scratch. Actually, he was the hero this night. Did you know he had bought a pistol?"

"Conrad?" she asked, her eyes wide. "My God. Conrad bought a pistol?"

"Yes."

"I had no idea. He's never fired a gun in his life."

"Well, he sure busted a few caps this night. He didn't kill anyone, but he sure gave a couple of those ole boys sitting over there on the boardwalk a fright." Frank couldn't help himself. He started laughing, and Vivian gave him a strange look.

"You find this funny, Frank?"

"Well, Viv," Frank said, wiping his eyes. "Yes, I do. If you'll pardon the crudeness, one of those attackers thought Conrad shot his . . . well, privates off."

Jimmy almost swallowed his chewing tobacco.

Vivian tried to look stern, but just couldn't pull it off. She fought back laughter. "Well," she finally managed to say, having a terrible time attempting to control her mirth. *"Did* he shoot the man's balls off?"

That did it for Jimmy. He swallowed his chew. "Mrs. Browning!" he gasped.

"No," Frank said. "But I have to say the man had a few anxious moments."

Jimmy got out of the carriage and was coughing and hacking and spitting.

"What's the matter with you, Jimmy?" Viv asked.

"Swallered my chew," Jimmy gasped.

"I'll get Conrad for you, ma'am," Jerry said. "And you can take him home. He's some shaky."

"Thank you, Deputy." Vivian looked at Frank in the flickering streetlamps. It was past time for them to be snuffed out. "I believe I've had quite enough excitement for one day, Frank."

"I agree, and I'm pretty sure Conrad will say the same."

"Quite. And another thing: I shall make sure he puts away that pistol."

Frank smiled. "That's wise, Vivian. At least until he puts in some long practice hours. Although I have to say it was his shooting that broke up the assault tonight."

"No, Frank. His days as a pistol shooter are over. He starts his second year at Harvard this fall. I'm tempted to send him back right now."

"That also might be wise. Viv, what about this Charles Dutton?"

"Here's Conrad. I'll talk to you about Charles tomorrow, Frank. And we must talk."

"All right. There are some things I want to tell you, Viv. No proof, just pure suspicion."

Frank watched the carriage until it was out of sight and then turned to Jerry. "Is Doc Bracken about through with those boys?"

"I think so. None of them was hurt bad."

"Let's lock them down and hit the sack."

"If I can get back to sleep," Jerry said with a smile.

"The way you saw logs, Jer, I don't think you'll have all that much trouble."

"Are you tellin' me I snore, Frank?"

"Either that, or there's a railroad runnin' through the office."

"Maybe it's my snorin' that wakes me up sometimes. You reckon?"

"Could be."

"Doc!" The voice carried to the men across the street.

"Are you sure I ain't been shot in the precious parts? It's all numb down there."

"On second thought," Frank said, "if he keeps that up, maybe you won't get much sleep."

"No, damn it, you haven't been shot in your parts. Good God, man. I've told you ten times. Why don't you look for yourself, you ninny?"

"I'm afeared to. Are you real sure, Doc?" the man persisted. "You won't lie to me about that now, would you?"

"If you don't shut up about it," Doc Bracken said, clearly irritated, "I can fix it so you won't have to worry about your precious parts ever again."

"How would you do that, Doc?"

"I'll cut the damn things off!"

The man started howling again, and that started the dogs in town answering him.

"Oh, Lord!" Jerry said. "It's gonna be a long night."

Eighteen

Just as dawn was coloring the skies over the mining town, Frank approached the tent where the four men were reported to be living. A man stepped out of a ramshackle building across the rutted trail and waved to Frank.

"Those ole boys pulled out late yesterday, Marshal. Packed up ever'thing and rode out. I'm glad to see them go, personal. Unfriendly bunch, they was."

"Did one of them have a bolt-action rifle?"

"A what?"

"A rifle with a piece of metal sticking out of the top of one side."

"Oh. Come to think of it, yeah, one did. That rifle had a telescope on it, too."

"They left their tent."

"Naw. That tent belongs to whoever claims it. It's been there for a long time. Ain't worth a damn. Leaks."

Frank pulled back the flap and looked inside the tent. The ill-fitting board floor was dirty and littered with bits of trash. The interior smelled foul. Frank backed out, wondering how anyone could live that way.

"Did any of them ever talk to you?" Frank asked the miner.

"Nope. Never said nothin' to nobody 'ceptin' themselves. They was a surly pack of yahoos. And I don't think they was up to no good, neither. Had a evil look about 'em. If you know what I mean."

Frank rode back into town and went into the Silver Spoon for breakfast. Jerry had already been in, getting breakfast for the prisoners—biscuits and gravy. Frank did not wish any conversation that morning, and took a table away from the other diners. He was edgy; in the back of his mind was the feeling that major trouble was looming just around the next bend in the road. And Frank had learned years back to pay close attention to his hunches.

He lingered over coffee, watching the town come alive. The smelter kicked into life, along with the steam whistle telling the workmen it was time for another day's labors to begin. Frank watched as two men rode into town. It wasn't the men who caught and held Frank's attention; it was their beautiful and rugged horses, bred for staying power. A few minutes later, two more men rode in, on the same type of horses.

Frank had wandered across the line onto the hoot owl trail several times in his life, and he knew what kind of horseflesh outlaws preferred: the type of horses he'd just seen, with plenty of bottom to them. Outlaws often rode for their very lives, and their horses had to be the best they could buy or steal.

Frank sipped his coffee and watched as two more men rode in on the same type of horses.

The Pine and Vanbergen gangs, he thought. *Part of them, at least. Coming in a few at a time. Getting ready to make their move . . . but what kind of move?*

Frank knew how Ned Pine and Vic Vanbergen operated. Neither one would risk coming into a town this size—now that there were more than a thousand people in and around it—and pulling anything. At least, he didn't think they would. But then, time marched on, and people changed. Lawmen around the country were getting better organized, telegraph wires were damn near everywhere, and if a bank was robbed in Springfield, Missouri, people in Dodge City, Kansas, and Louisville, Kentucky, would know about it within seconds.

So was this a breakaway part of the gangs, or some new gang that had just heard about the rumored gold strike and decided to pull a holdup . . . of what?

Frank sat straight up in his chair, his coffee forgotten and cooling.

The bank, of course.

"Damn," he whispered.

Frank pushed back his chair and stood up, reaching for his hat. He paid his tab and headed for the jail. He told Jerry, "Keep the rifles and the shotguns loaded up and within reach. Maybe stick another short gun behind your gunbelt. I think we've got some trouble riding in."

"I saw those men on the fine horses, Frank. The animals were a dead giveaway."

"Six of them so far. Might be more coming in. We'll keep our eyes open."

"I'll check the livery and hotel and the roomin' houses, try to pick up some names. Not that it will do much good."

"For a fact, they'll probably all be false." He glanced at the wall clock. "I've got to meet Mrs. Browning, Jer. I'll be over at her office if you need me."

"See you later."

Walking over to Viv's office, Frank noticed that the six men had all stabled their horses at the livery. *That means they're not going to pull anything immediately,* he decided. *They'll check on the town first. And maybe won't,* he amended.

Frank glanced at the bank building. He wondered how much cash Jenkins had in his bank. Thousands and thousands of dollars, for sure. It would be a tempting target for any outlaw gang. Jenkins had a bank guard, but the old man was more for show than effect. Frank doubted the man would be very effective against a well-planned bank holdup.

He couldn't go to Jenkins with a warning, for he had no proof. The six newcomers might well be looking to invest in mining property or some other business . . . but Frank felt in his guts they were outlaws.

Vivian was not in her office. The office manager said she had sent word she was not feeling well, and was staying home that morning. Conrad was staying home with her. He added that Conrad was still very shaken from the events of the past night.

Frank walked over to the livery and took a look at the horses the six men had ridden in. Fine horseflesh. Big and rangy, and bred for speed and endurance. The saddles were expensive. The men had, of course, taken their rifles and saddlebags with them. There was nothing else Frank could do, so he returned to the jail.

"Judge Pelmutter was called out of town," Jerry said. "He left on the stage about ten minutes ago . . . some sort of family emergency. Said he'd be back next week . . . on the Friday stage. Said unless you want to file charges against those two young punks who killed that man, cut them loose."

"I figured that much. How about the four we arrested last night?"

"Said to hold them."

"All right. Turn the two young hellions loose and tell them to hit the trail and don't come back here."

"Will do."

Frank looked out the front window of the jail office. Big Bob Mallory was sitting on a bench under a store awning across the street, staring at the jail.

"What the hell does he want?" Jerry asked, walking over to stand beside Frank.

"Me. I'm sure of that. And maybe Mrs. Browning. But he's got enough sense to know he'd better get rid of me first. He knows if he harmed Viv, I'd track him up to and through the gates of hell."

"Those six got rooms at Mrs. Harris's boardinghouse. Hotel is full up. She said they told her their names were Jones and Smith and Johnson, and so forth."

"Something is up, Jer. I just don't know what. All we can do is keep our eyes open and stay ready."

Frank left the office and began walking the town. After a while he walked over to the second livery that had just opened a week before. There were half a dozen fine-looking horses there he wanted to take another look at. They were beautiful animals that the owner had brought in with him. Several people had tried to buy them, but the livery owner had told each prospective buyer he was not yet ready to sell them.

Frank looked for the horses in the corral, but they were gone. He went inside the old barn and looked around for the owner. He was nowhere to be seen. The six horses were in stalls, all saddled up and ready to ride.

"What the hell?" Frank muttered.

Then it dawned on him. Six men ride into town on fine horses. They register at a rooming house under obviously false names. A livery man comes into town a week before, and brings six fine horses with him and opens for business, but won't sell the horses. Now those six animals are saddled up and ready to ride.

"Real good plan, boys," Frank whispered. "It almost worked out exactly as planned."

Frank walked swiftly back to the office. Jerry was out doing something. Frank paced the floor, thinking. He had no firm proof the six men were guilty of anything. Everything he had was suspicion, nothing more. He didn't want to alarm the bank personnel and have his suspicions turn out to be nothing. One of the six men was surely watching the bank, and if he spotted any panic, the robbery—if one was planned—would just be put off for another time . . . or if it went ahead, a lot of innocent people would be killed.

"Damn!" Frank muttered, gazing out the window. The town was already getting busy, even though it was still very early. Kids were playing, and women were shopping and standing on the boardwalk talking.

"All I can do is wait," he said. "Right now I'm between a rock and a hard place."

Frank walked over to the gun rack and put his hand on a rifle. Then he pulled it back. He shook his head. If the outlaw lookout spotted him carrying a rifle around town on this beautiful peaceful day, he would alert the others, and they would immediately suspect their plans had been queered.

Frank loaded up his pistols full, slipping a cartridge into the sixth chamber, which he usually kept empty; the hammer rested on that chamber. He walked out of the office and sat down on the bench on the boardwalk. All he could do was wait. He wondered where Jerry had gotten off to.

Ladies passed by, and Frank smiled and touched his hat in greeting. Most of them spoke; some did not. Frank did not take umbrage at being snubbed. He was a notorious gunfighter and a few residents of the town still felt a man of his dubious reputation should not be wearing a badge.

Jerry came strolling up and sat down beside Frank. "Anything happening, Frank?"

Frank explained briefly what he had found and what he suspected.

Jerry didn't question Frank's suspicions. "I'll get my other pistol," was all he said. When Jerry returned a moment later, he asked, "Do we alert some other men?"

"And tell them what, Jer? We don't have a shred of hard evidence to back up my suspicions. Way I see it, all we can do is wait."

Jerry was silent for a moment. "Frank, one of those six men just sat down across the street. Just to the right of the ladies' shop."

Frank cut his eyes without moving his head. "I see him. And yonder comes the livery man with one of those fine horses he's been stabling."

"The seventh man?"

"Has to be, Jer."

They watched as the stable owner looped the reins over a hitch rail just few yards from the bank's front door and walked slowly back toward his livery.

"Two or three of the horses will probably be led around to the alley behind the bank."

"I'll take me a stroll up the street to the end of the block, howdy doin' and chattin' along the way," Jerry said. "Then I'll cut across to the other side, go into the general store, and take me a look-see out the back door."

"OK. Stay over there. I think we're going to see some action in a few minutes."

"Bank's goin' to be crowded, Frank."

"Yes. Full of people. Let's don't get any innocent person hurt or killed."

Jerry paused in his rolling of a smoke. "That might be just wishful thinkin', Frank."

"I know. But we can try."

"Here comes one of those men ridin' up to the bank big as brass."

"And not a head on the street is turning in curiosity," Frank observed. "These ole boys are pretty damn sharp in their planning."

"It's goin' to happen soon, Frank."

"Yeah. Get going. Jer? Good luck."

Jerry smiled. "All in a day's work, Frank."

"Let's hope there aren't many days like this one."

Jerry walked off up the street, speaking to the ladies as he slowly strolled along.

Frank watched as the livery man rode another of the fine horses up the street and hitched him to a rail on the other side of the bank. Then Frank watched as two of the newcomers in question came strolling up, paused for a moment, then entered the bank.

OK, boys, Frank thought as he spotted another of the six men come riding up. *Let's do it and get it over with.*

Nineteen

Frank walked up the block to the corner before turning and crossing the street. He had already spotted the lookout, and kept on walking past the street intersection. He quickly cut into a very narrow alley and then surprised a couple of ladies who were shopping for bustles or corsets or dainties or something along that line.

"Pardon me, ladies," Frank said, quickly walking through the store. "There is apt to be a little trouble on the street in a few minutes, so please stay inside. Thank you." He exited the store as fast as possible. Being around a gaggle of women shopping for unmentionables always made Frank nervous.

Just as Frank closed the door behind him, he heard one woman say, "I think he's so *rugged,* don't you, Ophelia?"

"And so *capable,* too."

"Oh, Lord!" Frank muttered.

Frank eased up behind the lookout man and stuck the muzzle of a .45 in the man's back. "Take a hard right, hombre, and step into this store. That's a good boy. You try to give any type of signal and I'll blow your spine around your guts."

Frank stepped out of the store just in time to see three

more of the outlaws enter the bank. That left the livery owner still out somewhere. Frank and Jerry would have to worry about him later.

"What the hell is going on here, Marshal?" the man blustered as soon as Frank had him inside the store.

Frank relieved the outlaw of his guns, holstering his own .45. "Mr. Harvey!" Frank called, ignoring the outlaw's question.

"Marshal," the store owner replied.

"You have a gun?"

"I sure do."

"This man is part of a gang that is right now in the process of robbing the bank. If he tries to move or yell, shoot him. Will you do that for me?"

Harvey reached under the counter and came up with a Greener—a sawed-off, double-barreled shotgun. "Rob our bank? Why that sorry son of a bitch! You bet I'll keep him here and quiet. This here is loaded with nails and screws and bits of metal from the smithy's shop, Marshal. If that man tries to move, I'll spread him all over the store." Harvey jacked both hammers back with an ominous sound.

The outlaw paled. He wanted no trouble with a Greener. He cut his eyes to Frank. "How'd you make us, Marshal?"

"Just luck, hombre. Now you be very still and very quiet."

"I ain't movin' nothin'."

"Not if you're smart," Harvey warned. "I've fought Injuns and outlaws, and killed my share of both. One more wouldn't bother me one whit."

"I believe you, mister," the outlaw said. "I do believe you."

"Where is the man from the livery?" Frank asked.

The outlaw smiled. "He's out yonder somewheres. Chances are, he'll find you."

"Play it your way, hombre. See you in a little bit, Mr. Harvey."

"I'll sure be here, Marshal. And so will this one. Either standin' up or in pieces all over the store."

"Sit down on the floor and put your hands under your butt," Frank told the outlaw. "That's good. Now stay that way."

Stepping out of the store but staying on the stoop, Frank peeked around the corner of the stoop. He smiled when he saw the livery man standing in front of the bank, his thumbs hooked in his gunbelt. Frank stepped out and began walking toward the man, whistling a tune as he walked.

The livery man suddenly got really nervous as he saw Frank and no sign at all of his buddy, who was supposed to be standing in front of the store.

"Howdy, there, partner," Frank called cheerfully as he drew closer to the man. "Say, you don't have the time, do you?"

"Don't own no timepiece," the so-called livery man grumbled.

"Oh. Well. Too bad. Sure is a nice mornin', ain't it?"

"It'll do." The man cut his eyes to the bank.

"Bank's open if you're interested in opening an account," Frank told him. "Or maybe you're more interested in a withdrawal?"

"Huh? Naw. I'm just waitin' on a friend."

"Fine-looking animals there. All saddled up and ready to go, too. Got saddlebags all filled up with stuff, and bedrolls tied in place. But you have one too many horses."

"Huh? What are you talkin' 'bout, Marshal?"

"You have seven horses hitched up. There's only six of you."

Frank watched the man's eyes flick up the street toward the store where the lookout was supposed to be.

"He's not there, livery man," Frank told him.

"Huh? Who you talkin' 'bout?"

"Your friend. The rider of the seventh horse. He is, well, sort of occupied at this time."

The so-called livery man was even more nervous. Then he made the mistake of brushing back his coat and touching the butt of his pistol. Frank drove his left fist into the man's belly, knocking the air from him and doubling him over. Frank pushed him off the boardwalk, which was about two feet off the ground at this part of the street. The man bit the ground on his belly, which further knocked the wind from him.

Jerry ran up and jerked the man's pistol out of leather just as one of the bank robbers stepped into the doorway of the bank and looked out, a pistol in his hand. He leveled the pistol, taking a dead bead at Jerry.

Frank shot him, drilling the man in the center of his chest. The slug drove the man backward and knocked him into another bank—robber. Both of them staggered back and fell to the floor.

Frank jumped into the bank, both hands filled with .45's. "That's all!" he shouted. "Give it up. You can't get out of town."

One of the outlaws cussed him and swung his pistol in Frank's direction. Frank shot the man between the eyes. The bank robber died with a very peculiar expression on his face. He slumped to the floor and remained on his knees for a few seconds before toppling over on his face.

The others gave it up. They dropped their pistols and stood with their hands in the air. A short, stocky outlaw said, "Don't shoot, Marshal. We yield."

"Good God!" another bank robber whispered. "That's Frank Morgan!"

Jenkins and two of his tellers now had pistols in their hands, as did three men who were in the bank doing some early-morning transactions, and all were damn sure ready to use them.

"Outside," Frank told the outlaws. "And keep your hands in the air."

"Wonderful work, Marshal!" said Mayor Jenkins, the banker. "By God, it certainly was!"

What was left of the outlaw gang was marched over to the jail through a gathering crowd of citizens, a few of whom had ropes in their hands and were making crude suggestions as to what should be done with the would-be bank robbers . . . immediately.

"There'll be none of that!" Frank shouted, momentarily stilling the demands of the crowd. "These men are in my custody, and I'll see they'll get a fair trial. Now break this up and go on about your business."

"The marshal's right, folks," Mayor Jenkins shouted. "The excitement's over. Let's all settle down now."

Doc Bracken pushed through the crowd. "Anyone hurt over at the bank?"

"Two dead," Frank told him. "Somebody go fetch Mr. Malone and tell him he's got some business."

"I'm right here, Marshal," the undertaker called from

the rear of the crowd. "I'll see to the departed immediately."

Two well-dressed men stood on the boardwalk on opposite sides of the street. One was watching through very cold and cunning eyes. The other one was scribbling furiously in a notebook.

"Very impressive," said the man with the cold eyes. "Very impressive, indeed."

"What a story this will make," said the other man. "Where is the telegraph office, friend?" he asked a citizen standing next to him.

Frank and Jerry locked up the survivors of the attempted bank robbery and Jerry set about making a fresh pot of coffee while Frank logged the events of the morning in the jail book. The coffee was ready just about the time Frank finished his report, and the men settled down to enjoy a cup.

The door to the jail office opened and a short, stocky man wearing a suit stepped in. "Gentlemen," he said. "I'm Louis Pettigrew. Marshal Morgan, it is indeed a pleasure to meet you . . . finally."

"Finally?" Frank asked.

"I'm the author of the books about you, sir."

"Wonderful," Frank muttered.

Frank finally got rid of the writer after assuring him that he would give some thought to helping the man write the story of his life . . . something that Frank had absolutely no intention of doing.

"I've seen those books from time to time, Frank," Jerry said with a smile.

"Don't start, Jer."

Jerry laughed at him and got to his boots. "Maybe this writer fellow could arrange for you to go back east on a tour. You could do some trick shootin' and twirl your guns. That ought to give the folks back there a real thrill."

Frank picked up an inkwell and moved as if to throw it at Jerry. Laughing, Jerry left the office. Luckily for Frank, the inkwell was empty.

Frank locked up the office and walked over to the Henson Office building. He walked in just in time to see and hear a well-dressed man really browbeating one of the office workers. Frank listened for as long as he could take it and then walked up and deliberately bumped into the man, almost knocking him down.

The man caught his balance and turned on Frank. "You damned clumsy oaf!" he raged.

"Back off, mister," Frank warned him, "before you step into something you can't scrape off." He looked at the employee who had been the brunt of the Eastern man's rage. "You go get a cup of coffee and relax, partner."

"You stay right where you are, Leon!" the dude told the employee. "Now you see here, Marshal!" the man said, turning to Frank. "I am Charles Dutton, Mrs. Browning's attorney. And I resent your interference in a company matter."

Frank smiled and pulled out his second pistol. "You ever fired a pistol, Leon?"

"Yes, sir. During the war. I was a sergeant in a New York regiment."

"Take this pistol."

Leon took the pistol and held it gingerly.

"Now you go get a six-gun," Frank told Dutton.

"I beg your pardon?" the lawyer questioned.

"You speak to this man like he's some sort of poor cowed dog, mister, and you expect him to take it without him biting back or even showing his teeth in a snarl. That ain't the way it works out here. Now you go get a six-gun and meet this man in the street out front."

"I will not! Are you insane?"

Vivian's entrance into the building probably prevented Frank from knocking the Boston lawyer on his butt. Frank could not take an employer berating an employee in public. It was something that set him off like a fire-cracker.

Leon handed Frank's short-barreled .45 back to him, and Frank tucked it behind his gunbelt and turned to greet Vivian. The look that she gave Dutton was a combination of ice and fire.

"This is your friend, Vivian?" Dutton asked, referring to Frank. "This . . . bully with a badge?"

Vivian ignored that. When she spoke, it was to Leon. "What is the problem, Leon? Speak freely, please. Charles Dutton has no authority here."

"It, ah, concerned the weekly reports on the grade of silver being taken from mine number three, Mrs. Browning," Leon told her.

"The analysis of the purity of the silver?"

"Yes, ma'am."

"Give the reports to Mr. Dutton, Leon."

Leon held out the laboratory reports.

Dutton looked at the papers without taking them. "What is the meaning of this, Vivian?"

"The lab is about one mile out of town, Charles," Vivian told him. "Anyone can point the way. Why don't you go up there and tell the engineer in charge that you are taking over, and will personally run the tests? Can you do that, Charles?"

"I am your attorney, Vivian, not a chemist or an engineer."

"Can you do it, Charles?" Viv persisted.

"No. I cannot, Vivian."

"Then why don't you shut up and tend to your business? Stay in your area of expertise, and stay out of areas in which you have no knowledge."

For a moment, Frank thought Charles was going to pop his cork. He turned red in the face, and his eyes bugged out. He struggled to speak and then, with a very visible effort, calmed down. "As you wish, madam," he said, very slowly. "However, I was only trying to help."

"And any constructive help you might offer is certainly welcome, Charles. But I personally do not believe in berating employees in private, much less publicly."

"I shall certainly bear that in mind."

"Thank you, Charles."

"If by chance you should need me this afternoon, I will be at the hotel."

"I thought the hotel was full," said Viv.

"Not the luxury suites at the end of the hall. They have private baths. I insisted upon that."

Frank rolled his eyes and looked heavenward.

Viv caught his eye movement and fought back a smile. "Of course you did, Charles."

"It's so primitive out here," Dutton complained. "I don't understand how you tolerate these barbaric conditions, Vivian." He plopped his hat on his head and walked toward the front door without another word.

"Nice fellow," Frank remarked.

Leon muttered something under his breath that sounded suspiciously like 'He's a turdface!' *But surely not,* Frank thought.

"Frank," Vivian said. She had dropped the "Marshal Morgan" when addressing him. There was no point in any further pretense. The whole town knew they were seeing each other socially. "Could I see you in my office, please?"

Seated in Viv's office, Frank asked, "How's Conrad?"

"He's all right, but I insisted that he stay home today. I've just about convinced him that he should return east as soon as possible."

"I'm not sure about that now, Viv. As long as he stays here, there are plenty of us to keep an eye on him. Back there, he would have little if any protection."

Viv frowned, then slowly nodded her head in agreement. "You're right, Frank. I hadn't thought about that."

"Might be a good thing to keep him here until we get this situation straightened out and decide who's trying to kill us both. As if we didn't already know."

Before Viv could reply, they heard the sound of running boots in the outer offices. Jerry burst into the room. "Frank! Outlaws just hit the Lucky Seven. Got the payroll and killed the owner and his foreman."

Frank was on his boots instantly. "That's the mine about four miles from town, right?"

"That's it."

"Get a posse together. I'll get my horse and meet you at the office."

"Will do." Jerry left the office in a run.

"Be careful, Frank," Viv cautioned.

Frank winked at her. "Long as I got you to come back to, Viv."

"I'll be here."

Twenty

Frank looked at the bodies of the mine owner and his foreman and shook his head in disgust. The men had been shot to ribbons, each one more than a dozen times. Their faces had been deliberately shot away. He ordered the bodies taken back to town in a wagon.

"Marshal," said one of the men in the posse. "Those robbers used them men for target practice. They made a game of it."

"I know," Frank replied. "They shot them in the knees, then the arms, then in the belly. They tortured them for the fun of it." Jerry walked up and Frank asked him, "How about the workers—did any of them see anything?"

"One did," Jerry said. "The other three were in a secondary shaft of the mine . . . looking for gold," he added. "It was part of the Pine and Vanbergen gangs. The man is sure of that."

"How can he be sure?"

"He knows a couple of them. Was in jail with them once. They broke out, or was broke out. One or the other. He done his time for drunk and fighting, and hasn't been in trouble since."

"Those two gangs just keep getting more and more

vicious," Frank said. "This is not the first time they've done something like this. It's fortunate that no women were out here. We all know what happens to women they take captive. Which way did they head out of here?"

"Straight into the mountains, Marshal," a posse member said. "They're long gone through the pass now. And I ain't goin' into the pass."

Frank did not have to question any of the others about that. He knew without asking none of the men would be willing to enter the outlaw-controlled pass through the mountains. And he really didn't blame them one bit.

"Take the posse back to town, Jerry, and look after things until I get back. I'm going to prowl around some."

"You goin' to the pass, Frank?"

"I'm going to look it over, yes. I might not be back tonight. If that's the case, I'll see you late tomorrow."

After the posse was gone, Frank made sure his canteen was full of fresh water. Then he looped an ammo belt over his shoulder and across his chest. The belt was filled with .44-.40 rounds. Every loop in his gunbelt was full of .45 cartridges, and he had more rounds for the rifle and pistols in his saddlebags.

He began slowly tracking the outlaw gang through the rocky terrain. It wasn't that difficult, for the outlaws had made no effort to hide their tracks.

It took Frank a couple of slow-riding and very cautious hours to reach a good vantage spot about a hundred yards from the mouth of the pass. There he dismounted in a small patch of grass, eased the cinch strap, and let his horse blow and then graze. Frank took a pair of binoculars from his saddlebags, looped them around his neck, then slipped his .44-.40 from the boot. He climbed up the rocky ridge for about a hundred feet or so and settled himself in for a long, careful look-see.

What he saw was the nearly impassable entrance to the pass, and he had no doubts about it being guarded by at least two men around the clock. It was as he had been told: if you didn't know your way through, you would be in deep trouble. Even if you did know the tricky route, one of the Pine and Vanbergen guards would surely nail you if you tried.

The ways around the range were about forty miles east or west, and by the time a posse reached the outlaw stronghold they would be long gone.

"Damn," Frank muttered. He knew that north of the pass and the outlaw stronghold the terrain was badlands for miles and miles. A railroad spur line came down to a small town just north of the badlands, and that is where the mines in Barnwell's Crossing took their silver to be shipped out . . . providing they could get it to the spur line by wagons, which meant rolling right through outlaw territory on the single road that led to the tracks. Only about half of the silver-laden wagons had made it through thus far.

Frank watched the pass for half an hour before deciding he was accomplishing nothing by staying there. The only way the outlaw stronghold could be taken was with an army, and that would still mean a terrible loss of life.

Frank climbed down to his horse, tightened the cinch strap, and swung into the saddle, holding his rifle in his right hand, across the saddle horn. He headed back to town, feeling that he had accomplished very little with his long ride to the pass.

He rode into town just after dark, stabled his horse, and walked over to the jail. Jerry had fed the prisoners after Doc Bracken had made his daily visit to check on the wounded, and he had just made a fresh pot of coffee.

"Didn't expect to see you back this early, Frank."

"I looked over the entrance to the pass and decided this was not a good day to die," Frank said, pouring a mug of coffee. "The place is a death trap."

"The south entrance sure is. The best way in is from the north."

"But we don't have any authority up there," Frank told him. "I wonder why Colorado won't deal into this game with us?"

"I don't know if they've even been asked."

"I know there's a few small towns just north of the border with us. On the edge of the badlands. But Pine and Vanbergen are smart in that they don't pull anything up there, so they're not wanted in those areas."

It was a policy that was slowly dying out in the West, but for many years if a man was not wanted in a specific area or community, the local lawman would, in many instances, leave him alone as long as he did not cause trouble within that lawman's jurisdiction.

"Was either the mine owner or the foreman married?" Frank asked.

"Yes. Both of them. Wives are here. But neither of them had kids."

"That's good . . . that is, if anything about this mess can be called good."

"What about this Charles Dutton fellow, Frank? I just don't like that uppity bastard."

"Neither do I, Jer. I think something is going to break loose here in town very quickly now."

"Because this Dutton dude is here?"

"Yes. And Big Bob Mallory and Kid Moran, and those

four assassins who came after Viv and me, and all the rest of it. Dutton is tied in with it all. I'm sure of it. I just don't know the big picture yet."

"This is gettin' mighty complicated, Frank."

"A fellow named Sir Walter Scott wrote some verse once that went something like: 'O, what a tangled web we weave.' I don't remember the rest of it. But that much did stick in my mind."

"This mess is sure all tangled up, for a fact."

A citizen stuck his head in the office. "Marshal, sorry to disturb, but I thought you ought to know that Kid Moran is back in town. I was usin' the privy—just steppin' out, that is, after I—finished my business—when I seen him coming down the back way of the hotel. Usin' them steps that lead up to the fancy rooms. He was sort of slippin' down them, real quiet like, if you know what I mean."

"Thank you," Frank said. "I appreciate it."

"It's my pleasure, Marshal, for shore. If I see anything else suspicious like I think you should know about, I'll get right over to you with it."

"Thanks."

After the citizen had closed the door and walked on, Jerry asked, "What was that all about?"

"Charles Dutton has the most expensive suite in the hotel rented for his stay here."

"You think he's tied in with Kid Moran? A fancy Dan rich man like that?"

"It wouldn't surprise me any. Way this situation is shaping up here in town nothing would surprise me anymore."

"What was the line you recited? 'What a tangled web we weave?' I knew several families name of Scott back home when I was a kid. One of them was always quotin' that fellow Shakespeare. Like to have drove the rest of us goofy. You reckon they might be related to that poet?"

The next morning, Frank took a good bath and then carefully shaved. He blacked his boots and dressed in a new suit he'd bought just recently. No special occasion— he just felt like putting on some fancy duds.

He stepped out into a beautiful day in the high country: a blue, cloudless sky and warm temperature. He walked up to the Silver Spoon and took a seat, ordering a pot of coffee and breakfast. Kid Moran was seated across the room, staring at him, smiling at him. The Kid had taken no part in the attempted kidnapping of Conrad and the killing of Hal . . . at least, no part that could be proved. Kid Moran could come and go as he pleased.

Frank ate his breakfast and drank his coffee, ignoring The Kid. The Kid left the café before Frank, walking across the street and sitting down on a bench.

Angie came to Frank's table to clear off the breakfast dishes and said, "Be careful, Frank. There's something in the wind this morning."

Frank smiled up at her as he smoked his cigarette. "What do you think it is, Angie?"

"Killing you."

"You a fortune-teller? Maybe you can see the future?"

"Joke if you want to, Frank. But I've served half a dozen hard cases breakfast this morning."

"Sometimes it's difficult to tell a hired gun from a drifting cowboy, Angie."

"And sometimes it isn't." She refilled his coffee cup

and said, "You watch yourself today. This town's become a powder keg, and the fuse is lit."

She turned to leave, and Frank put out a hand. "Angie, what is it you're not telling me?"

"Nothing that I can prove. It's just a feeling I get every now and then. But over the years I've seen the best and the worst out here. I saw Jamie MacCallister go into action once. I've seen his son, Falcon, hook and draw. I personally know Smoke Jensen and Louis Longmont. I've been working in Western cafés since I was ten years old." She smiled. "And I'm no kid, Frank. I've got more than a few years behind me. You just be careful today, all right?"

"All right, Angie."

Frank looked out the window. The Kid was still sitting on the bench across the street, staring at the café.

Frank paid his tab and stepped out onto the boardwalk. None of his mental warning alarms had been silently clanging that morning, so what did Angie feel that he didn't? And why? The Kid was in town, probably to try to provoke a showdown with him. That was something that Frank had felt all along was bound to happen—no surprise there. And it might well come to a head on this day. If so, so be it.

The hard cases she had mentioned? Did she personally know those bad ole boys, or had she just recognized the hard case look? *Probably the latter,* Frank concluded. And Frank knew that many toughs wore the same look, or demeanor.

Frank walked one side of the main street looking at the horses at the hitch rails. There were some fine-looking animals there, and none of them wore the same brand. But what did that prove conclusively? Nothing. Nothing at all.

Frank cut his eyes. Kid Moran was pacing him on the other side of the street. Maybe it was time for Frank to settle this thing. He hated to push it, but damned if he was going to put up with being shadowed indefinitely. It was already beginning to get on his nerves.

He looked up the street. Damned if more newcomers weren't pulling into town. Two wagons coming in, four outriders per wagon. And Frank felt that was odd. Most Indian trouble was over, so what could the newcomers be hauling to warrant eight guards? The wagons weren't riding that heavy.

Frank paused for a moment to watch the wagons as they rolled slowly into town. One wagon stopped at one end of the street; the other one rolled on and stopped at the far end of the main street.

"What the hell?" Frank muttered. He looked over at the bank building. The guard was just unlocking the front door, getting ready for another business day.

" 'Mornin, Marshal," a citizen greeted Frank.

" 'Morning," Frank responded.

The citizen strolled on, whistling a tune.

Frank looked at Kid Moran. The Kid was standing on the boardwalk, directly across the street, staring at Frank, smiling at him. Even at that distance, Frank could tell the smile was taunting, challenging.

"What the hell is with you, boy?" Frank whispered. "What's going on here?"

Jerry walked up, smelling of bath soap and Bay Rum after-shave.

"Jerry," Frank greeted him.

"Frank," Jerry replied. "You're lookin' spiffy this mornin'. You're duded up mighty fancy."

"And you smell like you're goin' on a date," Frank said with a smile. "You got you a lady friend?"

Jerry laughed. "Well . . . me and Miss Angie might go for a walk this mornin'. We both been makin' goo-goo eyes at each other here of late. She's a nice lady."

"Yes, she is. And a damn good cook, too."

Jerry patted his belly. "I know!"

"Going to get serious, Jer?"

"I don't know. Maybe. Luckily we're both adults, and have been up and down the road a time or two. It isn't something new to either of us. So we're cautious." Jerry paused and looked at the wagons that had just rolled into town. "What the devil are those wagons doing, Frank? Looks to me like they're going to block both ends of Main Street. My God, they *are* blocking both ends."

Frank looked first at one end of the street, then the other. The wagons were not long enough to completely block off the wide streets, even with the teams, but it looked as if they were sure going to cause some major problems for other wagons trying to get past.

"Frank, they're folding back the canvas on both wagons. Heck, maybe it's some sort of circus come to town, or some minstrel show. You reckon?"

"I don't know what's going on, Jer. But I damn sure intend to find out."

"I'll take this end," Jerry said, pointing. "You take the other."

"Marshal Morgan," Jiggs said, walking up. "What in the world is happening? Those wagons are blocking the street. That can't be allowed."

"We were just about to straighten out this mess, Jiggs."

"I swear, Marshal, some people have no consideration for others, do they?"

Before Frank could reply, Jerry said, "Frank, what is that machinery those guys are uncovering? I never seen no minin' equipment that looked like that."

Frank looked and felt cold sweat break out on his face. He blinked, thinking he was surely mistaken. He stared. No doubt about it: his first look was correct. "Those are Gatling guns, Jer!"

"Gatling guns?" Jiggs blurted. "Good God! Are you joking?" He stared at first one wagon, then another. "By the Lord, you're right, Marshal. What are those people going to do? Put on some sort of a demonstration?"

A couple of seconds after Jiggs asked his question, a tremendous explosion rocked the town. A huge cloud of dust enveloped the road leading out of the main street and up to the mines. The immense explosion was so powerful it cracked windows and sent some people stumbling off the boardwalk and into the street.

"The road's blocked!" an excited man yelled from the other end of the street a few seconds after the explosion. Then he started coughing when the enormous cloud of dust began settling over the main part of town, covering everything.

The men in the wagons began cranking the Gatling guns, and lead started flying all up and down Main Street. Several men and women were hit and knocked spinning by the gunfire.

Pistol fire joined the rapid fire from the Gatling guns. On his belly on the boardwalk, Frank watched as half a dozen men, all carrying guns and cloth bags, entered the bank.

"Bank robbery!" Frank yelled, and rolled off the boardwalk and into the street just as the carriage from the Browning estate turned onto the main street from a side street. Frank could do nothing except stare in horror as a dozen rounds of lead raked the carriage. Vivian was knocked out of the carriage to lie still and bloody in the dirt.

Twenty-one

Frank snapped off a lucky shot that hit the gunner in one of the wagons in the shoulder, knocking him back. But in a heartbeat another man had taken his place and was cranking out the lead, spraying death in all directions. Frank tried to get up and make his way to Vivian, but the intense fire from the Gatling guns forced him back. He crawled behind a water trough as the bullets howled and whistled all around him.

Frank glanced over to where he'd last seen Jerry. The deputy was apparently all right, and had taken shelter in a store, returning the gunfire as best he could whenever the hail of bullets ceased for a few seconds. All the stores up and down the street, on both sides, were missing windows. The wounded were moaning, and many were crying out for help. There were men and women and a few children among them.

One of the bank clerks staggered out of the bank, his chest bloody, and fell facedown on the boardwalk. A young child, a girl, sat in the dirt beside her fallen mother and cried. Many of the horses that had been tied at hitch rails in front of various stores had broken loose and bolted. Others were badly wounded, screaming and thrashing on the ground, unable to get up because of their grievous wounds.

While the gunners were changing magazines on the Gatlings, Frank dropped one of the outlaws, who was exiting the bank with a bagful of money. Frank shot him twice, once in the belly, once in the chest, ending the man's outlawing days forever.

Jerry shot another one leaving the bank, shot him in the throat with a hurry-up shot. The .45 round almost took the man's head off. He fell back against the front of the bank building and lay kicking and jerking and trying to push words out of his ruined throat, the bag of money beside him forgotten in his horrible agony.

Frank rolled away from the trough and under the raised boardwalk, squirming his way a few yards closer to one of the death wagons. He shot the gunner in the head just as another charge of dynamite was lit and tossed. The barber shop exploded in a mass of splintered wood and broken glass. The peppermint-painted barber pole was blown a hundred feet into the air. It came down in the alley behind the barber shop and landed on the slant roof of a privy, crashing through and almost conking a man on the head who had taken refuge in there. He jumped out of the privy and took off, running toward the edge of town.

The main street was once more covered in dust and smoke and confusion. The Gatling guns resumed their spitting out of misery and destruction. Frank nailed another outlaw coming out of the bank, his shots turning the robber around and around in a macabre dance on the boardwalk. He dropped his bulging sack of money just before he slumped to the street and died beside the bag of money that cost him his life.

Frank heard a shotgun boom inside the bank, and an outlaw was knocked through the big front window, dead from the shotgun blast before he hit the boardwalk.

Frank took that time to jump up and make a run closer to one of the wagons. He made it to a dead horse and jerked the .44-.40 rifle from the saddle boot. Before he went belly down on the ground, he chanced a look toward Vivian. She had not moved. Frank was suddenly filled with a terrible rage. He levered a round into the chamber of the rifle and sighted in the new gunner cranking the Gatling gun. Frank shot him in the chest and knocked the man out of the wagon. No new gunner came forward to take his place. The bank robbers were running out of men.

Frank ran toward the wagon and jumped in. He swiveled the Gatling and began cranking, the rounds literally tearing the wagon at the end of the block to splinters, all mixed in with the blood and shattered bone of the two outlaws who were inside the wagon.

The outlaws who were not dead or wounded, or being held prisoner by various townspeople, were in the saddle and riding hell-for-leather out of town, toward the pass.

Doc Bracken was busy working on the wounded citizens, pointedly ignoring the calls for help from the wounded outlaws.

"Help me, Doc!" one called.

"Go to hell, you bastard," Doc Bracken told him without looking up from the bloody little girl he was working on in the middle of the street.

"I'm hard hit, Doc," the outlaw pleaded.

"Good," Bracken replied. "Go ahead and die. Rot in hell."

Frank hurried over to Vivian and knelt down. She had

taken two rounds in the chest from the big-bore Gatlings, but she was still breathing.

"Hang on, Viv," Frank said. "Doc Bracken's coming over soon as he can."

"Tell him not to waste his time, love. I'm all torn up inside."

"Hush, now, Viv. Don't talk like that."

"Talk while I have time to talk. I'm in no pain, Frank. It's all numb inside of me, but it's difficult to breathe. I've been lung shot, haven't I?"

Frank had seen the pinkish-looking fluid she'd coughed up. "I don't know for sure, Viv."

"I think I am. Let me talk while I still can, Frank. Don't interrupt, please?"

"I won't, Viv."

"You own five percent of Henson Enterprises, Frank. I saw to that just last week. The papers are filed, and it's all legal. Dutton can't do a thing about it except gripe. Money will be deposited in your name in a bank in Denver every month. It's all spelled out in the papers. Mayor Jenkins has them. He's a good, trustworthy man."

Frank waited while Vivian coughed up more fluid. It was pinkish in color. Holding her, he felt his hand at her back grow wet. He lifted one side of her jacket and found another bullet hole. He knew that unless the slug had veered off, it had probably blown right through a kidney.

"Is the sun going behind a cloud, Frank?" she asked. "It's getting darker."

"Yes, love. Clouds are moving in. It's going to rain, I reckon."

There was not a cloud in the sky.

Doc Bracken came over and looked at Vivian for a

few seconds. He lifted his gaze to Frank and shook his head. The doctor's eyes were filled with sorrow.

Frank felt as though an anvil had fallen on him.

"Look after Conrad, Frank," Vivian told him. "Promise me you'll do that."

"I will, Viv. I promise."

"He's home right now. I gave him a sedative. He probably slept right through the shooting."

"I'll do my best to take care of him, Viv."

"Let's get her to my office, Frank." Bracken had placed a cloth over Viv's major chest wound. "Stops the sucking, Frank. She might have a chance."

Bracken waved some men over and they gently picked Viv up and carried her away. Frank stood up and looked around him. The main street of town resembled a war zone. There were at least two dozen men, women, and children dead or wounded. There wasn't a window left intact. The barber shop was gone, and the buildings on either side of it were heavily damaged.

Jerry walked up, a bandage on his head. "You hurt bad?" Frank asked.

"Naw. I just got conked on the head by a flying board, that's all. Bled like crazy for a few seconds. Angie thought I was bad hurt. How's Mrs. Browning?"

Frank shook his head. "Real bad," he said softly. "She caught three bullets in the chest."

"I'm sorry, Frank. Jimmy?"

"Dead. That's him between the seats in the carriage."

"The driver is dead, too. He's on the other side of the carriage."

"Let's go see what we can do to help and get the prisoners over to the jail."

"We might have some trouble keeping a lynch mob from taking the prisoners."

"I couldn't blame them for trying," Frank replied. "But that's not going to happen in my town."

Frank and Jerry rounded up the surviving outlaws and marched them over to the jail and locked them down. "Stay here," he told Jerry. He left the office and walked up to a group of businessmen. "You're all deputized," he informed them. "Your job is to stay at the jail and guard the prisoners. You will prevent a lynching. Is that understood?"

It was, and the men agreed, although quite reluctantly.

"Fine. Get over to the jail and relieve Jerry. Tell him I need him out here, now. Move!"

Jerry joined him in the street and Frank said, "Let's get a tally of the dead and wounded. You start that while I find Jenkins and see how hard the bank was hit."

"Will do, Frank."

Men were shooting badly injured horses, putting them out of their misery.

"They didn't get away with a nickel," Jenkins told Frank. "We recovered every dollar. How many dead do we have?"

"I don't know yet. Jerry's checking on that now. But it's going to be high."

"Mrs. Browning?"

"Doc Bracken said she was still alive, but unconscious. She's hard hit."

"Was it the Pine and Vanbergen gangs that hit us, Frank?"

"Yes. Selected members. The rest of the gang was scheduled to pull something else."

"For God's sake, what? And where?"

"The one doing all the talking didn't know. Or said he didn't."

"You believe him?"

"He's pretty damned scared, Mayor. There's a chance he's telling the truth."

A citizen ran up to the men, nearly out of breath. "We've got over twenty dead so far, Mayor, Marshal," he gasped. "About that many wounded."

"Dear God!" Mayor Jenkins breathed. "How many of the wounded are critical?"

"Near'bouts all of them."

"All right, mister. Thanks," Frank told him. "Go sit down over yonder and catch your breath."

"No time," the citizen said. "One of the dynamite charges was tossed into Miss Rosie's place up on the hill. Some of her girls is still buried under the rubble. Maybe eight or ten of them. And Miss Rosie's missin', too."

"My wife's been griping and raising hell about that whorehouse for months," Jenkins said. "She wanted it gone, but not this way."

Frank swung into the saddle of the first horse he came to and rode up to Rosie's House of Delights, or what was left of the place, picking his way around the blocked road. There were dead and badly injured soiled doves on both sides and in front of the ruined old two-story home. There were plenty of men helping to search for and dig out those trapped, so Frank rode on.

No one had thought to look for dead or wounded at the small—mining claims that dotted the area around the town, and Frank had a hunch that had also been part of the gang's plan. Many of the men working the smaller mines had found pockets of gold, and did not trust the bank to hold it for them. They kept it in hidden places around their shacks. Ned Pine and Vic Vanbergen would have had spies working the town, buying drinks for thirsty miners, and would know some of the claims that were producing.

Frank's worst hunch paid off. The roar of the Gatling guns, the booming of the dynamite, and the screaming of the wounded had managed to cover the sound of the attack on a number of the small mines . . . and the attacks had been especially vicious. There were dead men and women nearly everywhere Frank looked.

Frank found one dazed but unhurt young man. "You have a horse, boy?"

"Yes, sir."

"Get on it and ride into town. Tell my deputy what's happened up here." Frank stared at the confused-looking teenager. "Do you understand what I just told you?"

The young man blinked a couple of times. "Ah . . . yes, sir."

"Move, boy!"

Frank did what he could for the wounded and waited for help from the town to arrive.

Soon Jerry rode up with about a dozen men, and for a moment they sat their horses and stared in disbelief at the carnage.

"A couple of you check out those mines up ahead for dead and wounded," Frank said. "Rest of you get down and help me identify these bodies."

"The telegraph is out, too, Frank," Jerry told him. "I guess the gangs pulled down the wires just as they were hitting the town."

"It was sure a well-thought-out plan, Jer, no doubt about that."

"They didn't care who they killed. I've never seen anything so vicious."

"The death count still rising?"

"Yes. By the minute, it seems like. A lot of women and kids were killed." Jerry shook his head. "Most of the stores on Main Street were damaged. Several of them will be closed for a long time while repairs are made."

"Some of them probably won't ever reopen. God!" Frank exclaimed. "Look at the bodies."

"We're going to have to match up the names of some of these people with records from the assayer's office."

Frank nodded his head. "We'll be lucky to match up half of them. Jerry, did you see Kid Moran do anything to aid the outlaws?".

"No. Not a thing. And he's gone. So is Big Bob Mallory."

"Figures. How about Charles Dutton?"

"I guess he's still in town. I haven't seen him."

"Any chance of getting Doc Bracken up here?"

"Not a chance, Frank. He's operating fast as he can, and the wounded keep piling up. He's moved his operatin' to the church buildin' on Willow Street."

"All right. See if you can get a couple of wagons. We'll move the wounded into town."

"How about the bodies?"

Frank sighed. "I guess we'll leave them where they fell for the time being. Let's see to the living first."

"Frank, I haven't seen Conrad Browning."

"Vivian told me she gave him a sedative this morning. He slept through the attack. I'd better go check on him and get him up and moving. He might not get another chance to see his mother alive."

"Don't give up on her, Frank. She's a strong woman with a powerful will to live."

"She took three rounds in the chest, Jer. Looks like one went through a lung and another punched through a kidney."

"But she's still alive."

"Yeah. Take over here, Jer. I'll be in town."

Frank rode into town and checked on Vivian. She was still clinging to life. He went to the Browning estate and got Conrad up and moving. He made coffee while Conrad washed his face and dressed. Then he told him what had happened.

The young man went white in the face with shock. "Mother?"

"She's still alive."

"Take me to her, Marshal."

"Of course."

Frank took Conrad to the doctor's office, where a local woman who was Bracken's nurse was sitting with Vivian. A very subdued Conrad took a chair by his mother's bed and reached out, touching her and finally taking her hand into his.

Frank slipped outside, leaving the mother and son together. He stood alone for a few moments, then carefully rolled a cigarette and smoked it, but he got no pleasure from it. The tobacco was bitter tasting on his tongue, all mixed up with the lonely feelings of sorrow and regret, for himself, for Conrad, and especially for Vivian. *And,* he thought with a sigh, forcing himself to admit it, *for all the things that might have been and now can never be. Never, ever be.*

Jerry rode up and dismounted, walking over to Frank. "How is she, Frank?"

"Doc Bracken says there is no hope, Jer. Conrad is in there with her now."

"How is he holdin' up?"

"Being a very strong and brave young man. But I don't think that's going to last for any length of time."

"They were real close, weren't they?"

"Yes."

"Frank, I hate to bring this up now, but I've got to. We've got forty-two people dead and seventy wounded, some of them real serious. We can't get word out, the telegraph is down, and the road is blocked by the outlaws about three miles out of town."

"What?"

"They want the money in the bank, Frank. All of it. We just got that word. And they know to a penny how much Jenkins had in his bank."

"How the hell could they know that?"

"One of the tellers was involved. Young man name of Dean Hill. His girlfriend came to the office and told me about him. She's over there now. Wants to talk to you."

"All right. Where is this Dean Hill now?"

"He rode out with the survivors of the holdup."

"I'll make you a wager. If he isn't dead by now, he will be very shortly."

"No bet. The young man has served his purpose. No point in keepin' him around. Those outlaws damn sure aren't goin' to share with him."

"Let's go see this girlfriend. Not that she'll be able to tell us much. How long do the outlaws think they'll be able to keep the pass closed?"

"Forever, Frank. She told me they plan on warning anyone wanting in that there is a smallpox epidemic in town. No one is allowed into town."

"Pretty good plan Vic and Ned worked out."

"Yeah. What are you goin' to do, Frank?"

"See this girl. Then I'm going to open the road . . . or die trying."

Twenty-two

Frank talked briefly with the frightened young lady in his office. She told him basically what she had told Jerry. She ended with, "What do you suppose will happen to Dean?"

Frank didn't want to tell her that her beau was probably already dead. "He'll have to stand trial, miss. I don't know what the judge will do." *If he is alive he'll spend the rest of his life in prison,* he thought.

After the young woman had left, Frank told Jerry, "Have a wagon hitched up. Transfer one of those Gatling guns over to it, and fill all the magazines."

Jerry looked at him.

"And some dynamite and caps, too," Frank added.

"Sounds like you're about to declare war, Frank."

"I am, Jer. For a fact."

Jerry left the office at a run, and Frank began putting together some gear. He was filling the empty loops in his ammo belt with .44-.40 cartridges when Mayor Jenkins came in.

"Coffee over there on the stove, Mayor," Frank told him. "It's fresh and hot. Help yourself."

"Good." Jenkins reached into his suit coat and pulled out some papers. "While I'm doing that, you sign these where I've put an X."

"What am I signing?"

"Some very important papers." He pushed a pen and inkwell across the desk. "Sign them and date them."

Frank scrawled his name, looked at the calendar and printed in the date, then pushed the papers away.

"I just spoke with Dr. Bracken, Frank. There is no change in Mrs. Browning's condition."

"I know."

"Doc Bracken is worried about Conrad. The boy is very shaky."

"He's learning that death is a part of living, Mayor. The kid is tougher than most people think. He'll be all right."

"I know you're about to do something. You want me to put a posse together, Frank?"

"No. This is something I have to handle myself. There has been enough loss of innocent life this day."

"One man against two large gangs?"

"If I decide I need help, Mayor, I'll send word back. What I would like for you to do is officially deputize some of those men I had guarding the prisoners earlier. They can take care of the town. I want Jerry with me at the blockade."

"I'll do that immediately."

"Thank you."

"Be careful, Frank."

"I won't promise that, Mayor."

Jenkins smiled his understanding, nodded his head, and picked up the papers. "I'll send over your copies in a few days. I want to have these recorded."

Frank finished filling the loops in both gunbelts, .44-.40 and .45, then filled up a large canteen with fresh water. Jerry walked in about the time he was finished.

"Got the Gatlin' gun loaded, Frank. Several cases of filled-up magazines."

"Dynamite?"

"Enough to blow up a mountain. You ever handled dynamite?"

"Plenty of times. One more thing: go over to Angie's and tell her to fix us some sandwiches to take with us."

"On my way."

Frank stowed his rifle and canteen in the wagon outside the office and looked over the team: good, powerfully built horses. Doc Bracken walked up. Frank guessed the doctor was taking a much needed break from his patients.

"Mrs. Browning is drifting in and out of consciousness, Marshal. She wants to see you. You'd better come now. I don't believe she can last much longer."

Frank walked over to the doctor's office and pushed open the door leading to the tiny clinic. Conrad was sitting by his mother's bed. He looked up at Frank.

"I'll leave you alone for a few minutes, Marshal," the young man said, standing up. "Then I'll be back. I have something to say to you."

"All right, son."

"I am not your son!"

"Yes, you are," Vivian whispered.

Conrad whirled around. "What did you say, Mother?"

"Frank Morgan is your father."

"Mother! You don't know what you're saying."

"Mr. Browning knew you weren't his own son, but he raised you as if you were. Frank and I were married in Colorado right after the war. I was pregnant with you when your grandfather drove him away."

Conrad stared at Frank for a moment, then charged out of the office.

Frank sat down in the chair beside Viv's bed and took her hand. "I guess he had to know, Viv."

"It was past time."

"You're going to pull through this, Viv."

"No, I'm not, Frank, and you know it. I can read that in Dr. Bracken's eyes, and yours."

Frank didn't know what to say. He held her hand.

"Listen to me, Frank. Please. I don't know how long I'm going to stay conscious. I don't want you to see me . . . die. I don't want that to be the last memory you have of me. I don't want that image to be the one you carry in your mind for the rest of your life. Do you understand that?"

"Of course I do, Viv."

"Promise me you'll take care of Conrad. Promise me you'll try to see him into manhood."

"I'll try, Viv. I'll do my best, if he'll let me. But if he won't . . . what can I do?"

"Nothing. If you'll try, that's all I ask."

Vivian closed her eyes, and Frank thought for a few seconds he had lost her. Then she took several ragged breaths and once again opened her eyes.

"Did you sign the papers Jenkins brought over to you?" she asked.

"What? Oh. Yes. I signed something this morning. He said it was important."

She tried a small smile. "They were very important, Frank. Thank you. How is Jimmy?"

"He's dead, Viv. And so is the servant."

"I'm so sorry. What a mess. It was a bank robbery, wasn't it?"

"Yes. They tried to rob the bank. They didn't get away with a nickel of the bank's money."

She stared at Frank for a moment. "You're going after them, aren't you?"

"It's my job, Viv."

"Frank?"

"I'm right here."

"I never stopped loving you. I want you to know that."

"Nor did I stop loving you, Viv."

"That makes dying so much easier, Frank."

"Now you stop that kind of talk. You hear me? You're going to pull through this, Viv. You are. You've got to try, honey. Try!"

"I'm awfully tired, Frank. And I'm suddenly at peace. I . . . really can't describe it."

"Viv!"

"Try to look after Conrad, Frank. Will you? Remember, you promised."

"I'll do my best, Viv."

Vivian closed her eyes.

"Viv! Viv!"

Conrad burst into the room, the nurse right behind him.

"Both of you get out!" the nurse commanded. "Right now! Move."

Conrad confronted Frank in the outer office. "I don't care what mother says. You're not my father!"

"But I am, boy. She spoke the truth. Let me tell you what happened."

"I don't want to hear anything you have to say. It's all a pack of lies!"

Frank checked himself before he could strike the young man. "Your mother is not a liar, boy."

"Of course she is!" Conrad came right back at him. "If what you say is true, she's lied to me for years. Now let me hear you deny that."

Before Frank could reply, Conrad said, "You can't, can you? No, because it's the truth."

"If you will just let me try to explain, Conrad—"

"I hope to God I never see you again," Conrad blurted. "All this tragedy is your fault. It never would have happened if you hadn't showed up here."

Frank struggled to grasp the logic behind the young man's words. What did his coming to town weeks back have to do with an attempted bank robbery? He shook his head. "Conrad, you're not thinking straight. I—"

"I don't want to hear anything you have to say. I just want you to leave. I don't wish to ever see you again."

"Boy, I made a promise to your mother that I would take care of you. I—"

"You!" Conrad hissed at him. *"You* take care of me? Oh, I think not. Get out and leave me alone."

Frank stared at his son for a few seconds. "All right, boy. But I'll be back. You can count on that. Then we'll talk more."

"Not if I have anything to say about it."

The nurse walked into the room, dabbing at her eyes. "One of you go get Dr. Bracken. Hurry."

"Mother?" Conrad blurted.

"Fading very fast. Hurry, boy."

Conrad ran out of the office. "Is she conscious?" Frank asked.

"No. My God, this has been a horrible day."

Frank recalled Viv's words: *I don't want you to see me die. I don't want that to be the last memory you have of me.*

"Yes, it certainly has been that."

The nurse gripped Frank's arm. "Kill those outlaws, Marshal. Kill every one of them. Avenge this town."

"I plan on bringing them to justice, ma'am."

The nurse looked at him for a moment and then turned away, walking back into the tiny clinic of Dr. Bracken without another word.

Frank touched the butt of his pistol. "Yes, I certainly plan on delivering justice, ma'am."

Frank headed for his office. Jerry was waiting on the boardwalk. "Is Mrs. Browning—" He could not bring himself to finish the question.

"It won't be long, Jer. You ready to go?"

"Ready. I put the sandwiches in the wagon."

"All right. You drive the team. I'll follow with our horses. What's the latest on the death count?"

"Still climbing."

"Let's go even the score."

Twenty-three

About half a mile from the blockade, Frank left Jerry with the wagon and rode up to take a very cautious look-see, walking the last hundred yards and peeping around the sheer rock wall on the left side of the road. The Pine and Vanbergen gangs had blocked the road with a heavy chain stretched across it and then stationed two wagons, tongue to rear, in back of that. They had two red flags on poles in front of the chain, signifying danger, and four men with rifles were on guard.

"Slick," Frank muttered. "Very slick." He looked up and shook his head. No way to get above the blockade, for the sheer rock face was several hundred feet high. Any assault would have to be a frontal one. And Frank guessed that the main body of the gangs was camped not too far off, so they would come running at the first sounds of trouble.

It had been suggested to Frank that a rider from town try to make it through the outlaw pass. He had smiled at that and asked for volunteers. When no one stepped forward that suggestion was dropped.

Frank rode back to Jerry now, and swung down from the saddle. "One way through, Jer."

"Straight ahead, right?"

"That's it."

"They're going to hear the wagon when we move it into place, for a fact," Jerry said. "But what the hell? Surely they know we're here."

"Oh, they know, all right. This is how we'll play it: I'll handle the Gatling, and you get the wagon in place, as close as you can without exposing yourself. There's a place to turn the team just before the curve."

"And then what?"

"Then I start cranking and clear the roadblock."

"And the gangs come on the run."

"Probably. But they're going to run right into our fire. You have a better idea?"

Jerry smiled and shook his bandaged head. "Can't say as I do. I'll get the wagon in place."

"I'll be at the curve with a rifle. As soon as they hear you they'll get ready to open fire. Just as soon as I get a target, I'll drop him."

"Sounds good to me."

"Good luck, Jer."

Jerry nodded his head and climbed into the wagon. Frank walked back to the curve and got into position. The guards had probably been warned by a lookout high above the road, for there was no one in sight.

As he waited for Jerry to get into place, Frank wondered if the four men who had ambushed him and Viv that sunny afternoon had been part of the two gangs. He didn't think they were. Dutton's men, he was sure.

Another man he damn sure had to deal with as soon as he got the road opened. And he would get the road open. Frank didn't have any doubts about that. Doubts about his ability to deal with any given situation were not something that plagued him. He just bulled ahead and got it done.

Jerry got the wagon into position and unhitched the team, leading them to safety, then came back and removed the cases of dynamite and caps, stashing them behind some rocks, well out of the line of fire. He returned to crouch beside the wagon, rifle in his hand.

"Ready for the dance?" Frank called.

"Play the fiddle, Frank. It's your tune."

Frank started cranking, the lead flying from the hand cranked machine gun. The heavy slugs tore into the wagons, knocking great chunks from the sideboards.

"I thought you said both them Gatlin's had been ruint?" someone called from the outlaw side.

"Yeah," another man yelled. "Damn shore don't sound like it to me."

Frank gave the outlaws another half a magazine and got lucky this time: a man staggered out, both hands holding his torn up belly. He collapsed on the rocky road and died.

"Jess is dead!" a man called.

"I see him, you idgit! I ain't blind."

"No, yore just stupid! That there is Frank Morgan, and I told you he wasn't gonna take this lyin' down."

"If you want your share of that money in the bank you'll shet your mouth and hold this here road."

"I want me some of them women in the town," another man said, his voice carrying clearly in the thin mountain air. "I got me a real powerful yearnin.' "

Frank gave the outlaws another half a magazine, and that ended conversation on their side for a few minutes.

While Frank was changing out the magazine, Jerry's rifle cracked and an outlaw screamed and fell to the hard road, one leg broken. The .44-.40 slug had busted his knee. Moaning in pain, the man dragged himself out of sight, behind some rocks on the side of the road.

Hundreds of feet above the road, some of the outlaw gang began hurling large rocks down at the road. But the top of the ridge angled outward, and rocks hit nowhere near the wagon. The outlaws gave up their rock throwing very quickly.

For a few moments, the siege became quiet, both sides apparently at an impasse.

Jerry edged closer to Frank. "How are we goin' to get the dynamite down to the blockade? We sure can't toss it down there. It's too far."

"I've been studying on that, Jer. I think we'll use the spare wheel off the wagon."

"A wheel?"

"Yes. It's a gentle slope down to the blockade, and the road is fairly smooth. We'll tie the charge to the wheel, light it, and roll it down there."

"And if it falls over, or rolls off the edge before it gets there?"

"There are four more wheels on the wagon. And we've got lots of dynamite. The trick is going to be cutting the fuse the right length."

"I'll get the wheel. You handle the charges. Me and dynamite made a bargain a long time back: it leaves me alone, and I do the same for it."

Frank smiled. He was an experienced hand with dynamite, and knew that it wasn't just the charges one should be cautious with, but the caps. He'd seen men lose fingers, hands, and entire arms after getting careless while capping dynamite.

Frank tied together a dozen sticks of explosives and

carefully capped the lethal bundle. Jerry rolled the big wheel up and squatted down, watching while Frank cut and inserted the fuse. Then Frank secured the charge to the wheel with a cord and looked at his deputy.

"You ready?"

"If that's a fast-burnin' fuse, we're in trouble," Jerry said.

Frank chuckled. "We'll soon know, won't we?"

"You don't know?"

"Nope. You got the dynamite and fuses. Didn't you ask?"

" 'Fraid not."

Frank struck a match and lit the fuse. "Roll it, Jer!"

Jerry was only too happy to start the wheel rolling. He breathed a sigh of relief when the wheel was on the road. The heavy wheel bounced and wobbled down the gently sloping road, the fuse sputtering and sparking as it rolled.

"Get the hell out of here!" an outlaw yelled. "That's dynamite comin' our way."

"Shoot the wheel and stop it!" another gang member shouted.

"You shoot the goddamn thing, Luke. I'm outta here."

For a few seconds it looked as though the wheel was going to topple over before it reached the blockade. Then it straightened up and picked up speed, rolling true.

At the blockade, outlaws were scrambling to get clear. They were running and cussing and slipping and sliding.

The wheel ran into a wagon and lodged under the wagon bed for a few seconds before exploding. It went off with a fury, sending bits and pieces of the wagon flying in all directions. The explosion lifted the second wagon up and over the edge of the road. The chain that had been stretched across the road was blown loose, and fell to the road. A huge dust cloud covered and obscured the area where the blockade had been. When the dust settled, the road was clear.

Several of the outlaws had not gotten clear: there were three men sprawled unconscious on the road. One of them was clearly dead, his neck twisted at an impossible angle. He had been picked up by the concussion and thrown against the cliff.

"Jesus!" Jerry said, his voice hushed. "How many sticks did you lash together, Frank?"

"Twelve."

Jerry cut his eyes to Frank and shook his head in awe. "Warn me next time, will you?"

"I hope there won't be a next time," Frank replied.

"It ain't over, Frank!" the shout came from high above the road. "You son of a bitch!"

"Vic Vanbergen," Frank said. "I recognize the voice."

"We'll meet again, you sorry son!" Vic yelled. "You can count on that."

"And that goes double in spades for me, Morgan!"

"Ned Pine," Frank said. "It's over here, Jer. They're making their brags and threats now."

"Watch your ass in town, Morgan," Vic yelled. "It ain't over by a long shot."

"He's tellin' you they've got men in town waitin' for you, Frank," Jerry said.

"Sure," Frank said calmly. "Big Bob Mallory will be back, and Kid Moran. Several others, I'm sure."

The lawmen waited on the road for several minutes more, but there was no more yelling from the top of the ridge. The Vanbergen and Pine gangs had pulled out.

Frank and Jerry made their way cautiously down to

the now wrecked blockade. Two of the outlaws who had not cleared the blast were dead, one with a clearly broken neck, the other with a massive head wound caused by the fallen debris. The others were gone.

"I'll hook up the team," Jerry said. "Bring the wagon down and we'll tote the dead back." He smiled. "Might be a reward on them."

"You're learning. I'll start clearing away some of this junk."

"Frank?"

"Yes?"

"Pine and Vanbergen knew they couldn't keep this road closed. Why did they even try?"

"I think they were counting on us being dead. Our coming out alive put a kink in their plans."

"You're really gonna have to watch your back careful in town, Frank."

"I've been doing that for many years. It's as automatic for me as breathing. Come on, let's get these bodies loaded up and get back to town."

Vivian was in a coma. Dr. Bracken told Frank that she might linger that way for hours, or even days. There was just no way to tell.

The two dead outlaws were both wanted and had a price on their heads. And they both carried some identification on them, which was a lucky break for the lawmen. Frank would wire the states where they were wanted as soon as the telegraph wires were repaired.

Frank filled out his daily report in the jail journal and then went on a walking inspection of the town. The main street was still a mess. The bodies of the dead had long been carried off, and the wounded were in makeshift hospitals. The undertaker had bodies stacked all over the place, overflowing out into the alley behind his parlor. There was just no time to embalm them all, nor did Malone have enough supplies to do so. The funerals were starting as soon as carpenters could knock together caskets.

Some of the caskets were tiny, and that was heartbreaking for anyone with a modicum of feeling.

Frank tried to talk with Conrad, but he refused to see him. After Frank tried twice and was rebuffed both times, he decided to leave his son alone. Frank would be in town and available when or if the young man wanted to talk.

Kid Moran and Big Bob Mallory were back in town. They were doing nothing to help out, just sitting and watching as the town struggled to pull itself out of the wreckage and cope with the heavy loss of life.

Frank didn't push the pair. There had been quite enough killing. But he knew they were there for a showdown. It was just a matter of time. With The Kid it was an ego thing. Kid Moran wanted a reputation. Frank still wasn't certain who was paying Big Bob, but Charles Dutton was at the top of his list.

Dutton was Conrad's shadow that day, all concern and sorrow and sympathy, and the young man was certainly receptive. Frank didn't, couldn't, blame the boy. Conrad didn't have any idea what was going on; apparently Vivian had never gotten around to talking with her son about her deep and dark feelings concerning Dutton.

And now it's too late, Frank thought with a silent sigh. *Too late for a lot of things.*

He was tired and taking a break, sitting on the bench

outside the marshal's office, having a cup of coffee. Late afternoon shadows were creeping about the streets of the mountain town, creating little pockets of darkness in hidden corners. This had always been one of Frank's favorite times of the day, when dusk was reaching out to slowly melt and mingle with sunlight. But on this day of tragedy he was filled with various emotions: a hard sense of loss, a feeling of impending doom, a sense that his time in the mining town was nearly over; other emotions that were strong but not yet identifiable. Well . . . one of the emotions was certainly familiar—the feeling that he had screwed up his life beyond salvaging.

Frank was a middle-aged man with a very dubious past, and not much of a future.

And damned if he knew how he could change it.

The voice of Dr. Bracken broke into his thoughts. "You mind some company, Marshal?"

Frank looked up. "Not at all, Doc. Glad to have some company." He scooted over on the bench. "Might improve my disposition."

Bracken looked at the cup in Frank's hand. "That coffee drinkable?"

"You bet. Hot and fresh." Frank started to rise. "I'll get you a cup."

Doc Bracken put a hand on his shoulder. "Sit still. I'll get it." He walked into the office. A moment later, a mug of coffee in his hand, Bracken sat down on the bench. "You were deep in thought, Marshal, your face a study in emotion. Anything you want to talk about?"

"Oh, not really, Doc. I guess I was just sitting here sort of feeling sorry for myself."

"You do that often?"

Frank smiled. "Not very often, Doc. Looking over the wreckage of this town brought it on, I suppose."

"That and Mrs. Browning," the doctor said softly.

"Yes. That, too."

"Frank, the West is still a small place, speaking in terms of population. Hell, man, half the town knew that you and Vivian Browning . . . ah, Henson . . . were once married. Many of those knew that old man Henson trumped up some false charges against you, and you had to leave. The story was all over the West back then. Newcomers, Johnny-come-latelies, don't know it, but we old-timers do. I've had people today, in the midst of all this tragedy, tell me that it's admirable how well you're holding up. Most of the people here in town, the regulars, the permanent residents . . . why, they like you, Frank. They've found that all your dark reputation is pure bunk. For whatever it's worth, the town is behind you."

"Doc, I'm going to hunt down that gang—every member—and I'm going to kill them, all of them. My reputation is about to get a lot darker."

"Only one man was cranking that Gatling gun, Frank."

"But they were all involved. And no one tried to stop that one man."

"I can't argue that point.

"Viv and me, Doc, we were picking up the pieces. We were going to start all over. Move to California, maybe, where very few people have even heard of me . . ."

That got Frank a quick, sharp look from Doc Bracken. Frank Morgan still didn't realize that most people over the age of eight had heard of him. He didn't know that there had been dozens and dozens of newspaper articles written about him. People knew about Frank Morgan's exploits from coast-to-coast and border-to-border. Now many in the press were beginning to call him the last gunfighter—Frank Morgan, the Last Gunfighter.

"All that's gone up in a few minutes of gunsmoke. Vivian is lying in a coma, dying. My"—Frank caught himself, but not before Dr. Bracken picked up on the hesitation—"her son won't speak to me. He blames me for all that's happened. Hell, maybe he's right. Not entirely, but partly. I accept it. What choice do I have?"

"That's nonsense, Frank. She got caught in the line of fire—that's what happened."

Frank sighed. "You don't know the whole story, Doc. And it's best you never do."

"If you say so, Frank." He took another sip of coffee. "Good. I needed that. It's been a long day, and it's going to be an even longer night."

"I'm sure."

Jerry walked up, a toothpick in his mouth. "Doc," he greeted Bracken. "You better go put on the feedbag, Frank. Angie's laid out quite a spread at the café."

"Yeah, that's a good idea. I am kinda hungry. Doc, how about you?"

"In a little while. I want to check on a couple of patients first."

When the doctor had gone, Jerry said, "Big Bob Mallory was seen leavin' the hotel about fifteen minutes ago, totin' his rifle."

"It's about time for the showdown, then. I've been feeling it coming for several hours. Where is Kid Moran?"

"Disappeared. I looked around and he was nowhere to be seen. Come on, I'll have coffee while you eat."

"Not looking a gunfight in the eyes, Jer. I changed my mind. A big meal slows you down. I'll eat later." Frank smiled. "Providing I still can eat, that is."

Twenty-four

With Jerry walking a dozen yards behind him, carrying a rifle and covering his back, Frank strolled down to the café. The front windows had been knocked out, and were now boarded up, but the horrible events of that day had not affected the quality of food. The delicious odors drifting out into the street made Frank's mouth water, bringing home the fact that he had not eaten all day. But he did not want to eat a large meal and then have to face a very fast gunslick. And Kid Moran was very fast.

Frank settled for a piece of pie with his cup of coffee. Then he had a cigarette with his second cup in the Silver Spoon Café. He was stubbing out the cigarette butt when Jerry came in and took a seat.

"Kid Moran's waiting for you, Frank. He's standing on the corner. He's got a third pistol shoved in his gunbelt."

"He must be figuring I'm going to be hard to put down," Frank said as he rolled another smoke.

"Don't forget he usually misses his first shot," Jerry reminded him.

"Yeah. And sometimes he doesn't. Always expect the unexpected in these things, Jerry. I've learned that the hard way over the years."

"I'll never have a stand up and hook and draw fight, Frank. I know better. I'm as slow as cold molasses."

"I hope you never do, Jer."

"Frank, let's you and me take him alive," Jerry suggested. "We'll get a couple of Greeners from the office and take him that way. How about it?"

"It wouldn't work."

"Why?"

"He'd fight, and we'd both run the risk of getting plugged. What he's calling for right now is still legal out here, and probably will be for some years to come. Have you seen Big Bob anywhere?"

"No. This smells like a setup to me, Frank."

"The Kid drawing me out, and Big Bob shooting me in the back?" Frank shook his head. "No. No, I don't think so. Bob Mallory works alone. Always has."

"There's always the first time."

Again, Frank shook his head. "No. The Kid's looking for a reputation, and Bob is getting paid by somebody— probably Dutton—to kill me." Frank paused in his lifting of his coffee cup. "Or maybe it's Conrad he's after. Jer, go check on Conrad. Keep an eye on him for me, will you?"

"If you order me to do so, Frank, I will."

"Do I have to order it done?"

"No. Of course not. I'm gone."

Frank finished his coffee and stood up, slipping the hammer thong off his .45. Angie was watching, and frowned.

"Frank, isn't there another way?"

"No, Angie. There isn't. Not with The Kid. He wants a reputation."

"He's lightning fast."

Frank smiled. "I'm no tenderfoot, Angie."

She returned the smile. "Of course, you're not. I didn't mean to imply—"

Frank held up a hand. "I know what you meant, Angie. Keep the coffee hot, will you?"

"Just for you and Jerry. And I'll have some supper for you, too."

Frank picked up his hat, settled it on his head, and stepped out of the café. He looked to his left. There was The Kid, waiting at the end of the block.

"Might as well get this over with," Frank said, thinking: *One way or the other.* He touched the brim of his hat in a salute to The Kid, a signal that he was ready, and stepped off the boardwalk and into the street.

Kid Moran did the same.

The word had spread about the pending gunfight. The main street was deserted of carpenters and other workmen. In only a few more years, stand up, hook and draw showdowns such as this would be mostly a thing of the past, but for now, it was still legal in most small towns in the West. If not legal, at least accepted by many.

Louis Pettigrew, the book writer from the East, was standing in the lobby of the hotel, watching it all and scribbling furiously in his notebook. He had written about dozens of shoot-outs, but this was the first actual gunfight he had ever witnessed. It was enthralling and exciting. What a book this would make: the aging king of gunfighters meeting a young, but fast, upstart prince in the dusty street for the title of the best of the fast guns. Wonderful!

Conrad was not watching the slow walk toward death in the street. He was sitting quietly beside his mother's bed.

Charles Dutton was watching from the hotel, a faint smile on his lips.

"Ride out of here, Kid," Frank called. "Don't throw your life away for nothing."

"It ain't nothin' to me, Morgan," The Kid called.

"Boy, the day of the gunfighter is nearly over. And as far as I'm concerned, it's past time."

"What's the matter, Morgan?" The Kid taunted. "You gettin' old and yeller?"

Getting old, for sure, Frank thought. *He's damn sure right on one count.* "Don't be a fool, boy. You know better than that."

"Frank Morgan done lost his nerve," The Kid yelled. "By God, it's true. You beg me to let you leave and you can ride out of here, Morgan. Beg for your life, old man."

The Kid's been drinking, Frank thought. *Where else would he get such a silly idea?* "Forget it, boy," Frank called. "That won't happen."

The distance between them was slowly closing. Little pockets of dust were popping up under their boots as they walked toward sudden death and destiny.

"Why don't you draw, old man?" The Kid yelled. "Come on, damn you. Pull on me!"

"It's your play, Kid," Frank said calmly. "You're the one challenging the law here in town. I'm ordering you to give this up and ride on out."

The Kid suddenly stopped in the middle of the street. Frank stopped his walking. There were maybe fifty or so feet between them. Plenty close enough.

"Suspenseful," Louis Pettigrew muttered. "I never knew it could be like this."

"Insane," Mayor Jenkins muttered, watching from inside his bank. "When is this going to stop?"

Angie stood in the doorway of her café, a just poured cup of coffee forgotten in her hand.

Undertaker Malone was watching from an alley. He was taking a much needed break from his work. The bodies of that day's tragic events were still stacked up inside his parlor and outside behind his establishment. Many had already been buried without benefit of Malone's services.

Willis was watching from his general store. He had sent his wife and kids into the rear of the store, safe from any stray bullets.

"Draw on me, you old bastard," Kid Moran yelled, "so's I can kill you and have done with this."

"Drag iron, son," Frank replied. "I told you this is your play."

The Kid stared at Frank, then shook his head. "You yeller son of a bitch!" The Kid hollered. "You're afeared of me. I knowed you had a yeller streak up your back."

Frank waited, silent and steady—a man alone in the middle of the street, the tin star on his coat twinkling faintly in the last rays of late-afternoon sun. Frank sensed The Kid was getting nervous, and that emotion would be a plus for him.

"What's the matter, boy?" Frank called. "You sound real edgy."

"Ain't nothin' the matter with me, you old fart! Are you gonna draw, or rattle that jaw of yourn?"

"I keep telling you, boy, it's your play. Are you deaf, or just plain stupid?"

"Goddamn you!"

Frank waited patiently.

Someone standing in the doorway of the saloon laughed.

The Kid cut his eyes away from Frank for just a split second. "Are you laughin' at me?"

Frank could have drawn and fired during the half second The Kid had averted his eyes. But he didn't. Frank really didn't want to kill The Kid. He knew, though, that The Kid wasn't about to give him any other option.

The Kid settled that quickly. "You damned yeller belly. I'm countin' to three. You better draw on me, Morgan. Sometime durin' the count. If you don't, that's your hard luck. It don't make no difference to me nohow. I'm gonna kill you anyways. I'm tared of all this jibber jabber."

"You're under arrest, Kid Moran," Frank called, making what he knew he had to do legal.

"Huh? I'm whut?"

"You're under arrest."

"Whut charge?"

"Threatening the life of a peace officer. Now come along peacefully or suffer the consequences."

"You go to hell, Morgan!"

"That's the last chance I'm giving you, boy."

Kid Moran cursed and grabbed iron. He just thought he was quick on the shoot. Frank beat him to the draw and shot him in the belly.

"Damn!" The Kid gasped, doubling over. But he held on to his gun.

"Drop your gun, boy!" Frank called.

"Hell with you, Morgan." The Kid lifted his .45 and jacked back the hammer.

Frank shot him again. The impact turned The Kid around in the street. He stumbled a couple of times, but he just wouldn't go down.

Kid Moran straightened up and grinned at Morgan.

"Now you're dead, Morgan," he gasped. "Now it's my turn."

The Kid lifted his pistol and Frank drilled him again. This time The Kid went to his knees, but didn't stay down long. He dropped his pistol and, bracing himself with that hand, struggled to his feet, drawing his second pistol.

"Damn you to hell, Morgan!" The Kid managed to spit out the words. Then he turned to one side and lifted and cocked his left-hand gun.

Frank dusted him with his fourth round, the bullet slamming into The Kid and blowing out the other side. This time Kid Moran went down and stayed down. He tried to rise, but just couldn't make it. His pistol slipped from his hand to lie in the dust.

Frank unconsciously twirled his pistol before holstering it. He walked over and looked down at the bullet-riddled young man. "Sorry about this, Kid. I really am."

"You really are . . . fast, Morgan. I never . . . seen nobody fast as you."

Frank knelt down beside The Kid.

Kid Moran struggled to speak, then gave it up, gasping for breath. "I'll get the doc, boy." Frank looked around. Dr. Bracken was walking toward the fallen Kid, his black bag in his hand.

Frank stood up and met the doc halfway. "I put four rounds in him, Doc. I don't see how he's still alive."

"I saw and heard it all, Frank. You gave him every opportunity to surrender. You only did what you had to do."

The men walked over to where The Kid lay. "Let me take a look at him," Bracken said.

"Forget it," The Kid gasped. "I'm done for and I know it. I'm fillin' up with blood. I feel it. Don't move me."

"All right, boy," Doc Bracken said.

"You got any kin, Kid?" Frank asked.

"Nobody that gives a damn."

"Your mother and father?"

"Wherever they are"—The Kid coughed up blood—"they can both go to hell!"

"You want some laudanum?" Doc Bracken asked.

The Kid didn't reply. His eyes were wide and staring in death.

Malone walked up. "I know The Kid had money," the undertaker said. "What do you want on his tombstone?"

Frank thought for a moment. Then he said, "Put on it: He died game."

Twenty-five

The bloody, bullet-riddled body of Kid Moran was carried off and stored with other bodies behind Malone's funeral parlor. The undertaker would get to Moran when time permitted.

Big Bob Mallory had been spotted leaving town. Frank checked his room at the hotel and found it bare. Big Bob was indeed gone, but where and for how long remained unanswered.

"Maybe he decided not to take the job," Jerry opined. He and Frank were sitting in the jail office, the day after the attack on the town.

"Don't count on that," Frank replied. "Big Bob demands money up front. If he takes the money, he'll finish the job."

"Wishful thinking on my part."

"You ready to take over the marshal's job, Jer?" Frank abruptly tossed the question at his deputy.

Jerry almost spilled his coffee down the front of his shirt. He stared at Frank, his mouth open; then he shook his head and said, "You goin' somewhere for a while, Frank?"

"As soon as it's . . . over for Mrs. Browning, I'm pulling out. I think you'll make a fine marshal, Jer." He smiled. "You and Angie will be assets to this community, for sure."

"You goin' after the Pine and Vanbergen gangs, Frank?"

"Yes."

"Alone?"

"Yes."

Jerry was silent for a moment, staring at the floor. He lifted his head and looked at Frank. "That's crazy, Frank. That's suicide."

"My mind is made up. You want the job, or not?"

"Well . . . sure, I do. If you leave, and the town council approves it."

"They'll approve it. You're a good, solid, steady man, Jerry. Both you and Angie are respected by the townspeople. You'll both do just fine."

"Maybe Mrs. Browning will pull through."

"I don't believe in miracles. Doc Bracken told me this morning her coma has deepened. She'll starve to death if she doesn't come out of it."

"What about the outlaws?"

"They're gone. Packed up, saddled up, and gone. Very doubtful they'll ever be back."

"Your mind's made up, isn't it?"

"All the way, Jer."

"Maybe something will happen that will change your mind. I'd like to see you stay."

Frank nodded his head in understanding and stood up. "I don't know what that would be, but thanks for saying it. The prisoners are all settled down. It's all quiet. Let's go walk the town."

"They put The Kid in the ground yet?"

"I don't think so. I don't think Malone's had time to fix him up yet."

"To be no bigger than he was, The Kid could sure soak up some lead."

"He did, for a fact. The Kid was as game as any man I ever faced."

The two lawmen walked the town, the sounds of sawing and hammering all around them, the smell of fresh-cut lumber strong in the air.

"This town might be here even when the mines play out," Jerry remarked.

"Could be. It sure wouldn't surprise me at all. Some cattlemen are gonna have to come in here. Maybe a few people raising horses. When the mines play out, the town will shrink down. But you've got a telegraph office and a bank, and some determined people. That's what it takes."

"Oh, hell!" Jerry said. "Here comes that writer fellow."

"Damn!" Frank muttered.

"Marshal Morgan," Louis Pettigrew called. "Might I have a word with you, sir?"

"Do I have a choice?" Frank whispered.

Jerry laughed. "I'll make the rounds. You two have a good time."

"Thanks, Jer. You're a real pal."

Jerry waved and walked on, leaving Frank with Pettigrew. Frank noticed Conrad and Charles Dutton walking up the boardwalk on the other side of the street. Even from that distance Frank could tell that Conrad appeared very pale. *Boy's under a hell of a strain,* Frank thought. *Dutton probably got him away from his mother's side to get him out for a walk and some fresh air. Or,* Frank amended, *maybe the bastard has something else up his sleeve, like setting the boy up for a kill.*

"Ah, Marshal . . ." Pettigrew said. "I would like to talk with you about doing your life's story. Would you be willing to discuss that?"

Frank looked at the Boston writer. "I beg your pardon? What did you say?"

Pettigrew looked pained. He sighed and said, "I wish to write your life story. There are a great many people back east who are clamoring for more information about Frank Morgan."

"Is that a fact?"

"Absolutely, Marshal. And it would be a very lucrative venture for you, I must say."

"I'll sure give it some thought, Mr. Pettigrew."

"Wonderful, Marshal. And let me say that the, ah, gunfight I witnessed yesterday out there in the street was a magnificent sight. Very dramatic."

Frank was watching Conrad and Dutton. They had stopped on the corner and were chatting. Conrad had his back to the street. "Dramatic, Mr. Pettigrew?"

"It certainly was. I can truthfully say I have never seen anything like it."

"You ever witnessed a hanging, Mr. Pettigrew?"

"Good heavens, no."

The morning stage was rumbling up the street, a day late due to the road being blocked the day before. The telegraph wires had been fixed, messages had been sent out that the reports of plague in the town were false, and the road had been reopened.

"A hanging can be very dramatic, Mr. Pettigrew. Especially when the neck isn't broken and the victim jerks around for several minutes, slowly choking to death. It's quite a sight." Frank said this with a very straight face.

Pettigrew was turning a bit green around the mouth. "I'll take your word for that, Marshal."

"I can probably arrange for you to witness an execution. If you would like that."

"Ah . . . thank you, Marshal, but no. Your description of the event is graphic enough."

Frank watched Dutton put his hands on the young man's shoulders and reposition him, fully presenting Conrad's back to the street, while Dutton was partly shielded by a post holding an oil-fueled streetlamp.

What the hell? Frank thought. *What's going on here? Very strange behavior on Dutton's part.*

"When would be a good time for us to get together for a long talk?" Pettigrew asked.

"Oh, sometime within the next couple of days, for sure," Frank responded.

"Wonderful. That will give me ample time to jot down pertinent questions. At your office, perhaps?"

"That will be fine."

"I'm so looking forward to it."

"Yeah, me, too," Frank replied with as much enthusiasm as possible, which was precious little. He had no intention of meeting with the writer. "I'll see you, Mr. Pettigrew. You have a nice day."

"Oh, I shall, Marshal. Thank you."

"You're welcome," Frank mumbled, as he began walking toward the corner. He stepped off the boardwalk and started crossing the street, his eyes on Conrad and Dutton.

"Hi, Marshal," a citizen yelled, catching Frank in the middle of the street.

Conrad spun around at the shouted greeting just as a rifle cracked somewhere behind Frank. Frank dropped into a crouch and turned around, snaking his .45 into his hand with a blurringly fast motion.

The rifle slug burned past Conrad, missing him by just a few inches. Had he not turned, the rifle bullet would have split his spinal cord. The slug slammed into a passerby who had just exited the newly arrived stage and was carrying his heavy traveling bag. The bullet meant for Conrad knocked the man off his boots and dropped him to the boardwalk, dead on impact with the dusty boards.

Frank triggered off a shot at a man in an upstairs window over a boarded-up shop, a man standing with a rifle in his hand, a faint finger of smoke leaking from the muzzle. The .45 round hit the man in his chest, just below his throat, and slammed him backward in the room.

"Conrad!" Frank yelled as rifle barrels began poking out of several second story windows. "Get out of here, boy. Someone is trying to kill you!"

Frank ran for the protection of the stage, but the driver was no stranger to gunfire, having experienced it many times in the past, and he wanted no more of it. He yelled at his team, and the six big horses took off.

Frank sprinted for the dubious protection of an open carriage in front of a shop, running and twisting to afford the snipers less of a target. Bullets howled all around him. Out of the corner of his eye he caught a glimpse of Dutton hightailing it alone around a corner. The fancy lawyer and so-called friend of the family was leaving Conrad to deal with the problem on his own. The young man seemed frozen in place on the boardwalk until Jerry came charging around the corner and grabbed him up and off his feet. Jerry turned, and a slug tore into his left leg, knocking him down. Just before he fell heavily, Jerry shoved Conrad to safety inside a corner shop.

Frank slid on his belly in the dirt and reached the rear of the carriage in time to see Jerry crawl into the shop, dragging his bloody leg, leaving a trail on the boardwalk. At least he was still alive, and Conrad was safe.

Frank knelt behind the boot of the carriage and began throwing lead at the upstairs windows. It was returned as fast as it was received. One rifle slug knocked Frank's hat off and sent it flying somewhere behind him. Another rifle slug burned a hot crease on his shoulder. The crease turned wet and sticky as the blood began to flow. Frank ignored the burning pain and jerked his second gun from behind his gunbelt.

Jerry opened up from the doorway of the shop, and at that point the hidden gunmen above the street decided they'd had enough. The gunfire ceased, and the street fell silent.

Horses tied at hitch rails had bolted in panic when the rifle fire began, running in all directions. One horse ran into Nannette's Boutique for the Discriminating Woman, and one lady (who was nearly the same size as the horse) ran out into the street dressed only in her bloomers, shrieking to high heaven. The sight of her stopped one man cold in his tracks.

"My Lord!" he hollered.

The panicked woman ran right over the man, knocking him into a horse trough. She kept right on running, and disappeared into the Silver Slipper Saloon. Men began exiting the saloon through all available avenues, preferring to face gunfire rather than confront the ominous presence of Mrs. Bertha Longthrower, wife of Reverend Otis Longthrower, pastor of Heaven's Grace Baptist Church . . . in her bloomers.

Bertha took one long look at her surroundings, her eyes lingering on the rather risqué painting on the wall behind the bar (which featured three naked ladies and a midget . . . in height only) and let out a whoop that would have shamed a Comanche Dog Soldier. She headed for the rear of the saloon, ran out the back door, and collided with a man just stepping out of the privy. Both of them were propelled back into the privy, which promptly turned over, trapping the scantily clad woman and the terrified man (who was certain he had been attacked by an enraged albino grizzly bear) in the narrow confines of the outhouse.

Back on the main street, Frank ran across the street and into an alley that led behind the line of shops, hurriedly reloading his guns. He caught a glimpse of a man with a rifle charging out of a back door, and yelled at him to halt. The man turned and fired at Frank, the bullet just missing his head. Frank drilled the man, the .45 slug striking the assassin in the chest, killing him instantly.

Frank cautiously made his way up to the downed and dead sniper. The rifle beside the body was a bolt-action Winchester-Hotchkiss. He had found one of the men who had ambushed him and Viv in the valley.

Two more of the men were still at large, but Frank suspected they were gone, having left ahead of the man on the ground. He picked up the rifle and walked back to the street. He wanted to have a long talk with Charles Dutton, but had no physical evidence at all with which to confront the man. Dutton was, so far, still in the clear.

Conrad was unhurt, and Jerry's wound, while painful, was not serious. The deputy would be off his feet for a few days, but was not in danger.

The passerby who had taken the bullet meant for Conrad was dead.

The horse who had invaded Nannette's had been led out and away, and the search was on for Mrs. Bertha Longthrower.

"Where is my wife?" Reverend Longthrower demanded.

"I think she's in the saloon," a citizen told him. "I seen her goin' in there . . . in her bloomers."

"In her what?" Reverend Longthrower thundered.

"Her drawers."

"Never!" the reverend roared.

"Hey, ever'body!" a man yelled from the saloon. "Otis is in the privy yellin' that he's bein' attacked by an albino bear. Come on."

Frank had a pretty good idea that the "bear" would turn out to be Mrs. Longthrower . . . in her drawers. That was not a sight he wished to see again. He told some men to get the body of the outlaw on the second floor and then went to check on Conrad and Jerry over at the doctor's makeshift hospital. Before he could cross the street Reverend Longthrower started hollering for his wife to get off of Otis.

"I imagine Otis would like that, too," Frank muttered.

Conrad had refused to lie down and rest for a while, choosing to go to the office. Frank sat down on the edge of the bunk and talked with Jerry for a few minutes.

"Doc says the bullet didn't bit nothin' vital," Jerry

said. "He says I just have to stay off my feet for a couple of days and rest."

"You take as long as you need, Jer." He smiled. "I imagine Angie will see that you're well fed."

Jerry blushed under his tan. "Yeah. I 'spect she will." He looked closer at Frank. "You been hit, Frank! Your shoulder's bleedin.' "

"It's just a scratch. I'm heading over to the office now to clean it up."

"Take off your shirt, Frank," Dr. Bracken said from behind him. "Let me take a look at that wound."

"It's nothing, Doc."

"Take off your shirt. That's an order. You get blood poisoning, you won't think nothing."

Doc Bracken cleaned and bandaged the wound, told Frank to take it easy for the rest of the day, and sent him on his way. Frank didn't want to tell the doctor he'd hurt himself worse than that peeling potatoes.

On his way back to the office, Frank ran into Louis Pettigrew. "Marshal," the writer said, "I have made up my mind."

"Oh?" Frank was staring at the man's bowler hat.

"Yes. I am going to write a series of books about you. Not just one, but perhaps a dozen."

Frank did not reply, just stared at the man in stunned disbelief. He couldn't keep his eyes off the man's dude hat.

"I have wired my publisher, and am now awaiting his reply. I shall make it my life's work."

"Your life's work?" Frank managed to say.

"Yes, sir. I shall outfit myself and follow you no matter where in the wilds you might decide to go. I shall chronicle the day to day living of the West's most celebrated but least known gunfighter. Won't that be grand?"

"Words fail me, Mr. Pettigrew." *I gotta get out of here, and do it quickly,* Frank thought.

"As soon as I receive word from my publisher I shall make preparations," Pettigrew said.

"To do what?" Frank asked.

"To make the West my home! I must say, this is very exciting."

I'll leave in the dead of night, Frank thought. *Slip away like a thief.*

"I just thought you would like to know about my decision, Marshal. And I hope you're as excited as I am."

"Oh, I am, Mr. Pettigrew. I can't begin to tell you how your decision has affected me."

Pettigrew patted Frank on the arm. "I'm so pleased, Marshal. I really didn't know how you would react to the news."

"I'm, ah, still trying to get used to the idea of you becoming a citizen of the West, Mr. Pettigrew."

"I'm really excited about it."

"I'm sure you are."

"Well, then, I'll see you later on. We'll make an appointment to meet and start work on the first installment. Ta ta, Marshal."

"Yeah," Frank mumbled. "Ta-ta to you, too."

"What is the writer so happy about?" Mayor Jenkins asked, walking up just as Pettigrew was leaving.

"He's going to become a permanent resident of the West."

"Really?"

"That's what he told me."

"Well, he's certainly welcome. I just hope he gets rid of that damn silly hat," the banker said, "before someone shoots it off his head."

Twenty-six

Frank had just finished a fresh cup of coffee and a smoke and had his feet propped up on the edge of the desk when a man walked into his office. "Sorry to bother you, Marshal, but I found me a body on the way into town."

Frank's boots hit the floor. "Where?"

"Just the other side of where them outlaws had the road blocked. I seen the buzzards circlin' and went to take a look. It's kind of bad, Marshal. The body's shore enough tore up somethin' awful. The ants has been workin' on it, as well as them damn buzzards."

"I'll head on out there. Thanks, mister."

"No problem."

Frank picked up a spare horse at the livery and headed out. He was not looking forward to bringing the body back. Several days in the hot sun would have the body bloated and stinking. The ants and buzzards, and probably coyotes and other animals, had been working on it and would have left it in a real mess.

Frank saw the buzzards long before he reached the body, about a hundred yards off the road, and up a natural game trail. Frank could tell by what was left of the clothing that it was more than likely the body of the young bank teller, Dean Hall, or Hill, or whatever his name was.

The body was a mess, not at all pleasant to look at, or smell. Buzzards and ants had been at the face and the eyes, and facial identification would be impossible. Buzzards, more than likely, had torn the stomach open, and intestines were stretched out for yards.

"Damn!" Frank said, trying to breathe through his mouth and not his nose. The stench was awful.

He found a big stick and beat off the buzzards, some of them so bloated from eating the putrid meat they could not fly. They waddled off and stared at Frank, giving him baleful looks, no fear in them.

He got the body on the tarp and rolled it up, securing it tightly with rope, closing both ends. That helped with the stench. It was going to be a real job getting the body tied down on the horse, for the animal was not liking the smell at all, and was trying to break loose and back off.

Frank didn't blame the horse at all.

Frank was securing a loose end of the tarp, one foot of the body sticking out, when he saw his own horse's head jerk up, the ears laid back, nostrils flared. Frank quickly jerked his rifle from the boot and grabbed the ammo belt he had looped over the horn. The tarp-wrapped body forgotten, Frank jumped for cover, thinking, *Setup!*

Someone, maybe Ned Pine and Vic Vanbergen, maybe Dutton, *somebody,* had set him up for sure. And the setup had worked to perfection. He was damn sure set up, and boxed in.

Frank had just bellied down behind the rocks when the bullets started flying all around him. All he could do for several minutes was keep his head down and hope that no bullet flattened out against the rocks and ricocheted into him.

He wriggled into better cover during a few seconds respite in the firing. He hadn't made any attempt to return the fire, for as yet he didn't have any idea where the gunmen were. He didn't know if there were two or ten of them. He knew only that if it lasted for very long he was in for one hell of a mighty dry fight. His canteen was on his horse, and the animal had wandered several dozen yards away—no way he could get to it. And there was little chance he could expect any help.

The firing began again, and this time Frank could pretty well add up the number of shooters he was facing, for not all of them were using the same caliber rifles. Five shooters, Frank figured. And several of them were slightly above him.

Two of the four assassins from the ambush in the valley and town were still alive; could they be a part of this?

Frank didn't believe so. But they could also very well be a part of a much larger picture. Maybe Dutton had hired an entire gang to rid himself of Vivian and Conrad. But why so much emphasis on him? Had Dutton found out that he was now a minor stockholder in the Henson Company?

"Damn," Frank muttered. "This is getting too complicated for a country boy."

Frank got lucky. He caught a quick glimpse of what looked like part of a man's arm sticking out from behind cover and snapped off a fast shot.

"Goddamn it!" he heard the man holler. "I'm hit. Oh, damn. I'm hit hard."

"Where you hit, Pat?"

"My elbow. It's busted. Can't use my arm at all."

"Hang on. I'm comin'."

The man who was heading to help his friend jumped up, and Frank dusted him, the .44-.40 round entering the man's body high up on one side and blowing out through his shoulder. The second shooter never made a sound. He folded like a house of cards and went down, his rifle clattering on the rocks.

Another voice was added. "Nick?"

Nick would never make another sound on this side of the misty vail.

"That bastard's got more luck than any man I ever seen," a third voice called.

"Yeah," a fourth voice shouted from off to Frank's left. "Let's get out of here, Mack. Let that damn lawyer fight his own battles. I'm done."

Frank waited for a few minutes, trying to pick up the sound of horses' hooves, but could hear nothing. They must have left their horses some distance away. Frank edged out of the rocks and ran a short distance to more cover. No shots came his way. He worked his way toward the higher ground cautiously. He found a blood trail that led off toward a clearing, but did not pursue it.

Working his way through the rocks, he found the dead man. He rolled the body over and went through the clothing, looking for some identification. He did find a wad of paper money . . . several hundred dollars. He shoved that in his back jeans pocket and dragged the man out of the rocks, then went back for the shooter's rifle. He began looking around for the man's horse, and after a few minutes found it. He led the animal back and hoisted the body belly down across the saddle, tying him securely with rope.

Frank managed to get the bank teller's tarp-wrapped body roped down in the pack frame, then headed back to town.

Townspeople paused on the boardwalk, watching Frank ride slowly up the main street. Doc Bracken came out of his office to meet Frank in front of the jail.

"The bank teller fellow's in the tarp," Frank told him. "I think it is, anyways. The other one is part of a gang that tried to ambush me. It was a setup to get me out of town. You seen that damn Charles Dutton fellow?"

"The Boston lawyer?"

"Yes."

"Not lately. Not since the shoot-out, I'm sure."

"I'll find him. How is Vivian?"

"Weaker, Frank. It's down to hours now, I'm sure."

"Conrad?"

"Finally accepting the fact that his mother is not going to make it."

"I'll get those bodies over to Malone." Frank reached in his back pocket and pulled out the wad of bills. "The shooter had this money on him."

"I'd give Malone twenty-five dollars and keep the rest, I was you."

"I'll give it to Jerry." Frank grinned. "For a wedding present."

"He and Angie have sure been making cow's eyes at one another of late."

"He'll make her a good husband, and she'll make him a good wife. Doc, you think this town is going to last after the mines play out?"

"Yes, I do, Frank. I just heard that a big cattle outfit

is going to come in. The town will lose about half its population when the mines go, maybe more than that, but the solid citizens will stay. Why do you ask?"

"I told you, Doc. I'm pulling out. Jerry will make a fine town marshal."

"We'll hate to see you go, Frank."

"I forget the name of the writer who wrote that line about all things coming to an end . . . something like that. It's almost time for me to move on."

Dr. Bracken's nurse came running out of his office and over to the men. "Doctor! Mrs. Browning just slipped away."

Doc Bracken looked at Frank.

"Correction, Doc," Frank said. "It's time to move on."

Twenty-seven

"Mr. Dutton left several hours ago, Marshal," the clerk at the hotel told Frank. "He had to make a very hurried business trip to Denver."

"Oh? How did he leave? There was no stage scheduled."

"Well, he had some rather rough-looking men escorting him. I'd never seen any of them before today."

"Thanks."

So much for Dutton, Frank thought, standing outside the hotel. *I'll deal with him when I find him . . . if I ever find him.* Frank had a hunch the Boston lawyer would never again set foot west of the Mississippi River.

The man who had told Frank about the body of the bank teller had hauled his butt out of town. No one had seen him before, and no one knew where he had gone. Another dead end. Undertaker Malone had stopped all other work to prepare Vivian's body. She was to be taken to the railroad spur line just across the border in Colorado and then to Denver. From there she would be transported back east for burial.

Conrad was to escort the body all the way back to Boston.

Frank walked over to Malone's funeral parlor. Conrad

was sitting alone in the waiting room. He did not look up as Frank entered.

Frank took off his hat, hung it on a rack, and sat down beside his son. "Don't you think we'd better talk?"

"We have nothing to discuss, Marshal."

"I'm your father, Conrad."

"Biologically speaking, I suppose I have to accept that as fact. I don't have to like it. Mr. Browning was my father. He raised me."

"And he did a fine job. I didn't know I had a son until your mother told me just a short time ago." *Just a few weeks back,* Frank thought. *And now she's gone . . . forever.* "I want you to believe that."

"I believe it, Marshal. But it doesn't change anything. I want you to believe that."

It's too soon to be discussing this, Frank thought. *I made a mistake coming over here. The boy is too filled with grief.*

"I know that mother left you a small percentage of the company, Marshal. I will honor her wishes. I won't contest it."

"I didn't ask her for any part of the company, Conrad."

"I believe that, too."

"You want me to leave you alone?"

"I don't care, Marshal. You have a right to be here."

"I loved her very much. I never stopped loving her." Conrad had nothing to say about that.

"Did Malone say when the"—Frank started to say "body" but he couldn't bring himself to form the word— "when people can stop by here to pay their respects?"

"In a few hours."

Frank stood up and snagged his hat off the rack. "I'll leave you alone for a time."

Conrad met Frank's eyes for the first time since Frank entered the waiting room. "I appreciate that, Marshal."

"Well, maybe I'll see you in a few hours."

"All right."

Frank was glad to leave the stuffy and strange-smelling waiting room of the funeral parlor. He had never liked those places. He stood on the boardwalk and took several deep breaths of fresh air, then looked up and down the street.

Another town I'll soon put behind me, Frank thought. *In a few months they will have forgotten all about me, at least for the most part. The town's residents will settle back into a regular way of life . . . and I'll do what I do best—drift.*

No, Frank amended. *Not just drift. I have a big job to do. I'll find the men responsible for your death, Viv. I promise you that. If it takes the rest of whatever life I have left, I'll do it.*

The news of Vivian Browning's death spread quickly through the town. People spoke in hushed, sorrowful tones to Frank as he walked back to his office. At his desk he wrote out a letter of resignation, effective when Jerry was able to return to work . . . which, according to Doc Bracken, would be in a couple of days. He dated and signed the notice, then sealed it in an envelope.

He checked on the prisoners, then walked over to his house and began packing up his possessions, leaving out a clean shirt, britches, socks, and longhandles. He went over to the livery and checked on his packhorse. The animal was glad to see him, perhaps sensing they would soon be again on the trail.

Frank stored his packed up possessions in the livery storeroom and then walked over to the café for a cup of coffee and perhaps a bite to eat. Angie took one look at Frank's expression and brought two cups and the coffee-pot over to his table and joined him.

She touched his hand. "I'm sorry, Frank."

"I have to think it was for the best, Angie. Better than her starving to death. It was just her time to follow the light."

"That's beautiful, Frank. Follow the light. Frank? How is her son taking it?"

"He's all right. He's tougher than he looks."

"And you?"

"Getting ready to pull out. Just as soon as Jerry is on his feet."

"That quick?"

"Yes. I have things to do."

"I don't have to ask what those things are. Is that what Mrs. Browning would want?"

"It's what I want."

She lowered her eyes from his cold stare. She struggled to suppress a shiver. Looking into his eyes that day was like looking into a cold, musty grave. Years back, Angie had surprised a big puma feasting on a fresh kill. The puma did not attack, but the eyes were the same as Frank's—cold and deadly. Angie backed away quickly and left the puma alone to eat.

Frank drank his coffee, declined the offer of food, and walked over to Willis's General Store. There he bought bacon, beans, flour, and coffee. He bought a new jacket for the trail, for his old one was patched and worn. He took everything back to the office. There, he sat and waited.

* * *

Frank did not return to the funeral parlor to view Vivian's body. He respected her wish that he not have that image in his brain.

The next morning, Jerry came limping into the office about ten o'clock.

"You supposed to be up, Jer?"

"Doc said it was all right long as I don't try to run any foot races. Mrs. Browning's body is being loaded into the wagon now, Frank, for transport to the rails."

"I know."

"You're not going over there?"

"No." Frank stood up. "You ready to be sworn in, Jer?"

"I reckon so, Frank. If that's what you want."

"Wait here." Frank walked over to the bank and got Mayor Jenkins. Ten minutes later, Frank had handed in his badge, and Jerry had been sworn in.

Frank shook hands with Jerry and the mayor and walked out of the office. He did not look back.

A half an hour later, he was on the trail. He didn't know where the Pine and Vanbergen gangs had gone, but he would find them. All of them. One at a time.

* * *

Look for Frank Morgan's next exciting adventure
THE LAST GUNFIGHTER: REPRISAL
coming in August 2000
wherever paperbacks are sold.

AFTERWORD

Notes from the Old West

In the small town where I grew up, there were two movie theaters. The Pavilion was one of those old-timey movie show palaces, built in the heyday of the Mary Pickford and Charlie Chaplin silent era of the 1920s. By the 1950s, when I was a kid, the Pavilion was a little worn around the edges, but it was still the premier theater in town. They played all those big Technicolor biblical Cecil B. DeMille epics and the corny MGM musicals. In Cinemascope, of course.

On the other side of town was the Gem, a somewhat shabby and rundown grindhouse with sticky floors and torn seats. Admission was a quarter. The Gem booked low-budget B pictures (remember the Bowery Boys?), war movies, horror flicks, and Westerns. I liked the Westerns best. I could usually be found every Saturday at the Gem, along with my best friend, Newton Trout, watching Westerns from 10 AM until my father came looking for me around suppertime. (Sometimes Newton's dad was dispatched to come fetch us.) One time, my dad came to get me, right in the middle of *Abilene Trail*, which featured the now-forgotten Whip Wilson. My father became so engrossed in the action, he sat down and watched the rest of it with us. We didn't get home until after dark, and my mother's meatloaf was a pan of gray ashes by the time we did. Though my father and I were both in the doghouse the next day, this remains one of my fondest childhood memories. There was Wild Bill Elliot, and Gene Autry, and Roy Rogers, and Tim Holt, and, a little later, Rod Cameron and Audie Murphy. Of these newcomers, I never missed an Audie Murphy Western, because Audie was sort of an anti-hero. Sure, he stood for law and order and was an honest man, but sometimes he had to go around the law to uphold it. If he didn't play fair, it was only because he felt hamstrung by the laws of the land. Whatever it took to get the bad guys, Audie did it. There were no finer points of law, no splitting of legal hairs. It was instant justice, devoid of long-winded lawyers, bored or biased jurors, or black-robed, often corrupt judges.

Steal a man's horse and you were the guest of honor at a necktie party.

Molesting a good woman meant a bullet in your heart or a rope around your gullet. Or at the very least, getting the crap beat out of you. Rob a bank and face a hail of bullets or the hangman's noose.

Saved a lot of time and money, did frontier justice.

That's all gone now, I'm sad to say. Now you hear, "Oh, but he had a bad childhood" or, "His mother didn't give him enough love" or, "The homecoming queen wouldn't give him a second look and he has an inferiority complex." Or cultural rage, as the politically correct bright boys refer to it. How many times have you heard some self-important defense attorney moan, "The poor kids were only venting their hostilities toward an uncaring society"?

Mule fritters, I say. Nowadays, you can't even call a punk a punk anymore. But don't get me started.

It was "howdy ma'am" time, too. The good guys, anti-hero or not, were always respectful to the ladies. They might shoot a bad guy five seconds after tipping their hat to a woman, but the code of the West demanded you be respectful to a lady.

Lots of things have changed since the heyday of the Wild West, haven't they? Some for the good, some for the bad.

I didn't have any idea at the time that I would some-day write about the West. I just knew that I was captivated by the Old West.

When I first got the itch to write, back in the early 1970s, I didn't write Westerns. I started by writing horror and action adventure novels. After more than two dozen novels, I began thinking about developing a western character. From those initial musings came the novel *The Last Mountain Man: Smoke Jensen.* That was followed by *Preacher: The First Mountain Man.* A few years later, I began developing the *Last Gunfighter* series. Frank Morgan is a legend in his own time, the fastest gun west of the Mississippi . . . a title and a reputation he never wanted, but can't get rid of.

For me, and for thousands—probably millions—of other people (although many will never publicly admit it), the old Wild West will always be a magic, mysterious place: a place we love to visit through the pages of books; characters we would like to know . . . from a safe distance; events we would love to take part in—again, from a safe distance. For the old Wild West was not a place for the faint of heart. It was a hard, tough, physically demanding time. There were no police to call if one faced adversity. One faced trouble alone, and handled it alone. It was rugged individualism: something that appeals to many of us.

I am certain that is something that appeals to most readers of Westerns.

I still do on-site research (whenever possible) before

starting a Western novel. I have wandered over much of the West, prowling what is left of ghost towns. Stand in the midst of the ruins of these old towns, use a little bit of imagination, and one can conjure up life as it used to be in the Wild West. The rowdy Saturday nights, the tinkling of a piano in a saloon, the laughter of cowboys and miners letting off steam after a week of hard work. Use a little more imagination and one can envision two men standing in the street, facing one another, seconds before the hook and draw of a gunfight. A moment later, one is dead and the other rides away.

The old wild untamed West.

There are still some ghost towns to visit, but they are rapidly vanishing as time and the elements take their toll. If you want to see them, make plans to do so as soon as possible, for in a few years, they will all be gone.

And so will we.

Stand in what is left of the Big Thicket country of east Texas and try to imagine how in the world the pioneers managed to get through that wild tangle. I have wondered that many times and marveled at the courage of the men and women who slowly pushed westward, facing dangers that we can only imagine.

Let me touch briefly on a subject that is very close to me: firearms. There are some so-called historians who are now claiming that firearms played only a very insignificant part in the settlers' lives. They claim that only a few were armed. What utter, stupid nonsense! What do these so-called historians think the pioneers did for food? Do they think the early settlers rode down to the nearest supermarket and bought their meat? Or maybe they think the settlers chased down deer or buffalo on foot and beat the animals to death with a club. I have a news flash for you so-called historians: the settlers used guns to shoot their game. They used guns to defend hearth and home against Indians on the warpath. They used guns to protect themselves from outlaws. Guns are a part of Americana. And always will be.

The mountains of the West and the remains of the ghost towns that dot these areas are some of my favorite subjects to write about. I have done extensive research on the various mountain ranges of the West and go back whenever time permits. I sometimes stand surrounded by the towering mountains and wonder how in the world the pioneers ever made it through. As hard as I try and as often as I try, I simply cannot imagine the hardships those men and women endured over the hard months of their incredible journey. None of us can. It is said that on the Oregon Trail alone, there are at least two bodies in lonely unmarked graves for every mile of that journey. Some students of the West say the number of dead is at least twice that. And nobody knows the exact number of wagons that impatiently started out alone and simply vanished on the way, along with their occupants, never to be seen or heard from again.

Just vanished.

The one-hundred-and-fifty-year-old ruts of the wagon wheels can still be seen in various places along the Oregon Trail. But if you plan to visit those places, do so quickly, for they are slowly disappearing. And when they are gone, they will be lost forever, except in the words of Western writers.

The West will live on as long as there are writers willing to write about it, and publishers willing to publish it. Writing about the West is wide open, just like the old Wild West. Characters abound, as plentiful as the wide-open spaces, as colorful as a sunset on the Painted Desert, as restless as the ever-sighing winds. All one has to do is use a bit of imagination. Take a stroll through the cemetery at Tombstone, Arizona; read the inscriptions. Then walk the main street of that once infamous town around midnight and you might catch a glimpse of the ghosts that still wander the town. They really do.

Just ask anyone who lives there. But don't be afraid of the apparitions—they won't hurt you. They're just out for a quiet stroll.

The West lives on. And as long as I am alive, it always will.

Here's an exciting preview of
The Last Gunfighter: Renegades
by William W. Johnstone

Coming in October 2005
wherever Pinnacle Books are sold

ONE

Brown County, Texas, and all the violence that had taken place there were a long way behind Frank Morgan now. He was riding southward toward the Rio Grande, taking his time, in no hurry to get where he was going . . . wherever that was. Someplace where his past might not catch up to him. A haven where he could go unrecognized.

But as idyllic as that sounded, Frank Morgan knew there wasn't much chance that he would ever find such a sanctuary.

It was hard to blend in when you were the last of the really fast guns.

Some of the others were still alive—Wyatt Earp, Bat Masterson, and Smoke Jensen were three that Frank could think of right off the top of his head. Somehow they had managed to settle down. John Wesley Hardin was still alive too, but he was in prison. Bill Hickok, Ben Thompson, Doc Holliday, Luke Short . . . They were all dead, along with most of the other shootists and pistoleers who had made a name for themselves at one time or another on the frontier.

It was a sad time, in a way. A dying time. But a man couldn't stop the march of progress and so-called civilization. Nor was Frank Morgan the sort of hombre to brood about it and cling to the fading shadows of what once had been. He looked to the future, not the past.

Now the future meant finding a warm, hospitable place

to spend the winter. It was November, and up north the snow and the frigid winds were already roaring down out of Canada to sweep across the mountains and the plains, all the way down to the Texas Panhandle. Hundreds of miles south of the Panhandle, however, here in the Rio Grande Valley of south Texas, the sky was blue, the sun was shining, and the temperature was quite pleasant. Frank even had the sleeves of his blue work shirt rolled up a couple of turns on his muscular forearms.

He was a lean, well-built man of middle years, with gray streaking the thick dark hair under his Stetson. His range clothes were of good quality, as was his saddle. A Colt .45 was holstered on his hip, and the stock of a Winchester stuck up from a saddle sheath under his right leg. He rode a fine-looking Appaloosa called Stormy and led a dun-colored packhorse. The big shaggy cur known as Dog padded alongside him as Frank rode down a trail that cut its way through the thick chaparral covering the mostly flat landscape.

Frank didn't know exactly where he was, but he thought he must be getting close to the Rio Grande. Some sleepy little border village would be a good spot to pass the winter, he mused. Cool beer, some tortillas and beans and chili, maybe a pretty señorita or two to keep him company . . . It sounded fine to Frank. Maybe not heaven, but likely as close as a gunfighter like him would ever get.

Into every heavenly vision, though, a little hell had to intrude. The distant popping of gunfire suddenly came to Frank's ears.

He reined in and frowned. The shots continued, coming fast and furious. They were still a ways off, but they were getting closer, without a doubt. He heard the rumble of hoofbeats too. Some sort of running gun battle, Frank decided.

And it was running straight toward him.

He had never been one to dodge trouble. There just wasn't any backing down in his nature. Instead he nudged his heels into Stormy's sides and sent the Appaloosa trotting forward. Whatever was coming at him, Frank Morgan would go right out to meet it.

Now he could see dust clouds boiling in the air ahead of him, kicked up by all the horses he heard. A moment later, the trail he was following intersected a road at a sharp angle. The pursuit was on the road itself, which was wide enough for a couple of wagons and a half-dozen or so riders.

Only one wagon came toward Frank, a buckboard that swayed and bounced as it careened along the road. The dust from the hooves of the team pulling it obscured the occupants to a certain extent, but Frank thought he saw two men on the buckboard, one handling the reins while the other twisted around on the seat and fired a rifle back at the men giving chase.

There were more than a dozen of those, Frank saw. He estimated the number at twenty. They rode bunched up, the ones in the lead banging away at the fleeing buckboard with six-guns. The gap between hunter and hunted was about fifty yards, too far for accurate handgun fire, especially from the saddle of a racing horse. But the rifleman on the buckboard didn't seem to be having much better luck. The group of riders surged on without slowing.

Frank had no idea who any of these men were and didn't know which side he ought to take in this fight. But he'd always had a natural sympathy for the underdog, so he didn't like the idea of two against twenty.

He liked it even less when one of the horses in the team suddenly went down, probably the result of stepping in a prairie-dog hole. The horse screamed in pain, a shrill sound that Frank heard even over the rattle of gunfire and the pounding of hoofbeats. Probably a broken leg, he thought in the instant before the fallen horse pulled down the other members of the team and caused the buckboard to overturn violently. The two men who had been in it flew through the air like rag dolls.

Frank sent Stormy surging forward at a gallop. He didn't know if the men had survived the wreck or not, but it was a cinch they were out of the fight, at least for the moment, and wouldn't survive the next few seconds unless somebody helped them. He drew the Winchester and guided Stormy with his knees as he brought the rifle to his shoulder and blazed away, firing as fast as he could work the repeater's lever.

He put the first couple of bullets over the heads of the pursuers to see if they would give up the chase. When they didn't but kept attacking instead, sending a couple of bullets whizzing past him, Frank had no choice but to lower his aim. Stormy's smooth gait and Frank's years of experience meant that he was a good shot even from the hurricane deck. His bullets laced into the crowd of gunmen in the road.

Frank was close enough now to see that most of the pursuers wore high-crowned, broad-brimmed sombreros. *Bandidos* from below the border, he thought. A few men in American range garb were mixed in the group, but that came as no surprise. Gringo outlaws sometimes crossed the Rio Grande and fell in with gangs of Mexican raiders. A man who was tough enough and ruthless enough—and good enough with a gun—could usually find a home for himself with others of his kind, no matter where he was.

Two of the bandits plunged off their horses as Frank's shots ripped through them, and a couple of others sagged in their saddles and dropped out of the fight, obviously wounded. The other men reined their mounts to skidding, sliding halts that made even more dust billow up from the hard-packed caliche surface of the road. Clearly, they hadn't expected to run into opposition like that which Frank was putting up now.

But the odds were still on their side, and after a moment of hesitation they attacked again, yelling curses and firing as they came toward the overturned wagon.

Both of the men who had been thrown from the wreck staggered to their feet as Frank came closer. He didn't know how badly they were hurt, but at least they were conscious and able to move around. They stumbled toward the shelter of the buckboard as bullets flew around them.

While Stormy was still galloping, Frank swung down from the saddle, as good a running dismount as anyone could make. He had the Winchester in his left hand. With his right, he slapped the Appaloosa on the rump and ordered, "Stormy, get out of here! You too, Dog!"

The horse veered off into the chaparral at the side of the road, finding an opening in the thorny stuff. The big cur was more reluctant, obviously hesitant to abandon his master in the middle of a fight. Frank didn't want to have to worry about him while he was battling for his life, though, so he added, "Dog, go!"

With a growl, Dog disappeared into the brush.

Frank ran to the wagon and joined the two men who were already crouched behind it, firing revolvers at the charging *bandidos*. The man who had been using the rifle earlier had lost the weapon when the buckboard flipped over. Both of them had managed to hang on to their handguns, though.

The buckboard was on its side, turned crossways in the road. The horses had struggled back to their feet, except for the one with the broken leg, and they lunged and reared in their traces, maddened by the gunfire and the reeking clouds of powder smoke that drifted through the air. A couple of them had been wounded by flying lead.

Frank rested his Winchester on the buckboard and opened fire again, placing his shots carefully now that he had a chance to aim. One of the raiders flipped backward out of the saddle as if he had been swatted by a giant hand, and another fell forward over his mount's neck before slipping off and landing under the horse's slashing hooves.

Bullets pounded into the buckboard like a deadly hailstorm of lead. The thick boards stopped most of them, but a few of the rounds punched through, luckily missing Frank and his two companions. The shots from the men fighting alongside him were taking a toll on the attackers as well. Less than half of the *bandidos* were unscathed so far. The others had been either killed or wounded.

The Winchester ran dry. Frank dropped it and drew his Colt. The range was plenty close enough now for an expert pistol shot like The Drifter. He triggered twice and was rewarded by the sight of another rider plummeting from the saddle.

The gang of *bandidos* had had enough. They wheeled their horses, still snapping shots at the buckboard as they did so, and then lit a shuck out of there. Frank and the two men threw a few shots after them to hurry them on their way, but the riders were out of pistol range in a matter of moments.

Frank holstered the Colt and picked up the Winchester, then proceeded to reload the rifle with cartridges from his pocket in case the raiders turned around and tried again. From the looks of it, though, the bandits had no intention of returning. The dust cloud their horses kicked up dwindled in the distance.

"Keep riding, you bastards!" growled the older of the two men from the buckboard as he shook a fist after the *bandidos*. "Don't stop until you get back across the border to hell, as far as I'm concerned!"

The man was stocky and grizzled, with a graying, close-cropped beard. Most of his head was bald. His hands and face had a weathered, leathery look, an indication that he had spent most of his life outdoors.

The second man was younger, taller, and clean-shaven,

but he bore a resemblance to the older man that Frank recognized right away. He pegged them as father and son, or perhaps uncle and nephew. Both men were dressed in well-kept range clothes that would have looked better if they hadn't been covered in trail dust. They had the appearance of successful cattlemen about them.

Frank spotted the other rifle lying on the ground about twenty feet away. He nodded toward it and said, "Better pick up that repeater, just in case they come back."

The older man snorted contemptuously. "They won't be back! Bunch of no-good, cowardly dogs! They travel in a pack and won't attack unless the odds are ten to one in their favor."

"And we cut those odds down in a hurry," the younger man said. He hurried over to retrieve the rifle anyway, Frank noted.

The riders had disappeared in the distance now, without even any dust showing. Deciding that they were truly gone, Frank walked out from behind the buckboard and went to check on the men who had fallen from their horses during the fight. He counted seven of them. Six were already dead, and the seventh was unconscious and badly wounded. Blood bubbled from his mouth in a crimson froth with every ragged breath he took, and Frank heard the air whistling through bullet-punctured lungs. The man dragged in one last breath and then let it out in a shuddery sigh, dying without regaining consciousness.

Frank's expression didn't change as he watched the man pass over the divide. *Any man's death diminishes me,* John Donne had written, and in a philosophical way Frank supposed there might be some truth to that. Donne, however, had never swapped lead with a *bandido*.

Five of the men were Mexicans, typical south-of-the-border hardcases. The other two were Americans of the same sort. Frank checked their pockets, found nothing but spare shells for their guns and some coins.

A pistol shot made him look around. The younger man had just put the injured horse out of its misery.

Frank walked back to the buckboard. The younger man began unhitching the team and trying to calm the horses. The older man met Frank with a suspicious look. He asked, "Who are you, mister? Why'd you jump into that fracas on our side?"

"My name's Morgan," Frank said, "and I just thought it looked like you could use a hand. I never have liked an unfair fight."

The man nodded and wiped the back of his hand across his nose, which was bleeding a little. That seemed to be the only injury either of them had suffered in the wreck of the buckboard. They had been mighty lucky.

"Well, the boy an' me are much obliged. My name's Cecil Tolliver. That's my son Ben."

Ben Tolliver paused in what he was doing to look over at Frank and nod. "Howdy." He turned back to the horses and then paused and looked at Frank again. "Wouldn't be Frank Morgan, would it? The one they call The Drifter?"

Frank tried not to sigh. Just once, he thought, he would like to ride in somewhere and not have somebody recognize him almost right away.

And it would have been nice too if nobody shot at him.

TWO

"Yes, I'm Frank Morgan," he admitted.

Cecil Tolliver frowned. "I don't mean to sound ignorant, mister, but I don't reckon I've heard of you."

Ben came over and held out his hand to Frank. "That's because you never read any dime novels," he explained to his father. "Mr. Morgan here is a famous gunfighter."

Tolliver grunted. "I never had time for such foolishness, boy. I was too busy tryin' to build the Rockin' T into a decent spread. You was the one who always had your nose in the *Police Gazette*."

Frank shook hands with both of them and said to Ben, "Most of what's been written about me in those dime novels and the illustrated weeklies was a pack of lies made up by gents who don't know much about the real West."

"You can't deny, though, that you've had your share of gunfights," Ben said.

Frank inclined his head in acknowledgment of that point. "More than my share," he allowed.

"Well, we're much obliged for the help, whether you're famous or not," Tolliver said. "If you hadn't come along when you did, I reckon Almanzar's boys would've done in me and Ben."

"Almanzar," Frank repeated. "I'm not familiar with the name. Is he the leader of that gang of *bandidos*?"

"You could call him that. He runs the rancho where those gunnies work."

Now it was Frank's turn to frown. He waved his left hand toward the sprawled bodies of the raiders and said, "Those don't look like vaqueros or cowhands to me."

"That's because Almanzar's a low-down skunk who hires killers rather than decent hombres."

"Sounds like you don't care for the man."

"I got no use for him," Tolliver said stiffly. "Him and me been feudin' ever since I came to this part of the country, nigh on to thirty years ago. Almanzar specializes in wet cattle, if you know what I mean."

Frank understood the term, all right. It referred to stock rustled from one side of the river and driven to the other. Down here in this border country, a lot of cattle had gotten their bellies wet over the past few decades, going in both directions across the Rio Grande.

Young Ben spoke up. "You don't know that Don Felipe has been rustling our cows, Pa."

"I know all I need to know," Tolliver replied with a disgusted snort. "Almanzar's a thief and a bloody-handed reiver, and this ain't the first time he's tried to have me killed!"

Obviously, there was trouble going on around here, Frank thought. Just as obviously, it was none of his business. But by taking a hand in this gun battle, he had probably dealt himself into the game, whether he wanted that or not. If Cecil Tolliver was correct about Don Felipe Almanzar sending those gunmen after him and his son, then Almanzar would be likely to want vengeance on Frank for killing several of his men.

"Another thing," Tolliver went on angrily to Ben. "I don't want to hear you callin' that bastard by his Christian name again. He ain't our friend and never has been."

"What about when you first settled here, before I was born?" Ben asked. "I've heard you say more than once, Pa, that without Señor Almanzar's help, the Comanches would have lifted your hair back in those days."

"That was a long time ago," Tolliver growled. "Things change."

Frank wasn't really interested in the history of the feud between Tolliver and Don Felipe Almanzar. He said, "Where were you men headed?"

"Back to the Rockin' T," Tolliver replied. "We'd been to San Rosa for supplies." He shook his head in disgust. "All the boxes done bounced out back along the road, when that bunch jumped us and we had to take off so fast. We're lucky the damn buckboard didn't rattle itself to pieces."

"San Rosa's the nearest town?"

"Yep, right on the river about five miles upstream from here. The name's fouled up—it ought to be Santa Rosa— but the fella who stuck the name on it didn't savvy Mex talk. Still a pretty nice place."

"I'll pay it a visit," Frank said. "I was looking for a place to get something to eat and somewhere to stay."

"You don't have to go to San Rosa for that." Tolliver jerked a thumb at the buckboard. "Help us set that wagon up, and then you can ride on to the Rockin' T with us. You'll be our guest for as long as you want to stay, Mr. Morgan."

"Call me Frank. And I wouldn't want to impose—"

"Impose, hell!" Tolliver had picked up his hat and now he slapped it against his leg to get some of the dust off. As he settled it on his head, he went on. "After what you done to help us, I'll consider it a personal insult if you don't let us feed you and put you up for a spell."

Frank smiled. "In that case, I accept."

He whistled and Stormy came out of the chaparral, followed by Dog. Tolliver and Ben looked with admiration at the big Appaloosa, but were more wary where Dog was concerned. "That critter looks a mite like a cross between a wolf and a grizzly bear," Tolliver commented.

"He's all dog," Frank said with a grin. "Just be sure

you've been introduced properly before you go to pet him. Unless you're a little kid," he added. "He'll let kids wool him around like he's still a pup."

Frank took his rope from the saddle and tied one end to the buckboard. Ben saw what he was doing and brought over the surviving three members of the team. The rope was tied to their harness, and the horses did the work as the buckboard was soon pulled upright again. Frank hitched Stormy into the empty spot in the team. The Appaloosa didn't care much for that, but he was willing to tolerate it if that was what Frank wanted him to do. Stormy turned a baleful eye on his master for a moment, though.

"I'd watch out for that horse if I was you, Mr. Morgan," Ben said. "He looks like he might sneak up on you sometime and take a nip out of your hide."

"I fully expect that he will," Frank agreed with a chuckle. He grew more sober as he gestured toward the bodies again. "What about them?"

"I'll be damned if I'm gonna get their blood all over my buckboard," Cecil Tolliver said. "When we get to the ranch, I'll send a rider to San Rosa to notify the law. In the meantime, a couple o' my hands can come back out with a work wagon to load up the carcasses. The undertaker can come to the ranch to get 'em for plantin'."

"There's law in San Rosa?"

"Yeah, a town marshal who don't amount to much. But there's a company of Rangers that's been usin' the town as their headquarters for a spell, while they try to track down some bandits who've been raisin' hell around here."

Frank's interest perked up at the mention of Texas Rangers. Over the past year or so he had shared several adventures with a young Ranger named Tyler Beaumont. Beaumont was back home with his wife in Weatherford now, recuperating from injuries he had received in that fence-cutting dustup in Brown County. Frank respected the Rangers a great deal as a force for law and order, even though his reputation as a gunfighter sometimes made the Rangers look on him with suspicion.

He wasn't looking for trouble down here along the border, though, so it was unlikely he would clash with the lawmen.

Tolliver and Ben climbed onto the seat of the buckboard. Frank tied his packhorse on at the back of the vehicle, then sat down with his legs dangling off the rear. When he snapped his fingers, Dog jumped onto the buckboard and settled down beside him. Tolliver got the team moving and drove on toward his ranch, the Rocking T.

Frank saw cattle in the chaparral as the buckboard rolled along. They were longhorns, the sort of tough, hardy breed that was required in this brushy country. Longhorns seemed to survive, even to thrive, in it where other breeds had fallen by the wayside. The ugly, dangerous brutes had been the beginning of the cattle industry in Texas, back in the days immediately following the Civil War. Animals that had been valuable only for their hide and tallow had suddenly become beef on the hoof, the source of a small fortune for the men daring enough and tough enough to round them up and make the long drive over the trails to the railhead in Kansas.

As a young cowboy, Frank had ridden along on more than one of those drives, pushing the balky cattle through dust and rain, heat and cold, and danger from Indians and outlaws. Since the railroads had reached Texas, the days of such cattle drives were over. Now a man seldom had to move his herds more than a hundred miles or so before reaching a shipping point. As much as he lamented some things about the settling of the West, Frank didn't miss those cattle drives. They had been long, arduous, perilous work.

With an arm looped around Dog's shaggy neck, he turned his head and asked the Tollivers, "How much stock have you been losing lately?"

"Not that much," Ben said.

His father snorted. "Not that much at one time, you mean. Half a dozen here, a dozen there. But it sure as hell adds up."

Frank knew what Tolliver meant. Rustlers could make a big raid on a ranch, or they could bleed it dry over time. Either method could prove devastating to a cattleman.

"The Rangers haven't been able to get a line on the wide-loopers?"

"They're too busy lookin' for the Black Scorpion."

"The Black Scorpion?" Frank repeated. "What's that?"

"You mean who's that. You recollect what I said about the Rangers huntin' for a gang of owlhoots? Well, the Black Scorpion is the boss outlaw, the son of a bitch who heads up that gang."

Ben laughed. "Now you're talking like the one who's been reading dime novels, Pa."

"The Black Scorpion's real, damn it," Tolliver said with a scowl. "Folks have seen him, dressed all in black and wearin' a mask, leadin' that bloodthirsty bunch o' desperadoes."

That sounded pretty far-fetched to Frank too, like the creation of one of those ink-stained wretches who made up stories about him. There might be some truth to it, though. The West had seen mysterious masked bandits before, such as Black Bart out in California. Frank was going to have to see this so-called Black Scorpion for himself, though, before he would really believe in such an individual.

Ben was equally skeptical, saying, "I'll believe it when I see it. It seems to me that Captain Wedge and the Rangers are wasting their time looking for phantoms when they ought to be hunting down rustlers."

"Well, I ain't gonna argue about that," his father said. "I wish they'd do something about the damn rustlers too."

Frank sat in the back of the buckboard and mulled over what he had heard. He had come down here to the border country looking for someplace warm and peaceful. It was warm, all right, but evidently far from peaceful, what with the feud between Cecil Tolliver and Don Felipe Almanzar, the rustlers plaguing the Rocking T, and another gang of bandits led by a mysterious masked figure. With all that going on, it seemed like trouble could crop up from any direction with little or no warning—or from several directions at once.

"Is it possible the Black Scorpion could be responsible for the rustling?" Frank asked.

"Folks have thought about that," Tolliver replied, "but me and some o' the other ranchers around here have lost stock on the same nights that the Black Scorpion's gang was reported to be maraudin' on the other side of the border. The varmint can't be in two places at the same time."

"No, I reckon not," Frank said, but he wasn't completely convinced. His instincts told him that there was even more going on around here than was readily apparent.

His instincts also told him that the smart thing to do would be to unhitch Stormy from the team, mount up, and light a shuck out of here. The troubles had nothing to do with him, and if he stayed around and was drawn deeper into them, his hopes for a quiet, relaxing winter might well be shattered.

On the other hand, he had never turned his back on trouble just to make it easier on himself, and he was a mite too old to start now. A leopard couldn't change its spots, nor a tiger its stripes.

The sun was low in the sky by the time the buckboard reached the headquarters of the Rocking T. Frank saw a large, whitewashed house sitting in the shade of several cottonwood trees. Behind it were a couple of barns, several corrals, a bunkhouse, a cookshack, a blacksmith shop, a chicken coop, and some storage buildings. There was a vegetable garden off to one side of the house and beyond it a small orchard filled with fruit trees. It was a mighty nice layout, Frank thought, the sort of spread that required years of hard work and dedication to build. He admired a man like Cecil Tolliver who could put down roots and create something lasting and worthwhile like this. For all of his accomplishments, Frank had never been able to achieve that. True, he had quite a few business interests scattered across the West, business interests that had made him a wealthy man, at least on paper, but he had inherited those things, not worked for them and built them himself. Most of the time, he felt as if all he truly owned were his guns and not much else. Stormy and Dog were friends, not possessions. And most of the time, that was all right. Frank didn't miss the rest of it except at moments such as this, when he looked at the Rocking T and wondered what his life would have been like if things had been different, if he hadn't been blessed—or cursed—with such blinding speed and uncanny accuracy with a gun.

Tolliver hauled back on the reins and brought the buckboard to a halt. "This is it," he said. "Welcome to the Rocking T, Mr. Morgan."

THREE

Their arrival hadn't gone unnoticed. A small black, brown, and tan dog came racing around the house, barking sharply at the buckboard. The dog stopped abruptly, however, when it spotted the big cur sitting next to Frank in the back of the vehicle. A growl rumbled deeply in Dog's throat and was echoed by the smaller animal, even though Dog was more than ten times his size.

"Don't get your back fur in an uproar there, Dobie," Tolliver called to the little dog. "This here's a friend."

"Behave yourself, Dog," Frank said firmly to the cur.

Dog jumped down from the buckboard. He and Dobie sniffed warily at each other, but neither of them snapped. After a moment, Dog strolled over to a clump of grass and hiked his leg to relieve himself on it. Dobie followed suit, establishing himself as the boss around here. Dog seemed to accept that, and if he'd been a human he would have shrugged, Frank thought as he watched the byplay between the two animals.

Dobie wasn't the only one to greet the newcomers. Several men walked out of one of the barns and came toward the buckboard. At the same time, the front door of the ranch house opened and four women emerged. Two of them were fairly young and had the same sandy-colored hair that Ben did. One of the older women had gray hair, while the other was a stunning brunette.

"Come on," Tolliver said as he climbed down from the wagon. "I'll introduce you to the womenfolk."

Frank slid off the back of the buckboard and followed Tolliver and Ben to the house. When he reached the bottom of the three steps that led up to the porch, he took off his hat.

"Ladies, this here is Mr. Frank Morgan," Tolliver said. With rough-hewn gallantry, he went on, "Mr. Morgan, allow me to present my wife Pegeen and our daughters Debra and Jessie. And this is Pegeen's sister Roanne."

Frank held his hat in front of him and nodded politely. "Ladies," he said. "The honor and the pleasure are mine."

"We're pleased to meet you, Mr. Morgan," Pegeen Tolliver said. She was oldest of the four women, the one with gray hair. She was still a handsome woman, though, and the same lines of timeless beauty to be found in her face were also present in the faces of her sister and her daughters. Roanne, who was around thirty, Frank estimated, was especially lovely. There wasn't that much age difference between her and her nieces, who were both between twenty and twenty-five, fine-looking young frontier women. And both already married too, judging by the rings on their fingers.

Frank noted that Roanne wore no ring at all, for whatever that was worth.

The men who had come out of the barn reached the house. Two of them stepped up onto the porch and moved next to Debra and Jessie. "My sons-in-law," Cecil Tolliver said, then introduced them. "That's Darrell Forrest with Jessie, and Nick Holmes with Debra. They're both top hands."

Frank shook hands with Darrell and Nick and said, "Glad to meet you, boys."

Darrell Forrest looked intently at Frank and said, "Frank Morgan . . . that was the name, sir?"

Before Frank could say anything, Ben Tolliver said, "That's right, Darrell. He's The Drifter."

Pegeen put a hand on her husband's arm and said, "Cecil, you went to town for supplies, but I don't see any in the buckboard. And one of the horses is missing. Does that spotted horse belong to Mr. Morgan?"

"That's right," Tolliver told her. His bearded face grew grim as he continued. "The supplies are scattered up and down the road this side o' San Rosa, where they got jolted out when we had to run from a bunch o' gunmen."

Pegeen's hand tightened on Tolliver's arm. "Are you or Ben hurt?"

"I reckon we'll have some bruises tomorrow. We got throwed off the buckboard when it turned over durin' the chase. But Mr. Morgan come along right about then and helped us fight off those bast—those no-good skunks." Tolliver looked at Nick Holmes. "Nick, send a rider to San Rosa to tell Flem Jarvis that we've got the bodies of seven o' them owlhoots out here waitin' for the undertaker."

"Seven bodies!" Nick exclaimed. "But I don't see—"

"That's because they're still out on the road right now. Once you've sent a man to town, you and Darrell take a couple of hands and a work wagon and go out to get the corpses."

The ladies all looked a little shaken by this casual discussion of corpses and an attack by a gang of outlaws. Being good frontier women, though, they remained calm and didn't waste time with a bunch of chattering questions. It took more than a little trouble to rattle a true woman of the West. And these were Texas women, which meant they had backbone second to none.

Pegeen turned to Frank and said, "Thank you for helping my husband and my son, Mr. Morgan. I hope you plan to stay for supper and spend the night with us. A little hospitality is the least we can do for you."

"Yes, ma'am," Frank said with a smile. "Your husband

already told me I'd be staying a while, and I sure appreciate the kindness."

"You're very welcome. Come on inside. I'll bet you could use a cup of coffee."

"Ma'am, coffee is one of my biggest weaknesses," Frank said, his smile widening into a grin. He went into the house with Tolliver, Ben, and the women, while Darrell and Nick hurried off to carry out Tolliver's orders.

The house was well appointed, with thick rugs on the floors and heavy, overstuffed furniture. A massive stone fireplace dominated one wall of the parlor. A tremendous spread of longhorns adorned the wall above the fireplace. Several sets of deer antlers were attached to the wall as well, and rifles and shotguns hung on pegs. A cavalry saber was also on display, and when Cecil Tolliver noticed Frank's interest in it, the rancher said, "I carried that when I rode with Jeb Stuart, Fitz Lee, and Mac Brannon during the war, Mr. Morgan. That was before I came out here to Texas."

"I thought I detected a hint of Virginia in your voice, sir," Frank said.

"Were you in the war?"

"I was . . . but that was a long time ago."

Tolliver clapped a hand on his shoulder. "Indeed it was. After supper, I'll break out a bottle of brandy I've been savin', and we'll drink to old times. They weren't the best of times, but they made us what we are."

"I reckon that's true enough," Frank agreed. Almost three decades had passed since the end of the war, but it remained the single biggest event in most men's lives.

A man couldn't spend all his time looking backward, though. As the women left Frank, Tolliver, and Ben in the parlor, Frank steered the conversation back to the here and now by saying, "I suppose you've had your hands riding patrol at night, trying to stop the rustling."

Tolliver nodded. "Damn right I have. All it's gotten me

is one puncher shot dead and another laid up with a bullet-busted shoulder."

"So the rustlers don't hesitate to shoot?"

"Not at all. Anyway, this is a big spread. It'd take an army to cover all of it at night." The frustration was easy to hear in Tolliver's voice. "But I can't just call in my men and throw the ranch wide open to the damn wide-loopers."

Frank shook his head. "No, you can't do that," he agreed.

"If you have any ideas, Mr. Morgan," Ben said, "we'd be glad to hear 'em."

Tolliver got a cigar from a box on a table next to a heavy divan and jabbed it toward Frank. "What I ought to do is hire some gunmen and ride across the Rio to wipe out Almanzar. I'll bet our rustlin' troubles would stop then!"

Ben frowned darkly, and Frank got the feeling that the young man didn't care for his father's idea at all. Ben wasn't the only one. Pegeen had come back into the room with her sister in time to hear her husband's angry pronouncement, and she said, "You'll do no such thing, Cecil Tolliver! You can't take the law into your own hands, and besides, you don't know that Don Felipe is behind the rustling."

Tolliver stuck the cigar in his mouth and chewed savagely on it for a moment before he said, "When we first come out here, Peg, there wasn't no law but what a man could carry in his own fist. We did all right in those days."

"We all nearly got killed more than once, fighting off Comanches and outlaws," she snapped. "You leave such things to the Rangers."

Tolliver just made a sound of disgust. He took another cigar from the box and offered it to Frank, who slipped it into his shirt pocket. "I'll save it for later, with that brandy," he said.

"Good idea. I got to gnaw on this one now, though,

to keep from sayin' things I hadn't ought to say." Tolliver crossed his arms and glared at the world in general.

His wife dared his wrath by saying, "I still need those supplies. Come morning, Cecil, you'll have to go back to town to replace the ones you lost."

"All right, all right," Tolliver muttered around the cigar. "But I'm takin' more of the boys with me next time, and if Almanzar sends his gun wolves after us again, they'll get even more of a fight than they got this time!"

Debra and Jessie came out of the kitchen carrying trays with cups and saucers on them. Steam lifted from the coffee in the cups, and Frank smiled in appreciation of the delicious aroma.

The coffee tasted as good as it smelled. Frank sat in a comfortable armchair and sipped from his cup. A time or two, he caught Roanne watching him with undisguised interest. He wondered if she was married or a widow or had never been hitched. An unmarried woman of her age was considered an old maid out here, but there was nothing old about her. To be honest, the boldness of her gaze wasn't very maidenly either. Frank returned her looks with an interest of his own. She was a mighty attractive lady.

They hadn't been sitting around the parlor for very long when a sudden rataplan of hoofbeats welled up outside. A large group of riders was approaching the ranch. Tolliver and Ben set their cups aside and stood up quickly. So did Frank. No shouts of alarm had sounded from the ranch hands, but these days, no one was taking a chance. With his hand on the butt of the Colt at his hip, Tolliver strode to the front door. Ben and Frank were right behind him.

As the three men stepped out onto the porch, they saw a group of about twenty-five men entering the ranch yard. The rider in the lead was a big, barrel-chested man with a raw-boned, hawklike face and a shock of white hair under a black Stetson. The last of the fading light revealed a badge pinned to his coat. Frank recognized it as a star set inside a circle, the emblem of the Texas Rangers.

"Captain Wedge!" Tolliver called out as the newcomers reined in, confirming the guess Frank had just made. "Good to see you and your boys. Could have used you around a little while ago."

The Ranger captain swung down from his saddle and curtly motioned for his men to dismount as well. "Why's that, Tolliver?" he asked as he turned to face the rancher.

"Because my boy an' me were jumped by a gang o' Almanzar's gunmen from across the border. If it wasn't for Frank Morgan here, Ben an' me would probably be buzzard bait by now."

Captain Wedge turned his dark eyes toward The Drifter and repeated the name. "Frank Morgan, eh?"

Frank knew there was no point in denying anything. It came as no surprise to him that a lawman had recognized his name. He said, "That's right."

"Heard of you," Wedge said with a curt nod. "Don't think there's any paper out on you right now, though."

"There never has been except on trumped-up charges that were proven false," Frank said.

Wedge nodded again. "Pretty much what I figured. Heard too that you've given the Rangers a hand now and then."

"I'm a law-abiding man," Frank explained. "I do what I can to help when I'm called on."

"Good to know." Wedge turned back to Cecil Tolliver. "What's this about you and the boy being attacked by Almanzar's riders?"

"They jumped us while we were comin' back to the ranch from San Rosa," Tolliver said. "We'd been to town to pick up some supplies. A whole bunch of 'em came on us suddenlike, yellin' and shootin'. We tried to get away and make a fight of it at the same time, but our buckboard turned over. Then Mr. Morgan rode up and took a hand in the game. We knocked down enough of the bastards so that the rest of 'em turned tail."

"Sounds like you're lucky to be alive," Wedge said.

"That's the way I figure it too."

The Ranger captain frowned. "How do you know the men who jumped you work for Almanzar?"

"Who else would have it in for me?" Tolliver demanded. "Almanzar and me been crossways with each other for a long time."

"What about the Black Scorpion?"

Tolliver looked surprised at Wedge's question. "What about him?"

"Could the men who attacked you have been part of the Scorpion's gang?"

Ben put in, "That thought crossed my mind too, even though I'm not sure I believe in the Black Scorpion."

"He's real enough," Wedge said.

Tolliver shook his head stubbornly. "I didn't see no sign of any masked man leadin' the gang. They were just a bunch of border toughs, the sort of hardcases Almanzar hires to make life miserable for me."

"The reason I ask is, the men and I have been trailing the Black Scorpion since yesterday. He and his gang raided a ranch on the other side of San Rosa. They were coming in this direction and it seems logical to me that they could have run into you and your son."

"Nope. Those gunnies worked for Almanzar."

Frank read the skepticism on Captain Wedge's face, and to tell the truth, he was beginning to have his doubts about Tolliver's belief too. From the looks of things, Tolliver's hatred of Don Felipe Almanzar was so deep-seated that the cattleman was quick to blame Almanzar for everything bad that happened, whether Almanzar had anything to do with it or not.

It appeared that Wedge might have argued the matter

further, but at that moment the women came out of the house onto the porch. The light was behind them and shone on their hair. Wedge took his hat off and nodded politely to them, saying, "Ladies. After a long day on the trail, you are sure a sight for sore eyes, if I may be so bold as to say so."

"You may," Pegeen Tolliver told him with a smile. "Hello, Captain. Will you and your men be staying to supper?"

"That sounds mighty nice, ma'am, but we're on the trail of some bad men—"

"You can't follow a trail very well at night," Tolliver put in. "Join us for supper, Captain. Your men can eat in the bunkhouse with the hands."

Wedge chuckled. "That Chinaman who cooks for you probably won't be very happy about having that many extra mouths to feed."

"He'll get over it. There's plenty of room for your men to bunk in the barn too, and we'll find a bed for you in the house."

The captain returned his black Stetson to his head. "I'm much obliged, Tolliver, and on behalf of my men, I accept." He turned and said to his troop of Rangers, "Light for a spell, boys. We're spending the night here on the Rocking T."

A grin creased Tolliver's leathery face. "I'd like to see Almanzar's nighthawks come a-raidin' now, with a couple dozen Rangers on the place! They'd get a mighty warm welcome if they did!"

THE LAST GUNFIGHTER SERIES BY
WILLIAM W. JOHNSTONE

__The Drifter
0-8217-6476-4   **$4.99US/$6.99**CAN

__Reprisal
0-7860-1295-1   **$5.99US/$7.99**CAN

__Ghost Valley
0-7860-1324-9   **$5.99US/$7.99**CAN

__The Forbidden
0-7860-1325-7   **$5.99US/$7.99**CAN

__Showdown
0-7860-1326-5   **$5.99US/$7.99**CAN

__Imposter
0-7860-1443-1   **$5.99US/$7.99**CAN

__Rescue
0-7860-1444-X   **$5.99US/$7.99**CAN

__The Burning
0-7860-1445-8   **$5.99US/$7.99**CAN

Available Wherever Books Are Sold!

Visit our website at www.kensingtonbooks.com

<u>BOOK YOUR PLACE ON OUR WEBSITE</u> AND MAKE THE <u>READING CONNECTION!</u>

We've created a customized website just for our very special readers, where you can get the inside scoop on everything that's going on with Zebra, Pinnacle and Kensington books.

When you come online, you'll have the exciting opportunity to:

- View covers of upcoming books
- Read sample chapters
- Learn about our future publishing schedule (listed by publication month *and author*)
- Find out when your favorite authors will be visiting a city near you
- Search for and order backlist books from our online catalog
- Check out author bios and background information
- Send e-mail to your favorite authors
- Meet the Kensington staff online
- Join us in weekly chats with authors, readers and other guests
- Get writing guidelines
- AND MUCH MORE!

**Visit our website at
http://www.kensingtonbooks.com**